THE DEADBEAT KILLER

A Charley Casey novel

Willow River Press is an imprint of Between the Lines Publishing. The Willow River Press name and logo are trademarks of Between the Lines Publishing.

Between the Lines Publishing
1769 Lexington Ave N, Ste 286
Roseville MN 55113
btwnthelines.com

First Published: September 2025

ISBN: (Paperback) 978-1-965059-58-6

ISBN: (eBook) 978-1-965059-59-3

Library of Congress Control Number: 2025942639

THE DEADBEAT KILLER

A Charley Casey novel

Michael Oldham

Jeff Oldham

DAY 1

CHAPTER 1

Charlie Casey just stared at the framed record. Eyeing his treasured 45 RPM was a longtime standing ritual of his that he did just before leaving to make a paycheck. The vinyl record, hung inside the hallway of his home, always worked its magic—getting his anger built up. During the last few years, he especially leaned on it for inspiration since the job of killing had begun to bore him.

A few minutes later, he was backing his Corolla out of his garage being careful not to nick it against his Porsche. The Toyota was used for work since in his profession drawing any attention while driving or otherwise was the last thing he wanted. As the front of his car cleared the garage door, he reached up and triggered the garage door device.

Out the driveway, he idled in the street as he watched the soft landing of the closing garage door. He took a split second to look over his hillside-hugging home, dimly lit up by several outside night lights. It was one that few people could afford yet it was unassuming. Perfect for his needs. He shook his head while remembering how thrilled he was when he bought it some 15 years back. Now, he couldn't imagine the purchase of any house being all that exciting. Lately, it seemed everything was losing its luster.

Glancing away from the house, Charlie shifted into drive. Weaving along a curving Astral Drive, he ignored the wee-hour lights of Los Angeles down below on his left. In the old days, while in his twenties, he would've gassed it and sped his way to Nichols Canyon Road. Back then, he would be imagining himself inside a Steve McQueen movie and cool as could be. But he now had a few decades of experience behind him, and he'd grown more cautious. Besides, he hadn't been in the mood lately to play out some imaginary McQueen role. Instead, at 53 years of age, he knew his life was more closely aligned with the role of Bronson's character in *The Mechanic*—a burned-out contract killer.

After winding his way through the canyon, he soon came to Sunset and made a left. Thirty minutes later, he turned off the boulevard and directly into Lew Holt Truck Rentals. He came to a stop with his headlights facing the business' locked chain-link fence gate. Leaving the car running, he got out and walked toward the gate while dangling a ring of keys.

He didn't like it when the car lights lit him up. But turning them off with the car in front of the gate would look more suspicious to any passing police cruiser. Still, if any cop cared to question him, he had an employee badge and Lew's cell number if they needed to confirm that he was simply running an early Monday morning errand for business' owner. Nothing, if Charlie could help it, was ever left to chance.

Charlie stopped a few feet short of the gate and looked through the fence to view the lot it was protecting. Between a couple of trucks, he spotted the Ford Taurus that Lew had left for him. What he didn't see or hear was just as important—dogs. Lew, after closing shop yesterday, had taken them to his home in the Valley for the night. Charlie smiled. He loved professionals like Lew who never made mistakes. If only the world had more of them.

CHAPTER 2

Some 15 miles away, as Charlie was inserting a key into the gate of Lew Holt Truck Rentals, Bixie Brown was unlocking her apartment door. Despite being in a hurry, she frowned after flipping on the light and looking at the years-old couch. Her frown remained as she scanned the tiny apartment space that made up her living room and kitchen area. She realized the couch and all her other banged up items belonged right where they were—inside a dump. Would she ever be able to afford a nice place?

Truth be told, she could afford a nicer place and newer furniture. But her Vicodin and bar-hopping habits were costly. Her finances were going to soon get worse. Men didn't pay good money for bodies over 30-years of age, unless they were exceptional, and hers wasn't much above average. At 28, she was past her peak earning power, at least according to her pimp, Zep Hill. And he hadn't helped the cause when he'd left her nose wider by a half inch after one of the many beatings he'd given her in the last few years.

Indeed, Bixie's ability to draw clients had been steadily declining in the last year. Zep had reminded her about it a few months back— *Bixie, requests for you are down to a trickle. For your own sake, you'd better spice things up for the tricks.* But, just a few weeks ago, Bixie gained something that gave her a way of spicing things up for her clients. All thanks to Zep's temper. After one of his recent physical outbursts, she needed dentures. She quickly learned that taking them off was something only a man could appreciate. Her hope was that Zep would soon be seeing an uptick in requests for the girl with dentures.

Putting her concerns aside for the moment, Bixie threw her purse down on the couch half expecting a cloud of dust to follow. Entering the kitchen, she found a scattering of her tiny and white elliptical-shaped friends. She threw one back with a chaser of water and looked at the clock—2:50 a.m. It was time to get ready for her next man.

Walking to the only bathroom in her one-bedroom unit, Bixie was thankful her client tonight was a man. Last night, Zep had sent her out on a call to a lipstick lesbian with a foot fetish. A few months back, of all his girls, he picked her for one of his transsexual clients. Zep used such dirty assignments for punishing any girl of his who got out of line. But Bixie knew that wasn't the reason she'd gotten those bad gigs. Zep no longer thought of her as a valued asset given that her body was getting flabbier by the month. This was worrisome to her as she stepped in front of the mirror to add some red, bronze, and blue to her face of black.

Charlie was back on Sunset, heading west in the Taurus that Lew had left him. He had parked his Corolla back at Lew's lot. Looking at the dash, he saw that the time was just past 3:00 a.m.—right on schedule. The way he figured, this was the time of night that the cops had already bagged their quota of bar-closing drunk drivers. Still, he had to be careful. It was too early for the larks of the world to be out, and Charlie knew any drivers on the road at this time may draw the police scrutiny.

A spell of Sunset Boulevard hypnosis took over. And Charlie found himself thinking about something that had been nagging at him for months—*What made me possible?*

Bixie backed away from the wall mirror, hoping her outfit would fit the specifics of what the client was after. A few nights back, Zep had told her what the man wanted—*a sixties go-go girl.* When she asked him what a go-go girl was, he answered back with, *how would I know…fucking google it.*

Zep never used to snap at her and only in the last few years had taken to beating her. But times had changed since she was the most-requested girl in his stable. That was nearly ten years ago. Back then, Bixie was a luscious 18-year-old—*you're my top bitch*, Zep would tell her. He would give her books to read, telling her she should be proud to work for a man that is well read and speaks good English. After her looks began to fade, he no longer gave her books. Instead, he gave her beatings for some meaningless offense or perceived slight.

She smiled at her rather simple outfit—a printed fringed dress and knee-high boots. It was probably not an exact replica of a sixties go-go girl, but it was close enough. Unless they were gay, men didn't know fashion styles from a hole in the wall. At least her three-inch high afro would fit the sixties theme.

Overall, Bixie was happy with her getup. She thought it would spice things up enough to ensure her client might request her by name, next time.

Her smile disappeared with a sigh as she caught a glimpse of her top dresser drawer, chipped and sagging from some broken hinge. Casting her eyes down, she realized after a few seconds she'd lost track of where she'd gotten it. Must have been on one of her many runs to Goodwill. But it could have been a hand-me-down from any number of people that had come in and gone quickly out of her life the last several years.

Bixie turned away from the mirror and vowed to somehow get a better place complete with new furnishings. Just before leaving her bedroom, she spotted her laptop complete with a dent on its top. The machine saddened her. It reminded her that she'd never formed a lasting romantic relationship with anyone. The laptop was the only vessel that she was ever able to pour out all her life stories, fears, and hopes.

A right turn on Fairfax interrupted Charlie's reverie and put him mentally back into job mode. The question—*What made me possible?*—would have to wait.

Passing Hollywood Boulevard, he came up a hill and stopped at a stop sign. Charlie turned left onto Hillside Avenue, and then made a quick right to get back onto another strip of Fairfax. He snaked around the street for a quarter of a block before steering the car to the left side of the street and between houses that were separated by huge lawns. Just before hitting the curb with the driver's side of his car, he stopped. He grabbed one of the dropcams he had brought. Opening his car door, he reached out a few inches and placed the dropcam rigged with a mobile hotspot and battery pack against the curb with its lens facing the street. He then gently closed his door and continued up the road.

Quickly coming to Fareholm Drive, he made a right. After a few seconds, he pulled over to a curb on his left. There, he deposited a second dropcam, where no houses were close by, and then continued up the street.

Less than a half minute later, Charlie came to a narrow private road to his left and stopped just after passing it. He backed into the private road and parked after his car cleared Fareholm.

Flipping off the headlights, he got out of the car with the engine idling. He left his door ajar, not wanting to create unnecessary noise.

Charlie had no fear that the open door would trigger his interior light. Nor did he have to worry about any pinging or dinging alarm sounds that go off from his open door or unbuckled seat belt. For Charlie knew Lew Holt never failed to prep the cars, all according to his particular needs, he sold to him.

Leaving the idling Taurus behind, Charlie walked the short distance to the point where he entered the private road off Fareholm. Looking around at the nearest homes, all featuring partially lit pieces of greenery, he watched. He saw no new lights go on and heard no odd sounds.

Charlie nodded to himself while his eyes were still moving in all directions. He turned back around.

With the real work about to begin, Charlie walked back to his idling car. He slipped inside, not fully shutting the door, and donned a pair of black latex gloves and a ski mask. Charlie adjusted its slits for his eyes and mouth. Save for the slits, a fuzzy spool of blackness was now hiding his short-cropped graying-black hair, crooked nose, and chiseled face.

When utilizing any items of disguise for a hit job, Charlie would put off wearing them until the last possible moment. Charlie knew that it was risky wearing them while driving or otherwise. Gloves and a ski mask would be difficult to explain to any police or security personnel.

Besides the gloves and mask, the only other clothing item meant to camouflage Charlie's actual physical features were the shoes he was wearing. They were a half-size larger than he normally wore. He'd put them on before leaving his home tonight.

Leaving his driver's side door still ajar, Charlie shifted the car back into reverse. He proceeded to cautiously continue reversing his car up the road that was barely wide enough for two cars.

It was 3:30 a.m. when Bixie pulled her faded-black Mazda Protege onto Fairfax, driving away from her faded pea-soup green apartment complex. Everything in Bixie's life was faded or fading.

At the moment, she herself wanted to fade into a deep sleep. She was tired but she had a job to perform. And she let out a moan as she thought about the task that awaited her. Sleep would have to wait a couple of hours. If the man was chatty, bedtime could be several hours away for her. Hopefully, given the odd hour he requested, he was just after a quick pick-me-up to get his day started before hurrying off to the office.

Tonight's trick, Bixie figured, was probably in his late 60s given his go-go girl request. If he needed the help of a little blue pill, hopefully he'd already taken it. She was in no mood to wait an extra hour for it to kick in.

Despite her impatient mood, she was going to put on a show for her client tonight. To that end, she paid a visit to Amoeba Music on Sunset earlier in the day and bought a greatest hits CD of a sixties group. It was a group she'd never heard of before, Zep had mentioned a song of theirs when discussing tonight's trick with her.

The CD had on it a song that the client had referred to when discussing with Zep, his needs for tonight. Bixie was going to surprise the client and strip to the song. It would be a special warm-up act. She would soon follow it with her crown jewel offering. The offering that required the removal of her dentures. She was determined to be requested back for at least one encore.

Passing under the Santa Monica Freeway, she slipped the CD into its player. She wanted to familiarize herself with the song. Cramming for a final was nothing new to Bixie. She quickly heard a line in the song that was a possible clue for why the trick had requested a black woman for tonight. Maybe he'd become tired of having the same flavor of women in bed. Well, after tonight, she'd make him want more of her chocolate.

CHAPTER 3

After backing his car up the private road about thirty yards, Charlie stopped when he came to a curve with an incline. Shutting off his engine, he looked at the two iPhones lying on his passenger seat. The phone screens offered him live feeds from the two dropcams he'd placed on the curbs. He saw from the screens that no cars were moving on Fairfax or Fareholm. Gently, he pushed the already-open car door out enough for him to exit the Taurus. He stepped out and left the door where it was positioned.

Standing next to the car door, he wet his lips while listening for noises other than nature sounds. None. Again he surveyed his surroundings. He liked that his car was between two small hills that created a canyon of sorts with the no houses in sight.

Getting back into the car, Charlie reached into the backseat. From a hidden compartment, he pulled out a rifle and an accompanying attachment. He quickly married the gun to its custom-made suppressor.

Charlie then reached back into the secret compartment, grabbing a gun sling. After clipping it on, he carefully eyed and handled the gun for some seconds. Satisfied, he slung its strap over his head.

The last item he brought out from the compartment was a bipod for the rifle. He laid the accessory on his lap. He reached into the glove compartment and pulled out a small case that held a pair of binoculars. As he hooked the case to his belt, he looked over at the two iPhones one last time. The phones screens showed the roads all clear. He hated to leave them behind in his journey outside the car. But he did not want to carry the phones with him since they emitted light which, no matter how remote a chance, might catch someone's attention.

Holding the bipod in one hand he exited the car, still leaving the car door ajar. He took one last look around his immediate area. Satisfied, he proceeded to walk up the now-uphill road and rounded the curve.

In less than a minute, slightly bent over and breathing heavier than he expected, Charlie came out of the curve but stopped as a side view of a lone three-story house came into view. It was straight ahead at the end of the road. Parts of the house and some pieces of its immediate surroundings were lit up by a multitude of lights shooting off from it. From forty-five yards out, the multilevel structure looked like a glowing flying saucer that had just landed. This was the house he was about to pay trouble to.

Staring at the house while catching his breath, he carefully spread the legs of the bipod out. He leaned it against the side of one of his legs. Next, he fumbled with the case attached to his belt. Soon he was holding the binocs to his eyes.

After focusing the lenses, he scanned the house and quickly landed his sights on his first target of the night—a dog. The German Shepherd was eyeing him from the vantage point of a top floor balcony but kept quiet. Charlie watched the dog lick its nose once while crouching down as if it were about to jump off the balcony and come after him. The stare down sent a chill up Charlie's spine. Animals were unpredictable foes.

But Charlie's main target tonight was not an animal. Rather a human. Over the years, Charlie counted his blessings that he was able to earn a lot of money capitalizing on the predictability of the human criminals he took out.

Tonight, that human criminal was the dog's master and the house's owner. His name was Alejandro Vargas.

Charlie had only been given a two-week notice on this assignment. And he was only able to familiarize himself with the house's layout three nights ago. This, after his cartel employer tipped him off that Vargas would be dinning out that particular night with a banking executive.

Scouting Vargas's house out that one night, Charlie was able to determine the German Shepard was trained to guard the home without barking. He also learned the dog had its limits as to how close one could get to the house before his well-disciplined training allowed him to sound off, or worse, to protect his master's domain. Charlie found the dog's limit to be about twenty-five yards. Tonight, he was going to breach the shepherd's barking perimeter. And that had created a problem.

Charlie moved the binocs away from his face. But his eyes remained on the dog, as it blurred in his vision. Despite being intimidated by the creature, he felt some sorrow for what was about to happen to the poor thing. Those were Charlie's thoughts as he continued to stare down the dog from afar while feeling around with his hands to put the binocs back in their case.

Next, Charlie grabbed the bipod and laid his six-foot frame down on the road. Facing the house upward at a 45-degree angle, he set the gun, with its strap still loose around his neck, on the bipod. He slivered his snake-thin frame into a comfortable shooting position while trying to ignore the bothersome pebbles sticking into his elbows.

Finally, using his right eye he looked through the scope of his favorite work tool—a Remington Model 700 ADL. After focusing the scope and using the benefit of the outside lights surrounding the house, he was able to look into the eyes of a dog that had no idea that he was breathing his last few breaths. The shepherd was peering through a foot-high space between wooden fence railings that wrapped around the outer part of the balcony. The dog was facing out from the side of the balcony with only air and hills behind it.

Charlie pulled the trigger. The dog dropped as silently as the gun's muffled sound.

Though long past savoring a successful hit, with the dropping of the dog, Charlie felt an emotion. It was not the thrill of joy. No. He felt for the shepherd. The animal was an innocent concern who had the bad luck of having a master who had gotten in the crosshairs of a drug cartel. The dog was just doing his job—protecting his master—and now he was another collateral damage victim of the drug trade.

Charlie had one more kill to make tonight. And this next one wouldn't be causing him any mental residue of guilt.

For Charlie, bumping off illicit drug-related money launderers was especially easy on his conscience. While he rarely felt sympathy for the drug dealers he'd hit over the years, he sometimes experienced some passing regret. But he never experienced any such regret when knocking off the men who funneled the money through a maze of financial filters.

The launderers, Charlie had found, had an air of sophistication about them whenever he mixed with them. They were bastards who thought of themselves as socially above the drug cartel leaders they provided financial services to. Services they traded for a slice of the illicit-drug profits their cartel clients were making.

The drug dealers chose their profession. And in general, especially below the top echelon, were down to earth. These players didn't carry an air of importance about themselves whenever Charlie had interacted with them.

But the money launderers always seemed to hold their noses up when Charlie had met them for business purposes. It irked him that these money cleaners thought of themselves as legitimate business professionals. Charlie respected the rest of the drug dealing crowd who at least had the honesty to admit they were criminals, plain and simple. On the other hand, the launderers, who loved pocketing their slice of the drug profits, never thought of themselves as criminals. Rather, just providing banking services.

Lifting his head up from the scope of the gun, Charlie eyed the home. He was watching for any possible reaction to his dropping of the dog. No additional inside lights came on. And he heard nothing. Not trusting his naked eyes, he brought out the binocs and resumed his gaze at the expensive house. While his eyes were on the house, his thoughts turned to the money launderer inside it.

Charlie had met Alejandro Vargas once. They'd had a meeting some weeks ago. An associate had recommended him to Charlie when he needed to move some large sums of money overseas.

During their meeting, Charlie had realized he never wanted to do business with the mustached and ever-smiling Vargas again. He found the thin Latin man repulsively cocky and dangerously lacking in the professional discretion that money men usually display. The dapperly dressed Vargas had managed to talk non-stop about himself and his thriving business. In less than an hour, Charlie had learned a lot about the money washer.

Vargas was born and raised in Costa Rica. He had wealthy parents. For college, his parents sent him to Harvard where he earned an MBA.

While at the University, he made connections that landed him a job in international banking in Los Angeles. Five years later, Vargas had gained the ranking of a vice president.

But Vargas's privileged upbringing had made even his above-average income seem like peanuts. The only thing worse than working for a few hundred thousand dollars a year would be to return home and work for his father. To Vargas, that was an unacceptable humiliation. Vargas wanted to become rich without the use of his family's money.

At age 45, Vargas had grown restless in his banking duties. He would quit. And using his international banking expertise, he launched a financial services company that handled a multitude of international banking transactions.

But Vargas found starting a business to be challenging. His firm struggled for several years. That is, until he began accepting clients with suspect backgrounds and shady business ties. Now, in his early 50s, he'd become the go-to man for Mexican cartels that'd begun to favor his unique trade-based money-laundering schemes.

Mexican cartels had a never-ending need to change their ill-gotten dollars into pesos. Vargas had a creative way to perform the currency exchange. He'd use the US drug profits to buy fruits and vegetables in the states. The goods would be shipped to one of the many food warehouses inside Mexico that he owned. The perishables would quickly be sold off to various Mexican companies which would pay Vargas in pesos, from which he would take his cut. And pass the remainder onto his cartel clients.

This scheme had quickly made Vargas wealthy in his own right. It also had recently landed him on the death list of his largest drug cartel client.

The issue that this large cartel client had with Vargas was simple—he'd become greedy. According to the man that hired Charlie to kill

Vargas, the money launderer was *eating more fruits and vegetables than was good for his health*. Vargas was apparently not satisfied with his standard ten percent cut.

Charlie had seen Vargas's game play out many times before. The Ivy-League educated suit servicing street-educated drug lords and thinking they could outsmart them. Vargas thought nobody would notice if he took a little more than his share of the profits here and there.

But someone had noticed.

And that *someone* made a phone call to Charlie and told him that Vargas had to go. Alejandro Vargas was insulting this cartel leader's trust and authority.

The money man's ending was to be a reminder to other launderers that taking any more than their agreed upon share of profits would get them a death sentence.

Bixie continued breezing along Fairfax Avenue, careful not to exceed the speed limit. In the wee hours of the morning, she had learned that without much traffic to guide you it was easy to exceed its flow and draw the attention of a police cruiser.

Getting a traffic ticket was one thing. But explaining where she was headed would be a problem, especially giving her outfit. She'd be tagged as a hooker before she could flash him a smile and some leg.

Passing Wilshire Boulevard, she turned down the CD player and reached for her phone. It was time to check in with the boss one last time before doing the job. Scrolling down her recent contacts, while stealing glances back up at the road ahead, she found Zep's name. After pressing her thumb on his name, Bixie put the phone on speaker.

Zep's line kept ringing and ringing. That was another thing that Bixie had noticed in the last year or two. Zep didn't communicate with her much anymore beyond what was necessary. Her aging body was costing her Zep's attention in a multitude of ways.

Finally, Zep picked up.

"Yes?"

She felt a rush of self-pity. Her employer had lately taken to skipping her name when he answered her calls.

"Zep, I just wanted to let you know that I'm about ten or so minutes from the man's house."

"Tell me his name."

Zep was big on his girls memorizing the first names, real or a given preferred alias, of the tricks they visited. This was one of his policies. He had once explained to Bixie that it makes the trick feel like a low life if his gal don't know his name. It also, Zep would stress, improved tips when a girl yells out the name of her man of the hour when she feigns a climax.

Tonight, like always, Bixie had memorized the name. She'd no clue or concern that tonight's trick had preferred to be called by his actual name.

When Bixie didn't answer quick enough, Zep repeated his question.

"Tell me his *fucking* name."

Bixie smiled sadly as she answered.

"Alejandro."

CHAPTER 4

Still on the ground, Charlie dropped the binocs away from his face. He closed his eyes and pinched them with his right thumb and index finger for a few seconds. Moving his head around, he felt the stiffness in his neck ease as he reset his mind back on the job of killing Vargas.

He brought the binocs back up to his eyes.

Looking through the binocs at Vargas's home again, Charlie saw that all the darkened windows he could see from his position remained as dark as they were before he'd finished off the dog. A couple of small inside lights were on but they had been on since he originally viewed the house tonight. Those lights appeared to be randomly lit for security reasons.

As he continued panning the house, he spotted a few CCTV cameras peering out from it. But they didn't concern him. A home alarm system was not going to trip him up tonight.

One of Charlie's discrete business contacts was a barrel-chested Armenian named Artie Abalian who he got hooked up with through a close friend. As an independent contractor, Abalian was skilled in the crafts of both locks and security alarms. The man did work for all of the major alarm security companies.

For a few thousand dollars, Abalian would provide Charlie information on any electronic security systems that a particular building may or may not have actively installed.

Yesterday, Charlie had found out from Abalian that the cameras, mounted at various spots, on Vargas's house and property were not to be of any concern. The cameras were not activated. They were there only for show.

Charlie had guessed this was going to be the case. He knew people in the drug trade all thought alike. The last thing Vargas would've wanted was any active alarm system tied to any security company or, worse, the local police. Vargas did not want to deal with the inevitable false alarms that home security systems set off.

The money man was more afraid of any police attention brought to his home by a false alarm than he was with protecting himself from an intruder. Besides, thieves were not what Vargas ever feared. Prowlers could be expected to occasionally try their luck at burgling a rich man's mansion.

Vargas feared his cartel contacts. One never knew what the cartels he skimmed profits from would do to him if they caught him in the act. And the money cleaner was smart enough to know that if any drug-related associates wanted him dead, no alarm system in the world was going to prevent it. So he'd passed on activating his home alarm system.

The only alarm system Vargas had in place was a dog. And Charlie had deactivated it.

With his elbows starting to feel the strain from him leaning on them from his grounded position, Charlie got to his knees. He quietly collapsed the bipod, laying it on the ground before standing up. He was done needing the instrument for the night.

With the rifle hanging on his side by its strap, he gently brushed himself off. Gazing straight ahead at Vargas's house, he took a deep breath and continued up the narrow road leading to it.

As he walked, Charlie tried to go over the plan in his head. But other thoughts were crowding his mind. Taking steps toward the house was like walking down a long hallway that would end with an execution—his own. He'd hoped that tonight's gig would shake the foreign feelings he'd been overcome with in the last several months. But he knew these feelings were here to stay at least until they were somehow dealt with.

Charlie sensed that dealing with these new intrusive thoughts would require more than just ending his profession of killing people. He'd have to find himself, and he realized that the first step in doing so was to answer the question that had been troubling him.

As he came within twenty yards of the house, Charlie once again forced himself back to his immediate issue—killing Vargas. He stepped left off the private road some ten feet and was now facing the middle of the side of the house. Looking to his left and up two stories he froze, as he spotted the bloody head of the dead dog. The animal was facing out toward his direction as if still on active guard duty. Charlie looked away and hoped his mind would soon forget the image.

He stilled himself and refocused on the job ahead of him.

Charlie looked to his right. Twenty-five feet away, he saw a piece of what he knew to be an expansive concrete driveway which the front of the home, hidden from his view, faced. He turned to his right and crept along. He went back over the road and came to a hill. He hiked twenty feet up the hill. He then turned around in a crouched position.

Facing the front of Vargas's home, Charlie caught his breath as quietly as he could. This, while he again looked for any new lights or movements inside the house. He knew that he'd be exposed to some outside lights, here and there. It was a risk that he'd anticipated, given his own scouting of the house.

Seeing nothing from inside giving him pause, Charlie continued his hike until he was positioned directly level with the second-floor master bedroom he was facing. The bedroom was on the far left corner of the house. This was the room where he knew Vargas was sleeping.

Using what moonlight was available, Charlie spotted the tiny slice of level ground he had found on his scouting trip, three nights back. It was a few feet away. He moved to it and crouched down, letting the rifle rest across his thighs.

Despite the outside house lights blinding him a bit, he nodded approvingly to himself as he studied the window of the master bedroom from thirty yards out. Charlie could see past enough of the window reflection to see that the curtains were drawn back. This was no surprise to him. Vargas had paid good money to wake up to a view of hills, rocks and the occasional small wildlife.

Charlie felt a sensation of goose pimples come over him as a cool breeze developed and sent a chill over his perspiring body. With all the clothing he had on, he was glad it was spring instead of summer as he reached into a pant pocket and pulled out a burner phone with string-wire headphones attached to it. He'd found the string-wire set easy to handle and difficult to lose, especially with gloved hands. Charlie had the brightness of the phone's screen set on a low dim level so it would be difficult to detect in the dark when in use.

After Charlie plugged the headphones into his ears, he placed the phone on the ground to his right. The phone was loaded with a single contact. He then lifted the rifle, pointing it toward the master bedroom window. And after focusing its scope to his liking, he let go a breath.

The scope of the gun had taken Charlie's sight through the window and onto the bed where he knew Vargas to be sleeping. He quickly spotted the dark outline of Vargas's body under covers. The headboard of the bed told Charlie that Vargas's feet were facing him.

Charlie was happy with his shooting position. And though he could start firing at Vargas now, he decided to stick to his plan. It would insure, beyond a doubt, that not only it was Vargas he was hitting but also offer him better odds of securing an opening kill shot to the head.

It was time to call and kill.

Charlie took a breath and looked around one more time to stretch his neck. He was thankful that Vargas had no close neighbors. He repositioned his right eye again on the scope. He now had his sights back on Vargas's bed. In a low voice, he broke the night air to instruct his phone to "call Vargas."

In a few seconds he began to hear intermittent rings in his ears. Like a cliché, Charlie saw the next few seconds in slow motion.

As the ringing continued in Charlie's ears, the covers on Vargas's bed began to show motion. With the crosshairs of the scope on the moving covers, Charlie watched. He saw an arm come out from under the covers. The arm reached out to a nightstand. From the nightstand, the person grabbed a now-glowing cell phone.

Finally, Charlie could see a man sit up in the bed and put the phone to his ear.

Charlie didn't notice the small smile he himself grew which was only from unconscious professional pride. His plan of using the target's phone to light up his head had worked.

But Charlie would still make sure that this obvious male was Vargas, saving him the trouble of going into the house to verify his kill. So he waited a split second longer. He heard the ringing in his ear replaced by the sound of someone clearing his throat.

"Bixie?" A groggy voice said in Charlie's ear.

This greeting threw Charlie off for a split second, but he quickly fell back on his plan.

Charlie tightened his grip on the rifle and said, "Alejandro?"

"Yes?"

With ID confirmed, Charlie fired at the well-lit head of Vargas. Instantly, Charlie's ears were filled with the sounds of Vargas's phone hitting the bed before falling onto the bedroom floor. At the same time, Charlie watched, through the gun scope, the light emanating from Vargas's glowing phone bounce around the walls of the room before settling and casting a faint, eerie glow in the room.

Keeping his sights still on Vargas's bedroom, he felt around and found his cell phone. He looked down at it just long enough to end the call to Vargas's phone. He quickly resumed scanning Vargas's bedroom through the gun's scope but found no movements.

Satisfied, Charlie finally allowed himself to lower the rifle. He continued to watch the faintly lit bedroom with his naked eyes as the glow of Vargas's phone screen suddenly faded out. Vargas's bedroom was dark once again.

With the kill finished, Charlie picked up his phone. There was no need to double check the kill. He'd killed Vargas with one hit.

Standing up, he took off the headset. He put them and the phone back into his pocket.

Given that he never touched the phone, Charlie would've preferred to have tossed it. But in these post-O.J. days, he had to be overly cautious since he couldn't possibly keep up with all that was inside LAPD's bag of CSI tricks. He'd take the phone with him to dispose of it later.

He began walking back toward the car, leaving a lot of cash and valuables behind in the home that he could've grabbed in minutes. Charlie knew other hired killers in the biz that routinely took from their victims, but he couldn't stomach such a thing. While he may not have respected a guy like Alejandro Vargas, he had an instinctual respect for the dead. He was no vulture, preying on them. Killing was his profession, and he considered stealing beneath him.

Bixie began to move her shoulders with the beat of a song while driving. The song that her soon-to-be client apparently liked was growing her. This Alejandro trick had good musical taste, Bixie told herself. She'd have no problem putting on a sexy show for the man while it played aloud.

But as she was driving past Hollywood Boulevard, her eyes looked up at the street name. Her car slowed a bit. But she didn't notice. And her own movements slowed too, as the song playing faded from her immediate attention.

Bixie's thoughts had begun to drift back in time. Had it really been over ten years since she first walked along the famed boulevard? She wondered.

She was 17 years old when she ran away from home. Bixie had left Wisconsin to escape the abuse of Skip Riggers. Her stepfather had started with pushes, then slaps. Eventually, Skip would simply slug her for some imagined disobedience.

From Wisconsin, Bixie had landed in Hollywood seeking a movie career. But Hollywood didn't offer the pretty, nobody girl fame and fortune. Instead, it handed her broken dreams and an empty purse.

After two short weeks in cheap motels, the money she'd lifted from her stepfather's stash of cash had run out. Bixie remembered walking on a cold and windy Hollywood Boulevard that first night without a bed to sleep in. She had nowhere to go when a car pulled alongside her. The passenger window came down. And a fat slob of a man wearing a white dress shirt with a loosened tie yelled out to her.

Three hours later she was closing the door of a warm hotel room after saying goodbye to the now-smiling fat man. The man had christened her as a street walker.

Bixie wondered what might have become of her if that slob had never pulled over. Maybe she'd have a nice home by now. A sadness came over her as she continued her reverie of the last decade.

Turning left onto Hillside Avenue, Bixie had a revelation that added to her sadness.

After she had run away to Hollywood, neither her mother nor her stepfather had ever tried to find her. All this time, she had thought of herself as a most-wanted runaway who had eluded capture. She now realized that was a fantasy. A fantasy drawn up from inside her mind to compensate for the self-doubts that had swirled around her subconscious all these years.

What a fool she'd been. As she drove, she shook her head at these thoughts.

As Bixie turned right, back onto Fairfax, she pushed the past out of mind and refocused on the job ahead of her tonight—pleasing Alejandro. With that mental shift, Bixie began to, once again, hear the CD and with it her mood improved.

With the touch of a finger, she brought her driver's side window down to give herself a kick of fresh air. The mix of the cool spring air and the now oncoming high of the Vicodin was hitting her.

Bixie was more than ready to meet her client.

CHAPTER 5

Charlie picked up the bipod he'd earlier left on the ground and continued walking. As he rounded the curve in the road, he felt a small burden lift from him. The dead dog was no longer facing his back.

But just before reaching his car, a familiar emotion came over him. He'd hoped the bad cloud would have waited till later to come back over him, but there it was again. The cloud was in the form of a thought that he'd pushed out of his mind earlier tonight—*What made me possible?*

Now at his car door, he knew there was no denying that he was done with his current life. Something was happening to him. And, as he removed his head cap, he resolved to find out what it was.

Charlie, still with the rifle and its strap around his neck, awkwardly slipped into the driver seat. He quickly put the bipod back in the hidden, backseat compartment. Twisting back around, movement on one of the iPhones on the passenger seat caught his attention. It was the phone connected to the first dropcam Charlie had placed on two streets on his way up to Vargas's place. He'd thought he saw something on its screen flash by.

He shot a look at the other iPhone that was tied to the dropcam he'd placed further up towards Vargas's house. It was located on Fareholm.

Charlie was hoping he wouldn't see any lights of an oncoming car, but he soon did.

A car was moving up Fareholm. He knew it was more than a safe bet the car would continue uphill, passing by the private road he was on and continuing toward one of the multitudes of homes dotting this section of Hollywood Hills. And normally something like this wouldn't trouble the professional killer.

But Charlie felt something in his gut that told him there may be trouble. At this wee hour of the morning, drivers should be heading out of these hills on their way to work. The car on his dropcam was going up towards a home in these hills.

With his car facing Fareholm, he'd be able to watch the car pass by. But he didn't want to waste even a few seconds leaving Vargas's property.

Charlie shrugged off what he thought was his own paranoia coming on from his aging mind. Continuing to unload his gear, he put the binocs away. The incriminating burner phone he'd used to call Vargas, was placed back into the hidden compartment. Just as he turned back around while unsnapping the strap from the rifle, a blinding light hit him. It was coming directly over the hood of his car.

Charlie snapped the rifle strap back on.

He froze as he studied the light source coming at him. Biting down on his lower lip, he discerned the light was from a pair of car headlights. The headlights were less than twenty-five yards ahead. They were coming slowly, but directly toward his car.

Charlie's mind barely registered some musical sounds emanating from the approaching vehicle. *Fuck me…a setup.*

Setup or no setup, Charlie couldn't afford to wait to find the answer. He knew what he had to do. Life offered no second chances if you're killed.

Shortly after Bixie turned onto the private road, she saw reflective lights flickering off the front of a car parked ahead of her. She slowed as she wondered if there'd be room enough for her to maneuver around the pair of headlights facing her.

When her headlights hit upon some shadowy movements coming from inside the parked car she slowed down some more. Squinting, Bixie tried to see what was going on inside the opposing car. She was about to turn down the music when she saw a flash of light burst from near the front window of the car. At the same time, she felt a bee sting sensation hit her right shoulder.

Another flash and another bee sting. This second one Bixie felt on her left shoulder.

Bixie hadn't noticed that she was no longer hearing the song still blasting out from the CD player. Somehow, she knew this life was now over for her. She only had time for one final thought before the next and final bullet hit her forehead. Would her next home be a nice one, she wondered.

After firing the third round, while hanging halfway out of his seat, Charlie jumped out of his car. He kept the rifle pointed at the car that'd been coming up towards his own car.

The stranger's headlights were no longer facing him. The car had drifted slightly sideways and backwards, coming to stop against a steep grade of hillside. Charlie could see that it was making repeated attempts to move forward and back up the road, as its engine was obviously still in drive. Charlie also now clearly noted a pulsating music coming from within the car.

Standing still some yards away, he focused on the inside of the now bullet-ridden car for any signs of movement. None.

Cautiously, but hurriedly, Charlie walked toward the car, ever conscious that time was ticking away. The noise of his bullets shattering the stranger's windshield might have woken up someone in the area. Noise travels in the still of the night, especially with no homes, save for Vargas's, within fifty yards of where he was standing.

Arriving at the driver's side door of the stranger's car, Charlie looked through the open window. He saw the dead driver lying on her right side, across the front seat. *Fuck me, twice.*

In all his years of killing, Charlie had never killed a female. A wave of revulsion was now engulfing his insides. He was finding it difficult to assess the situation. His emotions and thoughts were not clear, since they were all new to him.

But Charlie had to act on the information his mind was trying to professionally process. Or else, he would be in the ultimate trouble.

What Charlie did mentally process was that the dead female was not part of any setup. No. Given her looks, her outfit, and remembering the "Bixie" greeting Vargas had answered his phone with just thirty minutes ago, he concluded she was simply a prostitute.

Another wave of thoughts flooded Charlie's mind.

A single homicide of a money man for drug cartels would be one thing. But a double homicide—with the added twist of one of them being a hooker—was a juicy and newsworthy story. Charlie knew the crime scene he'd just created would draw out the white, black, yellow, and all other skin-type beauties of the local news channels, complete with live-from-the-scene reports. This type of publicity would make solving the killings a top priority of the LAPD who otherwise would be focusing on the latest gang drive-by shootout and the inevitable bystander-caught-in-the-crossfire story.

But Charlie's thoughts changed once again. Back to the realization that he had bumped off a woman.

Waking up Charlie from his dark thoughts was the song that continued to blare out from the woman's car. He recognized the tune. Under any other circumstances he might have smiled while reminiscing about the decades-old memories the song invoked for him. He hadn't heard the Box Tops hit in years. The irony of the song's lyrics didn't escape him. For the profession of the young lady he'd just killed, was the subject of the song he was hearing.

The victim's car was still in drive and continuing its meager attempts to inch forward. But it needed more power to climb the steep road. This was no imagined McQueen or Bronson movie. No. Charlie was inside a horror flick of his own making, complete with a soundtrack blasting away.

After expending a split second to look around, Charlie slung the rifle to his backside. And went to work.

Grimacing, he stuck his gloved hand through the car window and over the blood-soaked woman and shut off the engine, along with the Box Tops. With the smell of blood and cheap perfume attacking him, he eased the key out of the ignition. The key was attached to a ring with just one other key on it. Spotting a purse, he placed the key ring in it and snatched it off the passenger seat.

Holding the purse, he reached into his pocket. He grabbed his phone, which he had stored in the opposite pocket he'd used for the burner phone he used up the hill for killing Vargas.

CHAPTER 6

Patrol Officer Jim Sweeney was within six miles of the 8000 block of Fareholm Drive when he received the dispatch. It was about some loud music in the area. The 30-year veteran was wearing a half smile of pleasure. There was a huge home in that area where he used to fuck the brains out of a rich, but bored, and much older housewife.

Sweeney shook his head as he slowly made a U-turn and headed north toward Sunset. Had ten years already gone by since he'd seen Carol? Too bad she and her sugar daddy had relocated to a mansion in South Miami. He had no doubt the sexy older broad had picked up in Miami where she'd left off in Los Angeles. And gotten herself another young fuck buddy.

The officer stopped before making a turn onto Sunset. And while he looked forward to driving by the house where he'd met Carol for their flings all the years ago, he would take his time. He knew from experience the noise complaint would turn out to be nothing more than partying teenagers who pulled over their car on a side street. And he wanted to give the teens a fair chance to split the scene before he arrived.

The last thing Officer Sweeney was in the mood to do just before his shift was over was to be spending an hour or more booking a couple of glassy-eyed kids.

As Charlie walked away from the dead woman and her car, he had her purse in one hand and his own phone in the other. With the rifle against his back, and his gloves now removed, he managed to speed dial a number. He heard a faint ringing sound as he was bringing the phone up to his ear.

By the seventh ring, Charlie was seated in his car and growing angrier with every ring. As he finished putting away the rifle, a voice answered the phone.

"Bennie Densmore."

Charlie had to purposely relax his jaw to be able to talk.

"You didn't see my name on the screen?" Charlie said while placing the purse on the passenger side floorboard and tossing a jacket over it.

He started the engine.

"Charlie, I wasn't looking at the screen when—"

"You were paid to be awake," Charlie said while his car began moving downhill toward Fareholm Drive. He thanked himself for taking the time to back up into the tiny private road earlier, saving him now-precious seconds.

"I'm awake."

Promising himself to deal with the little prick later, Charlie went to the business end of the call. "Was there a cop dispatched anywhere near Fairfax and Hollywood?"

"When?"

Charlie was about to answer but he slipped into a momentary daze as he began to steer around the dead woman's car. He didn't notice that he had slowed his car to a crawl. His stomach churned, as he maneuvered around the crookedly parked Mazda.

Bennie tried again.

"Charlie?"

Blowing out a breath after turning onto Fareholm, Charlie was glad to no longer be looking back at his victim's Mazda in his rearview mirror. But by then, Bennie's voice had brought him back, full swing, to the mess he was in. Charlie tried to focus at the business at hand. He restated his question as he pulled over and got out of the car, the phone pressed against his right ear.

"Just tell me, Bennie, if any cops are heading anywhere near Fairfax and Hollywood," he said in a low voice while walking toward one of his dropcams.

With his right ear filled with the sounds of Bennie speed typing, Charlie reached down to retrieve the dropcam he placed on Fareholm earlier. When he touched it with his free hand a thought hit him—he'd planted the two dropcams tonight without gloves on.

Charlie had been debating picking up the other dropcam he'd laid down on Fairfax. But now he *had* to get it.

As he got back in the car, the typing sounds he was hearing come out of the phone were replaced by Bennie's voice.

"There was a cruiser dispatched to the 8000 block of Fareholm Drive to check out a noise complaint."

Charlie swallowed hard. Bennie continued.

"And, looking at the map, I would assume the cop car will be passing through the intersection of Fairfax and Hollywood…unless it happens to be currently patrolling the area for some reason."

"When was it dispatched?" Charlie said while driving away from the curb.

"Eight minutes ago."

"Where is the cruiser?"

A few seconds went by before Bennie's voice came back through the phone to reply.

"I don't have that information, Charlie."

Charlie could sense the pleasure Bennie took in stating that last piece of information. Someday the little pig would cross the wrong guy. Maybe that guy would be himself. But Charlie tossed those thoughts aside. Planning revenge on the hacker was far from a priority at the moment.

After ending the call, he put the phone away where its screen could not light up the car should someone call. Charlie then began to head towards Fairfax and the first dropcam he'd planted earlier. But his car moved barely twenty yards when his grip on the steering wheel tightened. He was seeing a glimpse of headlight beams originating just beyond the next curve in the road ahead of him. *Fuck.*

He pulled over in front of a house and cut the engine. His worst fears were confirmed as he saw the first half of a police cruiser twisting around the curve. Ducking down, he had two worries—the cop and the occupants of the home he'd just parked in front of.

Coming to a halt in front of the multi-storied Spanish-style mansion on Fareholm, Officer Sweeney looked straight out his passenger window. He whistled softly while staring at the front door. Carol had once answered his knock wearing nothing.

Turning his head, he looked over at a Taurus parked out front. Blowing out a snort from his nose, he remembered Carol had always parked her vintage sports car in that same spot, rather than keeping it in the garage. He laughed at the memory of how the sexy, older woman once explained that fancy cars are meant to be seen, not hidden. Yeah, she had an ego to feed not only with young bodies but with expensive toys.

CHAPTER 7

Charlie had been in plenty of precarious situations before, during his criminal history, but he couldn't think of a worse one than the present. Having killed two people within the last 45 minutes, he now found himself within feet of an idling cop car.

His mind was racing. He wondered if the Taurus he was hiding in fit into the Hollywood Hills neighborhood street where he was parked. Heck, he tried to remember if any other cars were parked along Fareholm or nearby streets. He couldn't remember. For all he figured, his Taurus could indeed be the lone car parked on the street. Worse still, he may even be parked illegally.

A sudden buzzing sound made Charlie jerk so violently he worried that it noticeably shook the car. Quickly realizing the buzzing was his phone vibrating from inside the glove compartment, where he'd half remembered placing it. He'd meant to set the phone to silent mode, but he must have selected the vibrate mode instead.

Looking at the buzzing glove compartment, Charlie knew who was calling. It was a man that went only by a single name—Laredo.

Charlie knew Laredo was getting more concerned and, no doubt, growing angrier with every ring he was hearing on his end. But Laredo would have to wait. And that, Charlie had learned years ago, was something the cartel enforcer didn't like doing.

Mercifully the buzzing finally stopped, and sound of the idling cruiser returned to Charlie's ears without interruption. He wondered what the officer was doing. Had the cop somehow spotted his headlights before he'd cut the engine? If so, were back up units now headed up here?

Forcing himself to take a breath, Charlie carefully reached under his seat for the Glock he'd placed there before leaving Lew's lot. The gun was to be both a backup piece for tonight's work, in case the rifle malfunctioned, or for such emergencies as he'd now found himself in.

Contemplating shooting a cop was crazy, he knew, but Charlie could think of no other way out, should the officer approach his car.

Feeling the plastic grip of the Glock, he brought it out from under the seat while listening for any sounds indicating the cop was leaving his cruiser.

Looking away from the Taurus, Officer Sweeney focused straight ahead and hit the gas pedal. Hopefully, the loud music-playing troublemakers had already split the scene. Lord knows he'd given them plenty of time to do so. Soon, his shift would be over.

As he heard the cruiser drive by him and continue up Fareholm, Charlie took a deep breath and then let it go. But he gave himself no time to relax or contemplate just what the cop had been doing in front of the house in the first place. Instead, he started the car. He quickly made it to Fairfax and was finally at the location of the second and last dropcam he needed to retrieve. He put the car in park.

To avoid the risk of being seen by getting out of the car, he reached over and opened the passenger door. Sliding himself a few inches, he managed to grab the dropcam off the street.

After shutting the passenger door, he straightened up in his seat. With both dropcams now collected, it was time to simply get the hell out of the area. Seeing no car lights either in his rearview mirror or any in front of him, he hit the gas.

Within a couple of minutes, he was on Sunset heading back to Lew Holt Truck Rentals to return the Taurus. By noon tomorrow, the car will have been torn apart, never to be seen again.

Reaching into the glove compartment, Charlie grabbed his phone. He confirmed that the last missed call was from Laredo, the cartel man, who would be paying him for killing the money launderer Vargas.

Charlie was afraid of few people. Laredo was not only among such few, he topped the list. Laredo could not only order him killed on the slightest whim of disappointment in his job performance but do the same for the slightest perceived act of disrespect.

Drug cartel enforcers had only two sources of power— the piles of money they can pay for the jobs they offer you and the ability to have you killed. To Charlie, it seemed that Laredo leaned toward the threat of killing you, and in the worse way, to keep you both under his control and on top of your game.

Laredo would brag about how he had disposed of this guy or even that girl. The enforcer would describe details of how they were tortured, not only for information they may be holding, but for the sheer enjoyment of cartel members like himself.

As Charlie passed through his third green light along Sunset, he looked down at his phone and pressed a finger to it. He waited for Laredo's voice to answer. In less than a single ring his call was answered by the heavily accented Hispanic voice he'd increasingly grown to fear.

"What happened to my last call?" Laredo's voice blared out of Charlie's earpiece.

Knowing Laredo was not one for small talk, Charlie skipped answering his question. Instead, he would play out this phone call in straight business talk. And he reminded himself that his mission with respect to the target, Vargas, was a success. Never mind that there was a complication.

Before answering Laredo's question, he also reminded himself he was on a cell phone and had to take precautions about what he said. One never knew when Big Brother was listening.

Charlie steeled himself and answered his cartel employer.

"The man we both know will not be eating anymore fruits or vegetables," he said driving through another green light that he only noticed subconsciously.

A few seconds went by. That told Charlie his opening statement was not the right one to make. Finally, Laredo spoke by repeating his opening question.

"What happened to my last call?"

Charlie had no time for this but wouldn't let himself forget who was on the line.

"I couldn't get to the phone," Charlie said. "I still need to—"

"Why couldn't you get to the phone?"

Charlie looked left, out his driver's side window. Whizzing by him were dusty and empty sidewalks. These fronted a multitude of small shops. Many had only darkened windows and were obviously empty like himself, he thought. A red light interrupted his poetic moment.

As Charlie came to a stop, he answered Laredo.

"Laredo, I'm sorry but I must finish some details concerning my job tonight. Then I will give you a complete report."

A long pause went by. Charlie sensed a growing tension in the conversation.

"Do whatever you're doing to finish up with tonight. I'll be tied up till lunchtime, your time. So, call me at 12:30." Laredo could be heard clearing his throat before adding, "Charlie, if something went wrong tonight, I want to know."

CHAPTER 8

Officer Sweeney hit the gas and continued ahead on Fareholm, leaving his ex-fling's former home behind. The man's eyes were sparkling as he remembered Carol bobbing on him smack in the middle of her expansive backyard lawn. He recalled the tingle of the late-night cold dew on his bare knees that felt nice when combined with the sensation going on higher up where Carol was doing her work.

As he drove, Sweeney realized he was hard as a rock and felt a tension headache coming on. The memories of his former fuck buddy were overpowering him.

Just as Charlie began to try to regroup mentally from Laredo's call and the disastrous scene he'd left back at Vargas's property, he felt a jolt in the form of a recovered memory. The memory was a simple sentence he recalled hearing—*Then there's Bixie, she's black as coal with a real nice shape.*

The next shock came within a split second as he remembered who had said that sentence to him—the pimp Zep. During the past several years, Zep had described "Bixie" a few times while giving him some female menu options over the phone. But Charlie would always leave

40

the girl choice up to Zep. Charlie took a splinter of comfort in the fact Zep had never sent Bixie over to him.

But whatever comfort not having slept with the girl he'd just killed gave him, it was quickly overshadowed from the realization of a new problem. Specifically, how police investigators would soon learn that Zep was Bixie's pimp. They'd surely track him down. And that, Charlie thought, could lead them to his own doorstep for a few basic reasons.

Charlie knew police investigators would bring Zep in for questioning concerning tonight's murders, since he'd be quickly tied to both Bixie and Vargas.

Besides Zep himself, anybody on his pimping client list would be a suspect. Maybe a jealous trick of Bixie's didn't want to share her with Vargas or anybody. This was just one of a multitude of reasons investigators would go over Zep's client list with a fine-tooth comb, especially after not coming up with other leads.

And, while Charlie never was visited by Bixie, he was sure that the investigators would be looking at all of Zep's clients.

Zep's phone records too would be combed over by police. But Charlie thanked his lucky stars that he always used disposable phones, as a precaution, when booking hookers. Still, Charlie believed Zep would have his client list on a computer file. Charlie knew such a file would have some kind of client profile on him. He knew that pimps could be paranoid about who was paying for their ladies. And though Charlie never used his real name when calling Zep, maybe the pimp had followed him from the various hotels where he met Zep's girls. Perhaps to his home.

Charlie knew that if Zep had ever gone to the trouble of finding out where he lived, he could be expected to have recorded it wherever he stored his client list. The police would soon get to it, and Charlie's profile would stand out from the other johns on such a list. Investigators would quickly run into trouble when trying to reconcile Charlie's high-dollar lifestyle with his lack of any reported income. This would be just the first of many reasons why they'd zero in on he himself, Charlie thought.

All this led Charlie to a troubling conclusion—Zep had to be eliminated.

As this sank in, Charlie was no longer conscious of the road ahead of him. Somehow, he managed to pull over.

The neon lights of a cheap Sunset Boulevard motel shined into Charlie's car interior. He found himself staring at the center of his steering wheel. Knowing he had to take out another innocent person tonight brought back that nagging thought—*What made me possible?*

But again, Charlie had to push this thought out of his conscious mind for the moment. He had an immediate problem on his hands. But before he'd act to solve it, he wanted to quickly double check himself and confirm the problem was real.

Charlie reached down to the passenger floor and grabbed, from under his jacket, the purse he'd retrieved earlier from the dead woman's car. It cost him another round of cheap perfume hitting him. This produced a sigh of sadness. Charlie wasn't used to having troubling emotions taking up valuable time on killing jobs. Steeling his emotions, he continued with the tasks at hand.

He rifled through the contents of the purse and quickly found a driver license with a photo matching the woman he'd just killed. Holding her license, he read the name on it—*Bixie Brown*. He raised his eyebrows and bobbed his head a bit, surprised that the woman used her real name while doing her business in her illegal profession. But it was helpful in putting things together, quickly.

Charlie was sure now that he had interrupted a sexual pay-to-play meetup between Alejandro Vargas and Bixie.

Next, he pulled out Bixie's phone and perused it. The last call she placed was to someone named Zep.

Charlie now had no doubt that the Zep he procured women from was Bixie's pimp.

Problem confirmed.

As Officer Sweeney continued driving along Fareholm, another pornographic scene co-starring Carol was playing on his mental screen. He was reliving the time he stopped by Carol's, in the wee hours, just after his shift for a quick cup of coffee before heading home.

Carol had welcomed him in and left him in the living room. She then went to the kitchen to make his coffee. When she returned holding the hot cup, she was wearing only a cherry-red top hat and matching red high heels. He remembered wondering at the time, if she was teasing him by playing out some Randy Newman song-related fantasy.

Sweeney whistled aloud at the memory as he looked around for any parked cars along Fareholm that could have been the source of the noise complaint. Seeing none, he continued slowly moving. He decided to take a peek up the private road coming up on his left. Sweeney knew the road was a long driveway of sorts. And he knew it'd be a perfect place to park and party since it would be dark and would have only the traffic of one home. Soon, he was turning onto the road.

Now on the private road, he grew a smile as a new sexual memory of Carol popped in his mind. But out of some subconscious sense of caution, that came with years of police experience, he stopped his patrol car. Continuing to dream and smile about Carol, he pointed a side unity spotlight up the darkened tiny drive. The powerful beam of light exposed a Mazda.

Officer Sweeney's smile dropped. All thoughts of Carol vanished.

Sweeney would tell friends that, when on patrol, he often knew when something was wrong in a major way even before pulling someone over for an otherwise routine traffic violation. It was a sixth sense that developed over many years of patrolling.

Here, the illuminated Mazda had given him not only bad vibes but also a couple of physical clues that spelled trouble. The car was parked at an odd angle, barely leaving enough room on the thin pathway for another vehicle to pass by.

Continuing to eye the Mazda that was some 30 yards ahead of him, Sweeney also noticed there was something missing that he was expecting. Usually, he would have been seeing teenage heads bobbing up and down inside the car trying to sneak a peek at the source of light while desperately trying to put their clothes back on. But he found no movements going on inside the car.

Maneuvering his side spotlight, he scanned the immediate perimeter around the Mazda. Nobody and no things.

He proceeded to drive the short distance to the car while the bad vibes he was sensing grew.

CHAPTER 9

As a few cars passed by him on Sunset Boulevard, Charlie allowed himself a precious minute to think. He knew he had to kill Zep and get his client list. And he had to do both tasks before any police investigators tied Bixie to Zep, her pimp.

But how to get to Zep? And fast.

He couldn't call Zep and ask to meet him somewhere. The pimp would think that odd and suspect something is up. But maybe Bixie could lure him to a place.

Reopening Bixie's purse, Charlie quickly relocated her driver license. Looking at it for the second time wasn't any easier than the first. But he forced himself to suppress another wave of bad feelings about killing the prostitute. He had to concentrate.

Charlie saw that Bixie's license had been renewed just a few weeks back, giving him confidence that the address on it was current. But he'd double check it with Bennie if time allowed. In less than fifteen minutes, he could easily be at Bixie's place on Fairfax Avenue.

Next, he grabbed Bixie's phone and reviewed it for text messages. Bixie and Zep had texted each other frequently. That was good. But what was better was that Zep's messages to Bixie were filled with curse words aimed at her. Especially if she didn't respond to him as he wished, for any given request.

Learning all this, Charlie now believed his plan had a better chance of succeeding.

He started the car and headed to Bixie's Fairfax apartment. As he turned onto Fairfax, he speed-dialed a number on his own phone. A few seconds later, he heard Bennie's voice.

"Yes, Charlie."

Watching the road ahead of him and making sure not to exceed the speed limit, Charlie spoke.

"If I give you a cell phone number, can you find me that person's address?"

"Easy as pie, Charlie my buddy. Very expensive, but easy."

"I didn't ask how fucking expensive it was."

Charlie then read out Zep's number to him.

Parking directly behind the Mazda, Officer Sweeney kept a spotlight on it as he stepped out of his cruiser. He continued to look for any signs of movement inside it. None.

With his eyes remaining on the Mazda, he pulled his flashlight out and turned it on. Using his free hand, he unsnapped and gripped his holstered gun.

Looking sideways at the Mazda, he proceeded to walk toward it. When he reached the driver's side door, his flashlight lit up the passenger seat and caught a large portion of a wiry black head of hair. The afro was splattered with a glistening liquid. As Sweeney's flashlight and eyes moved downward in sync, he saw the side of a female's face. He didn't notice that he'd stopped moving the flashlight as his eyes continued downward, hitting the woman's colorful mess of clothing. Now it was his eyes that were no longer moving.

Sweeney managed to speak into the night air.

"Holy shit."

Charlie parked a half block away from Bixie's apartment. He grabbed Bixie's phone and read through several threads of her and Zep's text messages to each other. He noted that Bixie would abbreviate or misspell often. Keeping the thread open, he typed out a message to Zep— *Sorry, but jus coldn't go thru with tonight's gig. Explan tomorow.*

Despite his nightmare of a night, Charlie smiled as Bixie's phone rang out with its screen showing Zep as the caller. The ringing stopped after it went to voicemail but quickly resumed. It was Zep calling again.

The pimp was pissed, Charlie thought.

All was going according to Charlie's plan as the ringing finally stopped and was quickly replaced by a single sharp sound that signaled a received text message.

After reading the profanity-laden message that ended with *where the fuck are you*, Charlie replied back—*at hom in bed.*

With that, Charlie tossed the phone aside and went back into Bixie's purse, retrieving the key ring, holding two keys, he earlier placed inside. One key was for Bixie's car, so the other had to be her apartment key.

Next, Charlie reached under his seat and grabbed the Glock. He then reached back under the seat, pulling out a suppressor and attached it to the gun.

Whoever called the police earlier to report some loud car music near the 8000 block of Fareholm Drive was hearing more noise now than before coming from the area. The noise was all due to Officer Sweeney calling in a report of a dead woman being found in a Mazda.

Police vehicles of all types and a couple of ambulances were lined nearly end-on-end starting at the opening of the small private road that began at Fareholm. This chain of cars ended at Alejandro Vargas's garage door. There was only enough room along the road for cars to drive single file in either direction.

Police had identified the Mazda, via its license plate, as belonging to a Bixie Brown. She had a DMV address listing on Fairfax Avenue.

CHAPTER 10

Charlie had gotten into Bixie's apartment utilizing a key on Bixie's key ring.

He was now inside her only bedroom and Charlie was feeling a slight chill. He looked left and studied the window he'd opened just a few minutes ago. He eyed its flimsy screen. Nearly a quarter of the screen was out of its channel, with the rest of it barely in it. The screen was so full of soot that the lights coming off from the covered parking spaces, just outside, created a tiny white star for each of the many holes it had.

Hearing a sound, he turned his head sideways and away from the window. He heard the roar of a sports car come to an end. Looking back over at the window, he heard the slamming of a car door. Besides the open window, Charlie's hearing was aided by the apartment's decades old paper-thin walls.

Zep had arrived, Charlie assumed. Nobody in this dumpy apartment building would own a sports car. And Charlie was glad the pimp had parked it close by. He even thought he could hear the pounding of Zep's feet movements, outside, as they stepped on the cracked and crumbling pathways of the complex.

Sitting on the floor, his back propped up against a cold metal bed frame with a single and torn-at-the-corners mattress stacked on it, Charlie prepared to meet the pimp. And being inside the bedroom of a woman he'd just killed a short while ago, he welcomed the diversion of escaping back into the hyper focused mindset his work required.

Still, killing Zep was a tall order for him. His only justification for it was that he had no choice, given his ties to the pimp. His guilt was somewhat lessened from the fact that Zep was in the underworld. And that was a world where one *takes your chances*. This was Charlie's thinking when his phone vibrated. After glimpsing its screen, he answered in a low voice.

"Go ahead, Bennie."

"The cops just got dispatched to the girl's apartment you asked about. And, yes Charlie, that is her current address. Anything else, my friend?"

Tightening the grip he had on his phone, it took Charlie all the patience he could muster not to shout back at Bennie. The hacker always threw the likes of "buddy," "friend," or "partner" at him. It especially irked Charlie knowing that Bennie Densmore cared for nobody but himself. So it was no small feat that Charlie was able to hold down his voice to a whisper.

"How close are they?"

"Charlie, I can't tell…I'm not able to see that, just now."

Hearing the squeak of the apartment front door that he'd purposely left ajar, Charlie clicked off his phone and raised the Glock. He had it pointed at the open bedroom doorway. Then he heard a vaguely familiar sounding voice shout out a command.

"Bixie, it's daddy Zep, and he's angry," the voice said. "How dare you stand up your trick. I'm going to teach you a lesson. So, get your fucking ass out of bed. Or I'll fuck up your mouth so bad that no dentures will ever be able to fix it."

This kind of talking was music to Charlie's ears. It made him angry. As angry as the framed 45 RPM he had back at his home. Zep's trash talk also allowed him to definitively justify taking him out. Taking out the pimp would be Charlie's way of making a down payment on the debt he figured he now owed Bixie for mistakenly killing her.

From the only bedroom in the apartment, Charlie sat in wait. He heard pant legs rubbing together. Charlie had never met Zep. He'd only talked to him on the phone while ordering a girl from him. But, hearing the sounds he was hearing, it just seemed to him that Zep was a big guy.

Now Charlie was hearing drawers being yanked out of kitchen cabinets. Next, he heard what sounded like utensils spilling out onto linoleum flooring. Finally, heavy steps and heavy breathing sounds were coming down the short hall and towards where Charlie was holed up.

The voice in the hallway made another statement.

"Bixie, after I get done with you, you'll never be able to walk the streets again."

Next thing Charlie witnessed was a rotund black man stop in his tracks, just inside Bixie's bedroom doorway. A bright red bandana was wrapped around the man's balding head. There was jewelry on his neck, hands, and wrists.

The stranger was holding a carving knife in one hand. His wide-opened eyes were dancing between the barrel of the Glock pointed at his chest and Charlie's eyes staring up at him.

Charlie spoke.

"Drop the knife."

As the knife was falling, Charlie watched the man's eyes glance at Bixie's outdated and banged up cell phone on the floor. The man's first words to Charlie showed he'd put two and two together.

"So, you're the one that's been texting me."

Silence.

"Who are you?" The man said while catching his breath.

"Bixie's friend."

The man's eyes narrowed, seemingly searching to recall if he'd ever seen the man who was pointing a gun at him.

"Bixie doesn't have any friends," the big man said.

Charlie lifted his head before answering.

"I'm a new one."

Sensing that this wasn't the first time that this man had faced a gun, Charlie continued speaking after resting the elbow of his gun hand on his upright knee.

"You'd best answer my questions truthfully."

The man slowly nodded, waiting for his next instructions.

"Who are you?"

"Zep."

Charlie raised his eyebrows, and Zep took the hint, answering again.

"Zep Hill," he said.

Charlie continued eyeing the pimp while he spoke an instruction.

"Take out your wallet and put it on the floor," he said. "Put it a foot in front of you. If

you do it too fast, the wallet will be the last thing you ever grab."

Charlie was thinking ahead. He despised going through the pockets of dead men, avoiding it at all costs.

Zep did as he was told.

Ignoring the wallet that was now a few feet in front of him, Charlie next ordered Zep to take out his car keys and phone and lay them down.

After these tasks were completed, Charlie instructed the pimp to remain still.

Carefully reaching out and grabbing Zep's phone with his gloved left hand, he laid it down next to him. Charlie continued to point the gun at Zep, using his right hand. Charlie removed his left-hand glove with his teeth.

Focusing on the pimp's phone lying on the discolored carpet of the Bixie's room, while still concentrating on any possible movement from Zep, Charlie was able to open the iPhone. This nearly brought a smile to his face, realizing he wouldn't have to spend precious time extracting the password out of the pimp. And, just in case he had a question or two for him after checking the contacts in the phone, he decided he would perform the task here and now. For Charlie knew Zep would soon not be able to answer any questions.

Using his left index finger, he began scanning Zep's phone's contacts list.

Charlie found neither his name nor an alias he often used were on it. He didn't bother checking any recent phone call activity of Zep's for his own number, since Charlie only used disposable phones whenever contacting pimps.

Pleased to be done with checking the phone, he put it down. Charlie was able to carefully slip his left glove back on his hand.

He picked up Zep's phone with his free hand and rubbed it all down with a still-moist shower towel that was on the floor. He finally tossed the phone aside.

Charlie, again, gripped his gun with both of his gloved hands. And addressed Zep, again.

"Where do you keep your client list?"

Zep looked confused.

"My client list?"

Zep was either playing dumb or was confused, Charlie figured. Remaining still, Charlie clarified his request.

"The list of guys that call for your girls. I want to know where you keep their names, phone numbers, and whatnot."

Zep shrugged. But quickly stilled himself while eyeing the gun.

"On my iPad." Zep seemed to perk up with this new dialog. Perhaps it was giving him some hope to get himself out of this possible deadly mess. "It's out front, in my car."

Charlie remained silent.

Zep offered him an eager-to-please look before talking again.

"It's the red Corvette, parked near the front gate."

Zep's face went blank, and he continued.

"Now, I know where I heard your voice. You're a trick…excuse me, a client."

The pimp must be stoned, Charlie thought. Why else would you tell your potential killer

that you know who he is? If Zep's boat wasn't sunk already, he'd have been helping to sink it.

"What about your home computer…does it have any client information?"

Zep shook his head.

"No sir. I'm a gamer, and that machine is only for gaming."

Charlie sensed the "sir" was because of his own age, not his gun. So, he stretched his gun arm out, bringing the gun closer to the much-younger pimp. He then continued his questioning.

"Any physical phone or record books listing your clients in them?"

Shaking his head again, Zep said, "No."

This was good, Charlie thought. If true, it'd save him a lot of time. And, more importantly, save him a lot of risk tonight. Since he'd avoid having to go over to Zep's place to retrieve the client list. Charlie believed Zep. He figured the pimp wouldn't gamble his life for a measly client list. Still, he knew himself well enough that he couldn't leave that loose end untied. Zep's house would be his next stop. He had Zep's wallet, and he presumed it would contain a driver's license. But he wanted to immediately double check the address he was given earlier by Bennie, after giving the hacker Zep's cell phone number.

With that in mind, Charlie asked another question.

"Where do you live?"

The pimp answered back with an address that matched the one that Charlie received from Bennie.

Charlie had one last question for Zep.

"Who's at your house, now?"

"Nobody. My woman is out this week."

Zep then made, what to Charlie, appeared to be a desperate attempt at bonding with his captor.

"Are you a gamer?" He said with a small smile on his face.

Charlie answered by way of a muffled sound.

Zep was no longer a pimp, tormentor, or gamer.

CHAPTER 11

With little more than 3 hours of sleep, Detective Daniel Harris of LAPD's Robbery Homicide Division had a double murder on his hands. He was tossing and turning when he got the call at 4:45 a.m. It took him 37 minutes after hanging up from his Westwood condo to shower and get to the scene of the killings.

Less than 30 minutes after Harris arrived, he'd paid visits to both murder victims at the crime scene that Officer Jim Sweeney had found, off Fareholm Drive.

Harris was standing on a balcony of the wooden mansion. The mansion was where, the top coroner at the scene had already speculated, the first of the two killings took place. Harris was staring down at a lifeless dog. Turning away from the bloodied German Shepherd, he started to go back into the house. But before he could, he was stopped in his tracks by a studious-looking male face.

Raising his eyebrows, Harris waited for the meticulously dressed male to say what he wanted to say to him.

Pushing up the pair of Gucci eyeglasses that fronted his thin face of olive complexion, he said, "I'm from the Coroner's office. Are you done with the dog victim? We'd like to zip him up."

Looking down and straight at him, Harris showed a forced smile on what he assumed was someone fresh out of grad school. The coroner's assistant had to be no more than half his 58 years of age. What was this world coming to? These were his thoughts before he addressed him.

"First, it's Detective Harris," he said. "Next, are you a member of PETA, or did I hear you correctly that you're with the coroner?"

"Sir?" He said, tilting his head.

"A dog is not a victim," he said, blowing out a breath. "It's fucking an animal."

Walking away from the man's blank stare and open mouth, Harris went back into the house. A minute later, he was carefully fitting his six-foot-two, bulky frame through its front door. He forged through the porch area, bumping his way around a small crowd of forensic personnel without muttering a single "excuse me."

Harris always believed that black people offered an "excuse me" or a "pardon me" and other such courtesies far too often. Let his brothers and sisters do that courtesy crap. He had no time for it.

Finally, Harris was standing out in the open air of the driveway. And glad to be hit with some fresh air again, as he lit up a smoke.

As the lead detective on the double homicide, Harris was taking advantage of finding himself alone to do a little thinking. He didn't have to do much thinking though to take a good stab at what the crime scene was telling him.

Harris quickly learned the dead man in the house was the owner of the home. The murder victim had been identified as Alejandro Vargas, a financier with suspected ties to Mexican drug cartels.

The dead woman, inside the Mazda, was Bixie Brown. She had a rap sheet filled with convictions ranging from prostitution to public intoxication.

Harris knew that Vargas was the target tonight and his prostitute was at the wrong gig at the wrong appointed time.

Blowing out his third cloud of smoke, Harris spotted a short and thin officer walking up the driveway of the house. The officer was headed directly toward him. When enough light hit the officer's face, Harris recognized him and quickly turned away in hopes that Sweeney would walk past him. He didn't.

Sweeney was smiling when he hit him on the shoulder and said, "Daniel, long time, no see."

Harris answered back while exhaling smoke, just missing hitting Sweeney directly in the face with it.

"I was hoping it would be longer."

The smile dropped from Sweeney's face.

"Look, Daniel," he began. "I only wanted to see if you had any questions before I leave. After all, I was the first on the scene."

Harris took a quick hit from his cigarette.

"I do have a couple of questions," Harris said with eyes that were difficult to read. "First, why'd it take you longer to get here from your squad car, a few miles away, than me from my bed in Westwood? I read when the noise complaint was dispatched to you."

Sweeney looked down and back up at the detective.

"Daniel, you're the same asshole you've always been," He shrugged. "It was a measly noise complaint."

Harris hated incompetence.

"Turned out it wasn't so measly." Harris looked around and back at him. "Maybe you stopped by that oldie-but-goodie lady's place for a quickie. As I recall, she lives around here."

Harris brought the cigarette to his mouth but stopped before taking another hit.

"While you took your time Sweeney, this crime scene was aging by the second."

Reading a worried look on the officer's face, Harris added to his comments.

"Don't worry Sweeney, I won't tell the Wizard. Besides, he's as blue as they come."

Lifting his chin up, Sweeney said, "Before I go, what was your second question?"

Rubbing his eyes, Harris answered.

"Do you know where the fucking coffee is getting poured around here?"

Looking down at Zep's lifeless body, Charlie only allowed himself enough time to vow that he was getting out of the killing-for-money business. From Bennie, he knew the cops were on their way over. He figured he had precious little time to leave Bixie's apartment and get the hell over to Zep's place.

So, he gathered up the pimp's wallet, car keys, and phone from the floor. Next, he spotted Bixie's laptop sitting on a table. He grabbed it.

He figured Bixie's laptop may have information on it that would allow police to quickly identify Zep's body. But Charlie certainly realized the police would know, after finding Bixie's body, they had a dead prostitute on their hands. And every prostitute has a pimp.

Once again, Charlie looked over Zep's lifeless body. He knew the cops would quickly guess the dead body as Bixie's probable pimp.

Charlie hoped to delay the police IDing Zep's body. In doing so, it would buy him time to make it over to Zep's house, before the police eventually would.

But Charlie was well practiced in not fooling himself. The cops could be at Zep's house now, having pulled up a police file on Bixie

Brown and her pimp. Going over to Zep's house would be a high-risk venture. One he had decided to take.

He also decided to take the extra precaution of leaving Bixie's ground floor apartment by climbing out of her bedroom window. After escaping the unit with Bixie's laptop tucked into the back of his pants, Charlie quickly located Zep's Corvette among the faded and dented compact cars lining the street. Using Zep's key, he climbed in and was glad to see an iPad on the passenger seat.

After starting the ignition, Charlie moved Zep's car up a block, parking it on a side street. He wanted to delay the eventuality of the police locating it since it too would hasten their ability to ID Zep.

A minute later, Charlie was pulling his Taurus away from the curb on Fairfax. While looking back in his rearview mirror, in the faint distance, he could just make out a mosaic of white, red, and blue police lights flashing.

Blowing out a breath, he was glad that Zep's house was his last stop tonight before heading back to Lew's yard. Then home.

DAY 2

It was 7:15 a.m. and Detective Daniel Harris was glancing back and forth between a police file photo on his phone and the heavyset dead man he was looking down on. Swiping away the photo, he went to his contacts and scrolled down to find the name of an LAPD intelligence analyst. Harris finally located Scott Nelson's name. He hit the send button.

With the phone pressed against an ear, he spied one more time at a small table close to a bed. He let out a breath of disappointment. The table had all the characteristics of a laptop station. Only it was missing a laptop.

After hearing a few rings in his ear, Harris left the bedroom. And walked down the hallway of what he'd recently learned was Bixie Brown's apartment. Finally, a voice sounded in his ear.

"Detective, did the picture work out?" Scott said.

"It's definitely Zep Hill," Harris said, as he entered the tiny living room of the apartment.

"The dead man?"

Harris stopped in his tracks.

"Who the fuck else were we talking about?" He barked into the phone. The police and various other crime scene personal mulling around him were now staring at him in silence. Harris paid no heed.

Scott's voice now softened in his ear.

"Detective Harris, I was just making sure. I'm still a newly minted investigative analyst. And—"

Harris broke in with, "Just get me the latest address listed for the pimp."

He then threw up a finger to a couple of police officers who were anxiously waiting to ask him something.

There was a pause before Scott's voice came back out of the receiver.

"Zep Hill?"

Rolling his eyes, Harris rang off and slid the phone into its holder attached to his belt. He eyed the two officers in front of him.

"Yes?" He said to the stockier of the two officers who took a step closer to him.

"Detective, are you done in the backroom?" The officer said.

He looked at the man's badge and said, "Officer Mitchell. I presume, that is, since you didn't introduce yourself."

"Oh, sorry sir—"

"Forget it. And yes, I'm done with the room. But leave it the fuck alone. Forensics and the coroner haven't gotten here."

The two officers looked at him with embarrassment.

With a shake of the head, Harris said to no one in particular, "The academy is just not what it used to be."

Harris turned toward the door but stopped in his tracks.

A slender Hispanic man sporting a neatly trimmed mustache and pressed suit stood in the doorway, looking up at him. The new man was wearing a bored expression despite all the busy activity around him. He gave Harris a nod. Harris dropped his shoulders while eyeing the man and spoke.

"Why are you here?"

Detective Alex Garcia showed Harris a small smile and said, "The Commander."

"Fucking Commander. Less than two hours into the case, he's already decided I need assistance from a rookie?"

"I have over a year of experience behind me now. And Daniel, with all due respect, it is a triple homicide. Maybe I can provide some help." Garcia caught a look from Harris and added, "In some small way. We worked well on that case a few months back."

"You haven't *worked* with me, you've *assisted* me," Harris said, walking toward Garcia. "But, lucky for me, I actually like you."

Harris walked past him and out the doorway.

"Well, I'm told I will soon get my own big case to handle," Garcia said while following Harris outside, careful not to bump into the police personnel who seemed to be everywhere.

"You deserve to," Harris said while fumbling to retrieve a match to light the cigarette he had in his mouth.

"Only because of what you have taught me."

Harris stopped his business with the match while taking in the compliment for a split second, then resumed lighting his cigarette.

Taking a puff, Harris caught a glimpse of the small crowd of gawking fellow residents gathered beyond the yellow police tape protecting some yardage beyond Bixie's front door.

Harris eyed Garcia through the haze of exhaled smoke in front of his face.

"What do you know about these murders?"

Garcia answered with, "I was just told to come to this apartment. The murder here, somehow relates to a double homicide at the home of a man named Alejandro Vargas. He was murdered along with a female."

Nodding, Harris said, "Go back inside to the bedroom before the coroner bags that body that's back there. If I am gonna be stuck with you on this case, you'd better get a look at it."

"Do we know the victim's name?"

"Zep Hill."

"Who is he and how does he fit in the murder string?"

"Hill is the pimp of Bixie Brown, the girl who was killed inside her car at the double-murder scene. Brown was renting this unit," Harris exhaled a small cloud of smoke and said, "We IDed Brown using the plates on her car. During a recent arrest, she'd named Zep Hill as her pimp."

"Got it," Garcia said but didn't start for the door, as he could see Harris wasn't finished.

"When you're done looking at the stiff...when you're done here...head over to the house of horrors off Fareholm. Look over the scene. Then call me. I'll let you know what's next."

With that, Garcia offered an "Okay" and went into the apartment.

After taking another hit of his cigarette, Harris went toward an officer guarding the crime scene. The officer pulled back a slice of yellow tape, making an opening for Harris to take his leave. Now away from the growing crowd of gawkers, Harris began to do something he considered a vital investigative tool—think.

Harris began to mentally line up the timeline of the killings. And by the time Harris had extinguished his cigarette butt with his right wingtip, he had an appreciation for the skills of the, what most likely would turn out to be a single, killer. The killer had killed a man, then his visiting prostitute, and then the pimp of the prostitute. All in quick succession. All one step ahead of the police.

Charlie opened the laundry room door that led to his garage. He fingered a nearby wall switch.

Standing still, he cautiously watched the driveway and the sunlight grow with each jerk the garage door made until it was fully up. Feeling a rush of relief come over him, he realized he was half-expecting to see police cars and an army of guns facing him. He tried to tell himself he was paranoid. But he knew a triple killer is hunted with a special sense of urgency.

Finally stepping into the garage, he shut the house door behind him and checked its lock with a gentle twist and pull of its handle. Satisfied, he walked around the front of the Toyota feeling the warmth its engine was still emitting from its journey home from Lew Holt Truck Rentals a short time ago.

Since he wasn't going on a work-related venture this Monday morning, Charlie slipped into his Porsche.

He sunk into the soft, cold leather upholstery of the seat and thought for a split second he could fall asleep. But he knew sleep wouldn't come, even though he'd been up for a day. And that's why he'd jumped from his bed several minutes ago and decided to go to one of the last refuges of peace and tranquility in his troubled existence.

Charlie backed out of the driveway for the second time this morning. Just hours ago, he was heading to the Hollywood Hills to kill a money launderer. Now, he was headed to a gravesite in Orange County. The drive would take him an hour or so, depending on the undependable traffic flow of the Southland freeways.

Within 20 minutes, he was on the 101 Southbound. Glancing at the radio dial, he grimaced. He'd force himself to turn it on and hear about the misery he'd caused last night. He needed to find out what the police knew about possible motives and suspects.

Still, Charlie knew investigators always knew more than what they enjoyed feeding to the young, short-skirted, and gullible local reporters.

He tuned into the news channel. Immediately, as if a demonic presence was tormenting him, the newswoman announced she was recapping *this morning's top story: The LAPD has confirmed that three bodies killed in the wee hours of today may indeed share the same killer or killers, making it a triple homicide. LAPD spokesperson Shane Caldron did confirm that the yet-to-be identified victims are two males and a female...*

Charlie turned the radio off, before he could hear the full report. It proved too difficult of a task.

Before hearing the word "female," he was listening to the report as if someone else had done the crimes. But he knew he was the killer of the "female." And he knew who the female was. Her name was Bixie Brown. And that brought the report to him, personally.

In thinking of Bixie, something else was triggered in his mind. It was about another female, a former girlfriend who has been floating around in his mind for the past few decades.

Thoughts of Laura Hadley always brought Charlie's periods of high spirits back down and his low periods, such as today, down further. What Bixie and Laura had in common, he didn't exactly see the connection. But he knew, things weren't exactly adding up for him at the moment. Too many of his thoughts were being squeezed into too short of a time period.

Charlie also knew the now-frequent nagging question — *What made me possible?* — somehow needed to be answered. Above all, these thoughts confirmed to him that he did indeed need to go to the place where he was headed. Within an hour or so, he'd be at the side of his mother's grave. He figured he needed a little heaven before a lot of hell. As the midday phone call he owed Laredo was approaching.

Ten minutes after Charlie Casey had turned off his radio, the man who was in charge of investigating his killing spree tuned into the news on the radio. Detective Daniel Harris was inside his department-issued Crown Victoria. He always kept abreast of what police information the news people were spilling out over the public airways about the crimes he was working on, at any given time. Listening to such reports was about as enjoyable as a school homework assignment.

Harris was driving over to Zep Hill's home. The address of which Scott Nelson had retrieved for him from one of the multitude of databases the investigative assistant had at his disposal.

He turned up the radio sound dial as the newsman was telling the listeners *of a new development in the triple killing that began in the Hollywood Hills. According to an unknown police source, the killings were done by a single killer. The police source said that there was only one pair of footprints found at the two crime scenes and...*

As he shook his head, Harris turned the dial down. He always wondered how the rats of his own police force could leak unauthorized information—stuff they knew could help the bad guys they were tracking down—and sleep at night. But he knew why they did it—ego. For whatever reason, dishing out tidbits of information to news scoundrels, as Harris thought of most reporters, made certain types of people feel important.

Harris never felt the need to get an ego kick by chatting it up with a local TV reporter with a pretty face. Sure, he would talk to the press on rare occasions. But only when he felt the need to either protect the public, by letting them know of a dangerous person or persons to be aware of, or when asking for their help in finding or identifying a suspect that was on the run. Otherwise, he brushed off press inquiries. As such, the local media didn't much like him. And that was fine with him since reporters seemed to be all take and no give.

So when Harris turned the corner and saw the pack of reporters mulling around the front yard of a house, he said, "Fuck" out loud to himself. It sure seemed to him that this case had a police tipster in need of an ego boost.

No longer needing to bother with checking the address that Nelson had given him, Harris pulled over. He parked in the street, just to the side of a car parked along the curb. When he shut his car door behind him, he was confronted by a well-known local male TV reporter he was acquainted with from a multitude of previous crime scenes. The man was standing in the middle of the street, between Harris's car and Zep's house. Harris almost laughed. He could never get used to heavy pancake makeup, lipstick, and the hairspray-coated mop of hair on TV men.

"Detective Harris, what's the motive for the killings?" The reporter asked.

Harris started toward the man and Zep's house without responding. The reporter then got mad and continued talking.

"Detective, that's my car you just boxed in."

Just before passing the reporter, Harris nodded toward the crowd of press personnel that had gathered on Zep's lawn.

"And that is my crime scene that you and your fellow press rats have blocked my ease of access to."

Harris quickly reached Zep's lawn and began working his way through the crowd. He ignored several other questions shouted at him from the press people pointing mics at him while chasing after him.

He asked the first police officer he ran into, "where the fuck is the yellow tape?" Before the officer could answer, Harris was past him and through the door of Zep's house.

Once inside, he locked eyes with an old white-haired friend. Jim Lambert was one of the more-senior patrol officers on the LAPD. And, though they hadn't seen each other in several months, Lambert was all business after he crossed the room and spoke to Harris.

"Daniel, I just got here. We're gonna rope off those guys out front in a minute," Lambert said. "We had to secure the inside of the house first. The press showed up here at the same time we did."

Harris gave the officer a smile, while noting his posture had become more stooped since he last saw him. Poor guy, Harris thought, must have only months till they force him out.

"Someone obviously leaked the pimp's address to the pack of scoundrels outside," Harris said. "Probably the same rat that told them about the single set of footprints found at the murder sites."

Lambert motioned his agreement.

Harris began looking around. On his immediate right, he spotted a desktop computer in a side room that looked like a home office. He sighed as he realized the computer's tower was lying on its side. Walking a beeline to the computer, he hadn't noticed Lambert followed him.

Reaching the computer tower, Harris leaned down and confirmed his fears that the hard drive had been ripped out. From behind him, Lambert spoke up.

"That's the only computer in the house."

Still keeping his eyes on the tower, Harris straightened himself back up. He looked back at Lambert.

"Thanks, Jim," he said, before turning his head and eyeing the computer tower again. "Somebody wanted that hard drive awfully bad."

Harris was glad that Lambert was the only one within earshot of him. He vented to one of the few people in his police circles he trusted.

"This killer knows how to clean up his messes."

CHAPTER 13

A few blocks below the always-busy Sunset Strip of West Hollywood, Bennie Densmore was playing out his morning ritual. He was sitting inside the soothing warm water of his sunken hot tub, holding a cup of his beloved lemongrass herbal tea. His back was facing his sliding-glass patio door. With his eyes just above ground level, he was looking past the steaming bubbles in front of him and onto a green lawn. He glanced at the multitude of colorful flowers encircling the perfectly trimmed grass, dripping with a fresh coat of cold dew.

The picture-perfect backyard was designed by his domestic partner who had spent countless hours toiling under the sun to plant and care for it. Still, Bennie wasn't appreciating his partner's lawn and garden creations. His mind was doing what it did best and most often—networking and scheming. Both of which had one purpose—to gain him money.

All other things in Bennie's life were second to his financial goals, even his lover. And though he enjoyed hanging around with his much-younger mate of several months, Bennie thought of Scott Nelson as nothing more than a boy who was a toy. And, more strategically, a boy who was naïve and could be manipulated.

Bennie never hid from his lover the fact that he hacked databases for a living. But what he did hide from Scott were the types of clients he serviced and how some of them were more than a little shady.

The computer hacker also never told Scott the main reason he even expressed an initial romantic interest in him after the two shared a dance together at their favorite club, Micky's. No. Scott would be devastated to know that it was his job inside the LAPD that was Bennie's main attraction to him. The kid had no clue that Bennie considered him half an informational tool and half a sex toy.

Taking a sip of tea, Bennie grew a smile as he thought of the agitation in Charlie Casey last night. Maybe his client was in a heap of trouble. And client troubles generated billings.

The ring of his cell phone, lying nearby on the patio, interrupted Bennie's happy thoughts. Grabbing the phone, the hacker frowned when he realized it was not a client who was calling but his mate. He would have preferred to start his week with a client calling with a paying gig. Still, he told himself to be of good cheer. For keeping tabs on his sources, especially his best one, was part of his job.

Bennie answered his phone with, "Is this Scott Nelson, the cutest police analyst in the world, calling?"

CHAPTER 14

Charlie knew the city of Santa Ana could trace the origins of its name to an effort to give honor to Saint Anne. Several times a month, Charlie came to Santa Ana to pay his respects to someone he considered a saint and who was named Anne.

Prior to most of his visits to his mother's grave, he purchased flowers at a particular flower shop in the city. At 9:35 a.m., he pulled his car up to the shop.

Looking over the hood of his car, Charlie was able to read the cardboard clock on the shop door of Valdez's Roses—*9:40*. He was able to make out the caption above the clock—*Be back at*.

He shut off his engine, and in his rearview mirror caught sight of a Honda Accord. It pulled up several spaces behind him. Still, he was able to notice the color of the aging Honda's bent hood didn't match its other body parts.

Charlie continued to watch the Honda as a tall, middle-aged woman emerged from it. Soon, the slender woman he knew to be Velinda Valdez, was waving at him as she walked past his car on the way to her shop.

Nodding back to her, he watched as she unlocked the shop door with the sunlight glistening off her long jet-black hair. After opening the door, she looked back at his car wearing a smile and sunglasses, before going inside. Charlie smiled back at her without realizing it. He thought about how Velinda looked like some sort of celebrity in what, he figured, had to be drugstore-bought sunglasses. Charlie didn't know cheap sunglasses from a fashionable pair, but he did know Velinda was a single mother with little income.

Not wanting to risk making Velinda feel self-conscious, Charlie removed his own sunglasses as he climbed out of his car. Before shutting his door, he tossed the stylish name-brand pair of shades onto his passenger seat.

Walking into the shop, he found Velinda standing at a flower cutting table. Behind her was a bank of glassed-walled refrigerators displaying shelves of greenery and colorful flower arrangements. She eyed him and offered him the usual personalized greeting she gave him whenever he paid her shop a visit.

"What is the flower count today?" Velinda said.

"Thirty," he said, from behind the cash register counter.

Velinda nodded at Charlie and went to work.

Ten minutes later, she had a bouquet of 30 yellow roses wrapped in cellophane with all the stems neatly tucked inside a plastic cemetery vase. She had temporarily put the vase inside a holder and placed it in front of Charlie.

He gently placed three one-hundred-dollar bills on the counter and said, "Thank you."

Velinda looked up at him, slowly shaking her head. A few seconds of silence passed before she spoke.

"You've been coming here for several years. Each time you tip more than the cost of the flowers. A few hundred dollars more."

"I haven't paid attention."

"Well, I have," she said. "You're very generous…and you don't really know me."

Charlie swallowed.

"I know your name is Velinda. You came here from Mexico with your husband, and you have a daughter in high school." Charlie paused while eyeing her and said, "And I know your husband has been living in Mexico."

"Jorge is now my ex-husband," she said matter-of-factly.

"I see."

"And, yes, Jorge has been living in Zamora for over six years with a much-younger woman than I." She smiled before continuing with, "Who I've heard enjoys nights out and dancing."

Charlie looked down.

"Oh, I'm over it," she said without a trace of bitterness. "But I don't think my daughter will ever get over her daddy abandoning her. Poor thing, she's a gifted girl and has her heart set on medical school. I've tried to tell her we won't be able to afford it."

She continued as Charlie looked back up at her.

"Since Jorge left, it's been a struggle just to pay rent. But, you probably guessed that from my car." She laughed, but soon grew a blank face as she continued to look up at him. "How did you know those things about me?"

Charlie shrugged.

"Just listening whenever I'm in here, picking up flowers."

She examined his face with her eyes and said, "I know some things about you."

He remained silent as she continued.

"Besides being generous, I know you're wealthy." She looked past Charlie and eyed his car, then back at him. "And it's not just the car you drive or the tips you give me. I can just tell."

Looking down again, Charlie felt a new wave of emptiness come over him as he realized something about himself. With his head still down, he eyed her.

"You can be proud of how you make your money," he said.

She raised her eyebrows. "And you can't?"

"No."

She grew still.

"What do you do?" she said.

He paused. "I'd rather not say."

She nodded but held his eyes.

"Are you married?" She asked.

"No."

"Any kids?"

He shook his head. Grabbing the flowers, he turned to leave when Velinda's voice stopped him.

"May I ask your name?"

For a split second, the happenings of last night had disappeared from him. He turned back to her and answered.

"Charlie."

She brightened.

"Well, Charlie. At the risk of sounding nosy I'm going to ask you another question."

He tensed up. But didn't stop her from continuing.

"Ever since you've been coming here, the number of roses you buy changes by one with every additional year, I believe. It's been thirty for some months now. Before that, you were purchasing twenty-nine." She stopped and blinked, before asking her question. "What does the flower count mean?"

After answering Velinda that his mother had passed away 30 years ago, Charlie could tell from the look on her face she now understood the meaning of the flower count.

Charlie could also read from Velinda's face, coupled with her interest in his personal life, that she'd taken a liking to him. But he knew when he chose his profession that romance could not play a part in his world. Besides, whenever some woman did show interest in him it only served as a reminder that his long-lost flame, Laura Hadley, was never going to be a part of his life again.

But five minutes after leaving Velinda's shop, he let these negative thoughts go as he turned into the cemetery where his mother rested. After passing through the wrought-iron gates, he looked to his right and caught a glimpse of the chapel. Inside its stone walls was where his mother's funeral was held. Winding his way through the narrow roads of the grounds, he thought back about that day.

Plenty of mourners had come to the service to pay their respects to his mother, but only a few stood out to Charlie now. There were his close buddies—Tim Dagel, Bruce William, Brad Chen, and Kenny Briers. In the front row with him, Laura had sat to his left, with his best friend Tab Smith on his right. In thinking about these people, Charlie wondered where the last three decades had gone.

He also wondered why he and all these friends, save for Laura, had become tragic figures. Charlie thought about the club he had started with these five male buddies of his.

The Deadbeat Club offered a way for Charlie and his friends to have some fun with the idea that they all had fathers that had split the domestic home scene, long forgetting about them.

Charlie thought about how the Deadbeat Club membership seemingly became a ticket to a life of crime. Ending in either a jail cell, or death. Indeed, only Bruce William and himself were still alive.

This all made Charlie wonder something about himself and his club buddies—*What made all of us possible?*

What Charlie didn't want to revisit, at the moment, was why one club member in particular—Tab Smith—was dead. It was a secret he'd kept to himself. But he forced away the memory of his best buddy as he left the chapel in his rearview mirror. His limits on pain intake were currently overloaded.

A minute later, Charlie rolled to a stop, some 40 yards past his mother's curbside grave. He didn't feel comfortable parking the Porsche too close to her resting place. As he knew his mother would've never approved of how he obtained the car. When the car fell silent, he spent a few seconds clearing his mind before reaching into a backseat compartment for a book of poems. It was one of the many poetry books his mother had spent years collecting.

Looking at the book, Charlie managed a smile while fondly remembering his mother desperately trying for years to get him to acquire an ear for poems. He never did. But he was determined that she might continue to enjoy poems from beyond the grave.

After grabbing the bouquet of 30 flowers, he left the car.

A short time later, Charlie found himself standing over his mother's gravestone. Inches from his feet, and spiked into the ground, was the cemetery vase holding the yellow roses he'd brought. He finished reading three short poems aloud in a whispered voice, and he closed the book.

He turned back around and began walking back to his car. Looking at his watch, he saw that only thirty-five minutes remained before he had to make his scheduled 12:30 p.m. call. Charlie shook his head. He really hadn't thought much about what he was going to say to Laredo. And the cartel enforcer, he knew, was going to want a complete explanation about last night's fuckup back at Alejandro Vargas house.

Reaching his car, Charlie was glad he'd left enough time to spare to allow him to get out of the cemetery before making his call. The last thing he wanted was to stink up the resting place of his mother with the doings of his dirty business.

Minutes later, he was exiting the gates of the cemetery and feeling the comfy warmth of his mother leaving him. As he straightened his car out onto the road, he felt the fear of Laredo creeping into his consciousness. Nothing good, even when things were going smoothly in his killing work for the enforcer, ever came from talking to him.

Down the road, Charlie turned into a nearly deserted parking lot of a dying strip mall featuring a decades-old hamburger drive-thru as its anchor attraction. With a few minutes to spare before he had to make his call, he cut the Porsche's engine and leaned his seat back. He had to quickly think about what he was going to tell the cartel enforcer. As his head hit the back of the seat, Charlie felt an onslaught of exhaustion overtake him.

CHAPTER 15

Det. Harris stepped back from the red Corvette to gather his thoughts. The car was registered to Zep Hill, and it stood out like a sore thumb on this side street, just off Fairfax Avenue. It was parked a block away from Bixie Brown's apartment. But when police questioned the residents of Bixie's apartment building, one of them reported seeing the Corvette parked in front of the complex early in the morning.

Harris broke off from a couple of officers and started toward his own car when his phone chirped. He answered the phone without looking at the screen.

"Harris," he said into his receiver as he reached his Crown Victoria.

"Daniel, it's Alex," the caller said. "I'm just leaving the Hollywood Hills crime scene."

Fumbling with his free hand for his car keys, Harris said, "Meet me at Canter's for lunch."

A knocking sound jerked Charlie out of his slumber. Startled, he looked left as he straightened himself up in his car seat.

Charlie saw a smiling man looking at him through his driver's side window. As Charlie moved his left hand to hit the window switch, he stopped himself. This was no time to let down his guard.

Looking a few feet past the bloated man wearing sunglasses, Charlie saw an empty small car with some security company name on it. Next, he looked around the nearly empty parking lot of the strip mall. He could find no police presence.

Charlie, at last, lowered the window a bit and let out a "yes?"

"You're triple parked, sir," the security guard said. "Plus, I noticed you're parked in the middle of the lot. I'm worried about someone carelessly hitting you if they're not paying attention. I've seen it happen before."

"Thank you," Charlie said, as went to power his window back up. "I'll repark."

Starting his car, Charlie felt a panic taking over him as he caught the dash clock. It read 1:15 p.m. He was supposed to have called Laredo 45 minutes ago. He hit the gas. Pulling up a few car lengths away from the hamburger drive-thru, he cut the engine.

Groggy from less than an hour of sleep in the last 36 hours, he contemplated getting a cup of coffee before making the call. But each minute he delayed the call was risking something that would make his tardiness an even worse matter—Laredo calling him. Charlie had to be the one who made the call.

Grabbing his phone, he felt stifled by a sudden stuffiness that came over him. He needed some ventilation. After starting up the engine, he adjusted the air and began to feel a renewed sense of alertness.

He placed the call to Laredo. And after a few rings, the man's voice answered.

"Charlie," Laredo said on the other end. "You're late in calling, and that's not good."

"Laredo, I feel asleep and—"

"Is that sound I hear the drone of your car, Charlie?" Laredo said, cutting him off.

Putting the phone down on his lap, Charlie cut the engine and quickly picked the phone back up. Laredo's voice broke the split second of silence that had taken over the car.

"That's better," he said, then pausing before speaking again. "You're famous, Charlie."

Hearing this jolted Charlie, but he said nothing.

"Charlie, did you hear me? Last night's job made the news."

Noting the dark tone of Laredo's voice and the subtle but clear message of danger it carried, Charlie wet his lips before replying.

"Look, last night I finished the Vargas job. While I was leaving his place, a prostitute...," Charlie grimaced for a split second at hearing himself callously say this last word in reference to a woman he shot dead. "A prostitute named Bixie Brown—"

"Did you get that name from the news?" Laredo said, interrupting him.

"No. I took her purse."

"After you killed her?"

Charlie swallowed.

"Yes," he said.

"Why'd you kill this whore?"

Hearing it voiced that he had killed a female shook Charlie again. It took him some seconds to gather himself.

"Laredo, it was an accident. The girl showed up in a car at Vargas's place just as I was leaving. I didn't know it was a female in the car."

"So, why'd you call it an accident?"

Anger hit Charlie, and he snapped back at his employer.

"Laredo, you know I don't do ladies."

"As of last night, that's no longer true."

Laredo paused.

Charlie sensed Laredo was enjoying himself.

"The news report I just heard, Charlie, had the pimp of the whore being shot last night, as well. They said his name was Zep Hill."

Charlie stiffened. Laredo had taken down or memorized Zep's name. And that told Charlie the cartel enforcer considered last night's disaster an important matter. He didn't interrupt Laredo, as his employer continued.

"The police are looking for a triple killer, Charlie. You explained why you killed the hooker but why her pimp?"

Charlie knew the reason why he had killed Zep last night was not going to go over well with Laredo. But, as risky as the truth was going to be to his personal safety, he knew the punishment for lying to the enforcer would be fatal. So Charlie went with the truth.

"I had a personal connection with the pimp."

A loud laugh came out of the phone and into Charlie's ear. Instinctively, he jerked the phone away from his head. Looking at the phone, he felt belittled. He put the phone back to his ear as he heard the laughter stop. Laredo's voice was speaking words, again.

"I see," Laredo said, dropping any hint of humor. "You were a client of this dead pimp. And, he must've had some kind of information on you. So, you decided to kill him before the police got to him."

A few seconds of silence passed. Charlie wondered where this conversation was ultimately heading.

"But Charlie you're tied to a lot of pimps. We've seen you making visits plenty of times to that suite at the Beverly Hills Hotel. What do you locals call that place? The Pink Palace? It's nice. I stayed there a few years back. But, I wonder why you don't take your whores somewhere closer to your home." Laredo paused before adding, "Surely there are nice hotels closer to Astral Drive."

Charlie had always assumed that Laredo knew where he lived. That was expected from the likes of drug cartel people. They were paranoid by nature and didn't trust anyone, even those inside their own criminal organization. These types would want to have the home addresses of all their underlings in case they needed to eliminate one or more of them on short notice. As was the case with the money launderer Vargas.

But now Charlie realized that Laredo had his minions following him around town, while he was doing his own private things. And this, Charlie considered a breach of expected personal privacy. Still, he knew now was not the time to put up a protest. So he ignored Laredo's last question.

"Laredo, I did my job last night. What happened was unfortunate, but I can't let it distract—"

"I wasn't finished with your mess last night," Laredo said, cutting him off again and waiting a few seconds before asking his next question. "So, I take it that you now need to kill off every pimp that you've ever used in LA?"

"No," Charlie said while keeping still, in his car seat.

"Why not? Surely, all the pimps you have used have your contact info somewhere. And, the cops are bound to speak to them all."

Alone in his car, Charlie unconsciously shook his head before answering.

"Zep was the only pimp I gave my name to. And, even with him, it was only my first name and only in the beginning of our contact with each other. It was years ago. But, he may have had my name in some old file."

Another few seconds of silence, with Charlie thinking this whole thing was not going over well. But he had expected that.

Laredo cleared his throat.

"Charlie, you being tied to this pimp puts the cartel at risk. If the cops get to you, they may somehow get to me."

As Laredo paused again, Charlie looked out over his car hood and up at the hamburger drive-thru's signage. The fear in him lifted briefly, just enough for him to remember a specific time that he'd patronized the place as a teenager. Once back then, he had pulled up through the drive-thru window with his best buddy Tab Smith in the passenger seat. Both of them were laughing over something stupid.

Now Tab was dead, and Charlie found himself making a living as a killer for hire. He shook his head, trying to reconcile the turn of events in both of their lives. But these thoughts vanished as Laredo's voice brought him back to the present, back to the feeling of fear.

"Seems to me, Charlie, you've had a new attitude these last few months. You put me off last night until lunch today. Then 12:30 rolls around, and I don't hear from you. It was past 1:00 when you finally called." Laredo's voice grew as he continued. "You don't seem to care much about the work, anymore. And people who don't care anymore in your type of profession, Charlie, are dangerous. Because they make mistakes. And, last night, you made a big one."

Charlie answered back in a flat voice.

"Like I said, Laredo, I did my job last night."

Laredo let go a laugh.

"What you did last night was to make the news," he said. "This has fucked me up with my superiors."

Charlie rubbed his forehead with one hand and tightened his grip on the phone with the other. He had nothing to say to Laredo's last statement. It was a relief when Laredo continued.

"So, Charlie, I'm going to test your attitude. I want you to meet me in LA to talk about a job I have for you."

Pressing his lips together, Charlie knew this was a bad sign. But he had to go along with Laredo's plan, at least on the phone. Given his exhausted state of mind, he didn't trust his memory. So he reached for a pen in a small, open compartment to his right. Next, he spotted a receipt on his passenger seat and grabbed it. He flipped it over onto its blank side.

Now holding his phone with his left hand, Charlie was finally ready to take a date and time down.

"Laredo, when do you want to meet?"

"Tomorrow night."

Charlie looked up from the still-blank piece of paper. Everything was going in a warp speed since he shot Alejandro Vargas.

CHAPTER 16

Finishing the last of the tea, Bennie Densmore stepped out of the hot tub. He heard the happy sounds of water droplets falling off his slippery, wet body as he stretched and yawned. Just as the droplets were becoming a trickle, he reached down and grabbed at small parcels of the Speedo swimsuit he had on, squeezing water out of them. The computer hacker hated wearing them, but due to an annoying neighbor he had no choice.

Looking over his shoulder, Bennie eyed the home of the neighbor in question and muttered a curse word. He'd always gone nude in the hot tub until a few months ago. That was when his hated neighbor complained to him that his small kids could see him from their second-story window. If he took another dip in the nude, the neighbor told him he'd call the police.

Bennie only readily agreed to wear a swimsuit since drawing police attention of any kind, given his line of work, was to be avoided at all costs.

The hacker took a few steps toward the pool towel rack he'd recently purchased for his patio. Just before grabbing his terry cloth robe off the wooden rack, he caught sight of his 5-foot, 2-inch plump frame reflecting off the sliding-glass door. He wasn't sitting, but he still thought that he had the look of a rotund buddha statue. Holding the robe, he paused to take a further physical inventory of himself.

Sure, Bennie knew he was a short man. And he was teased about it throughout his school years on the playground. He would never forget how he was called every derogatory name in the book for short people. But, as his thoughts drifted toward his form of revenge on all those teasing schoolyard kids, he smiled and nodded to himself in the reflection of the window.

Bennie's form of revenge on his old school mates was financial in nature. At 41 years of age, Bennie had more money than most, if not all, of his former teasing classmates. He figured he had the last laugh of all those fucking pricks. Most of them were losers toiling away each weekday in some partitioned-off, cramped office cubicle, surrounded by a sea of yellow square notes they'd stuck on their half-sized walls of cheap fabric.

Turning sideways toward the window, Bennie looked at his pillow-size belly and realized it had grown at least half an inch in the last few months. Maybe it was that red wine habit Scott introduced to him on the night they met, last summer. Yeah, maybe his boy toy gave him a new bad habit, but along with it came the wealth of LAPD data he provided.

Maybe he'll drop the wine habit when he drops Scott, he thought as he snuggled into his robe with a shrug of his shoulders and a shiver.

After tying his robe shut with its fabric belt, he untangled his tight-fitting swimsuit from his layers of flab and climbed out of it. He hung the now-mangled piece of swimwear on the rack to dry.

Next, Bennie slipped into his nearby pair of slippers he'd laid out, earlier. Comfortable, he opened the sliding-glass door and stepped into the living room.

Finding the TV remote, he aimed it across the room at the huge TV screen and brought it to life. He went to move but was stopped in his tracks by what he was hearing and seeing on the screen. The TV was spewing out the local news, complete with a red colored box announcing that there was a breaking news story.

Bennie froze as he read the news story title announcing a triple killing that happened last night. His hand, holding the remote, dropped to his side. He took on a deer-in-the-headlights stare while watching the has-been male senior news anchor speak about the killings of two males and a female.

After listing a few facts about the crime spree, the news anchor handed over the broadcast to a brunette reporter on location at a Hollywood Hills home. The female reporter, whose expansive cleavage seemed to be holding her microphone in its place, was standing on the entrance of the home's long driveway.

She launched into her report while pointing up the narrow driveway and explaining that "a female prostitute named Bixie Brown, and a male named Alejandro Vargas were found shot to death at this multimillion-dollar property. I am told, this home was apparently owned by the male victim, Vargas. Alejandro Vargas was, according to our police sources, a financier of sorts for drug cartels."

Leaning his head toward the TV, Bennie continued to listen to the reporter who was telling her TV viewers that "just in the last few minutes, we have learned the identity of the man found shot to death at Bixie Brown's Fairfax Avenue apartment complex. His name is Zep Hill. A police source referred to him as a well-known pimp who Brown apparently had been working under. Here is a live shot of that Fairfax Avenue apartment complex…"

This is when the voice of the reporter began to fade from Bennie's senses, while his eyes nearly crossed for a flash as they moved away from the TV screen and focused on nothing in particular. Bennie's mind though was focusing on something in particular—a scheme that could land him the biggest payday of his shady career. The scheme involved Charlie Casey.

Bennie knew the information Charlie had requested last night lined up with the TV news reports he'd just heard. It didn't take much for Bennie to conclude that Charlie was responsible for the murder carnage of last night. A killing carnage that began in the Hollywood Hills and ended inside a dumpy apartment on Fairfax. No wonder Charlie was so agitated last night. Bennie now knew his client was indeed in a heap of trouble.

To Bennie's thinking, Charlie and his misadventures may have created the perfect storm of an opportunity. Never one to miss an opportunity, especially one of this potential size, Bennie turned the TV off and put the remote down. He started toward his home office. It was time to do some research on Charlie Casey.

Inside his home office, Bennie Densmore's belly jiggled as he pulled his chair closer to the computer screen on his desk. Using his mouse, he quickly located the file he had built on a particular client of his. The name of the file was Charlie Casey.

Opening the file with a double click, Bennie was surprised to find how little personal information he had on Charlie. This, despite seeing that they'd been doing business together dating back several years. Charlie was the most secretive client he had. The man never offered any small talk to him. Bennie couldn't guess if Charlie was a Lakers fan or a beer lover.

Continuing to eye his notes in Charlie's file, Bennie was reminded of the fact that nobody had ever actually told him what line of work Charlie was involved in. Still, over the years, Bennie had come to realize that Charlie Casey was a hired gun. He eventually deduced this after he realized that every person connected to any phone number, vehicle license plate, or home address that Charlie had asked him to research had ended up dead.

He clicked off Charlie's file. It was time to find out how much society knew about Charlie Casey.

Bennie already knew the hitman was well hidden in the police world, at least inside his home base of Los Angeles. He'd gotten this information this morning from his lover Scott Nelson, who once again risked his job and more, by searching every LAPD database he could access from his analyst's desk inside the department walls.

The fact that Charlie was a ghost to the LAPD didn't surprise Bennie, given the nature of his dealings over the years with him.

To find out more about Charlie, Bennie would utilize his computer hacking expertise and perform an unconventional internet search. A search that would take him into the world of the dark web.

Bennie began to furiously type away on his keyboard, all in an effort to uncover an enigma named Charlie Casey.

But after a few hours of hacking into the usual and not-so-usual databases he fished around in for his trade, Bennie realized that Charlie was a unique case study among his criminal clients. He confirmed that Charlie was well hidden, not only in the police world, but also in the everyday world and the underworld.

Under the name Charlie Casey, the man had no credit cards, no real estate, no cars, no bank accounts or investments, and no driver's license.

Bennie concluded, in society, Charlie was a nonentity.

While backing away from the glare of the computer screen, Bennie kept his eyes focused on the last database search result he'd gotten for Charlie Casey—*no such person found*. He felt a giddiness overtaking him. This all would fit into his scheme of making a huge payday. For he knew, a man like Charlie would pay a lot of money to remain a ghost in this world. And given Charlie's 3-person slaughter last night, Bennie figured the man would pay almost anything to insure his societal ghosthood.

Looking down on the dark laminate wood floor of his home office, Bennie spotted several cracks and chips. He began to simmer with anger, as he knew complaining to his bitchy and tight-ass landlord wouldn't get the floor repaired and certainly not replaced. But he quickly realized his anger was directed inward, towards himself. He knew he was not satisfied where he was at, in life.

Sure, he could afford to buy a decent condo and pay cash for it. But he never allowed himself to do so since such a move might draw scrutiny from some tax authorities or worse. To the IRS, he was a computer consultant, pulling down thirty odd thousand dollars a year. Bennie made sure his lifestyle matched closely with this stated income.

Bennie's life plan called for homeownership only when he had enough to retire, outside of the U.S. He'd buy a property with a beachside home on some foreign island where, for small payments to the right people, no questions about sources of income would be asked of him. At his age though, Bennie thought by now he'd already be sticking his toes into the sand of a warm tropical beach while enjoying an early retirement.

But he wasn't on a beach nor retired.

And it was this realization, this morning, that made up his mind concerning Charlie Casey. Bennie wondered why he hadn't previously leveraged Charlie's growing list of kills. Well, live and learn. It was time to request a meeting with Charlie.

Bennie knew it was risky to attempt a shakedown of a contract killer. But a payout so big that it could fund his retirement was worth the potential hazards.

Of course, he would take precautions and arrange the meetup at a public place. He would park his car with the utmost of care, making sure Charlie wouldn't see him arrive or leave.

Bennie got up from his squeaky chair. He smiled at the thought of all the money and freedom he would soon have, thanks to Charlie. Retirement was just around the corner and with it a new life for himself. He'd dispense of Scott, who was lately becoming too needy for his taste.

Indeed, Bennie would leave every ounce of his current life behind when he boarded a plane out of the bad old USA, for good. He couldn't wait to see the big and final deposit confirmation, from Charlie's money wire transfer, on his offshore numbered account.

Bennie reached for his phone but stopped. He would wait a couple days for things to settle down for Charlie before calling him. Besides, he wanted to also wait for wire payment, due for last night's work he'd done for him, to hit his numbered account. Unlike many of his other clients, who often stiffed him or fucked him over, Charlie was dependable and always paid on time.

Seated at a table inside Canter's, Harris pushed the menu in front of him aside. Detective Alex Garcia took the clue and did not pick up his menu. He'd learned that Harris was a man on a mission when any active murder case was fresh. Especially one involving females.

A waitress appeared and dropped off the coffee the two detectives had ordered. The heavyset and sloppy much-older woman sensed that the customers wanted some time before they ordered. She scurried off.

Harris eyed Garcia.

"Summarize what you know so far about the case. If I am stuck with you assisting me on it, I want you on the same page as me." He looked about and added, "And Alex, let's keep our voices down."

Garcia nodded and pulled out a notepad and pen. Using the tip of the pen to guide him down his notes, the detective swallowed and spoke.

"The first victim shot was Alejandro Vargas, a money launderer for Mexican drug cartels. The next victim was Bixie Brown, a prostitute. She was apparently on her way to turn a trick with Vargas. The last victim, at least that we know of, is a pimp named Zep Hill. Hill was Brown's pimp." He looked up at Harris, then back down at his notes before continuing with, "Vargas and Brown were shot with the same weapon—a rifle—while Hill was shot with a handgun."

Harris interjected.

"Well, according to the coroner, the first *victim* was Vargas's dog. And, that's important."

"Why?" Garcia said.

"Because the manner in which the dog was shot—a perfect hit to the head. And, from a long distance away. This told me the killer knew the dog was going to be there. The dog was probably shot before he got off a single bark. No neighbors heard any barks."

Alex smiled while taking a sip from his coffee. Harris continued.

"The crime scene all adds up." Harris poured cream into his coffee but never took his eyes off Garcia and continued. "Vargas was shot while in his bed after answering his phone. So, the killer had cased Vargas's house before doing his deeds last night. Or, the killer already knew about Vargas and his living and sleeping arrangements. The killer even knew the perfect spot and position to park his car along the private road leading to the house."

Harris grabbed onto his coffee cup and paused just as he lifted it up.

"Add to all of this, that during last night's killing spree, the killer used two types of guns—a rifle and handgun."

Harris finally took a sip of coffee. He swallowed and put the cup back down on the shiny table.

"Alex, this all tells me this was a professional hit. An experienced killer would have an arsenal of more than one type of gun on him, as a precaution against the unexpected. And, the unexpected did happen in this case."

Garcia narrowed his eyes.

"How so?" he said.

Spreading his fingers open, Harris answered him.

"After shooting Vargas, the killer was either leaving the scene or packing up his car when he was surprised by Bixie Brown. She was coming up the private road in her Mazda. At that juncture, the killer had no choice but to kill Brown."

Garcia began to mess with his mustache, while continuing to listen.

"The killer then grabbed Brown's purse and phone from her car. Her phone must have been used somehow by the killer to track down Zep Hill."

Letting go of his mustache, Garcia interrupted.

"But Daniel, why did the killer then bother tracking down Bixie Brown's pimp and offing him?"

Harris leaned into the table.

"Alex, the killer did more than track down and kill Zep Hill. After he shot Zep Hill, he took steps such as moving Zep's car to delay us from being able to ID him. It's obvious to me, the killer wanted to beat us to Hill's house. And, he did." He took another gulp from his coffee. "The killer risked a lot to not only kill the pimp but to get his cell phone and any electronic files he had at his home or in his car. And, he did all this after a double murder where only a single murder had been planned."

Shaking his head, Garcia said, "Daniel, the killer was after some kind of information that had to be important to him."

Now Harris leaned back against his chair.

"That's the capstone of this discussion," he said. "Alex, the killer is tied to the pimp."

Pausing, Harris let that sink in, before continuing.

"The killer must have used Zep Hill for hookers. He may even have been a client of Bixie Brown's. No matter, Brown's pimp was Hill, which the killer found out from her phone." Harris spread his hands apart. "The killer risked getting caught to get at both Brown's and Hill's computers and phones before we got to them. He must have believed that one or both of these two people had some information on one or more of their devices on him personally. Something that could lead to him."

After glancing down at his notepad, Garcia looked up.

"There were no computers at Vargas's house, and the killer had to know that," he said, as if having a sudden realization. "And the killer knew the contacts on Vargas's phone would be useless for anyone looking for his killer. Otherwise, he would have entered the house before or after the killing to get at them. And, it looks like he didn't."

Nodding, Harris said, "A money launderer like Vargas is too smart to keep any electronic files concerning his illegal business dealings at home. Those files are somewhere in Los Angeles, but they are probably being deleted as we speak by the cartel members who ordered the hit on him."

"Right."

The waitress reappeared. And Harris looked up and told her, "It's just gonna be the coffee today."

The waitress took her leave. Harris eyed Garcia.

"But the killer has tipped his hand by killing the pimp."

Garcia waited for an explanation.

"Alex. We now can assume the killer uses hookers. He may do so by calling a pimp or simply picking them up off the streets. But, since our killer is a professional hitman, my guess is that he calls pimps directly to arrange his girls, not wanting to risk an arrest for soliciting a prostitute. Zep Hill can't be the only pimp that our killer does business with, either directly or by using his hookers."

Harris took a second to look at his watch, before continuing.

"That's why I'm meeting with a pimp in about 20 minutes. And Alex, I want you to go off and meet with a couple of other ones. I'm having Scott Nelson email you some names and addresses of some of our well-known local pimps. I want you to ask them all if they have any clients that seem especially cautious or different."

Harris spotted the check the waitress had put down on their table without either of them noticing. He pulled out his wallet and laid some bills down on top of the check.

"And Alex, call Rob Johnson in ballistics. Ask him if he'd quickly take a look at the bullets from the three victims. Maybe the same gun was used in a prior shooting." Harris looked grim. "Or a future one."

Harris stood up. Garcia followed his lead. Once outside, Garcia got Harris's attention.

"I'll talk to Johnson in ballistics," Garcia said. "But I'm not sure pimps will be offering up information on their johns to me so easily."

"The pimp I am meeting will," Harris said. "He's a CI."

Harris turned toward his car. But stopped when Garcia pressed a point to him.

"Yes Daniel, but the pimps I will be tracking down will not be confidential informants. They will have no reason to talk to me."

Harris stared down at Garcia.

"Give them a fucking reason," he said. "Tell them you either need suspects or information. And, it's up to them which one you bring back to the station."

Garcia smiled. "Got it."

"And Alex," Harris said, while retrieving his car keys from his pocket. "You better tell these pimps you see to be careful. We don't know if our killer may wish to eliminate any and all pimps he's had dealings with."

"Okay." Garcia hesitated for a split second before saying something more. "Daniel. You never actually said the obvious. So, just to be sure. You have concluded that we are looking for a male killer. A solo male."

"Yes."

Garcia put on his sunglasses and smiled.

"And Daniel, our killer seems like a smart one."

Harris, paused in thought, at this comment. And Garcia dropped his smile. Harris looked away and lowered his voice, almost talking to himself.

"This guy's different."

CHAPTER 17

Charlie Casey was seated in front of his computer inside his home office. As the computer was waking up, he shook his head as he read the time of 8:12 p.m. showing on the screen. He meant to avoid learning how little sleep he'd gotten since returning home from his mother's gravesite and Laredo's call. The nap he'd just woken up from had been a battle between his efforts to get some rest and fighting the urge to give up on it, altogether.

Knowing he'd killed a woman last night, Charlie wondered if he'd ever sleep well again.

Certainly, his talk with Laredo this afternoon added to his more immediate worries. But concerning himself with Laredo could wait. At least till tomorrow night when he was scheduled to meet up with the cartel enforcer.

Tonight, Charlie would focus on the hard drive and iPad he took last night from Zep Hill's home and car, respectively. His freedom might depend on what was stored on them.

The data on Zep's computer devices would tell Charlie if the pimp had ever found out if his client, named Ron Wendell, was actually Charlie Casey. If so, Charlie knew he'd have to disappear somewhere, as fast as possible. For he could not gamble that Zep had stored his client files only on one or both of the devices he now possessed. And, if that were the case, the police would eventually run across his name on Zep's client list and come after him.

Despite Zep telling him that he kept his client lists on his iPad, Charlie first reached for the pimp's hard drive. He figured Zep wouldn't have carried an incriminated list of johns on an iPad he'd kept in his car.

Fifteen minutes later, he disconnected Zep's hard drive from his computer. He'd found nothing but game programs and related files loaded on it. Zep had been truthful, after all.

Now Charlie was hoping the pimp was truthful that his client list was stored on his iPad. He grabbed it and turned it on, glad that he'd remembered to check it last night to make sure the "Find My iPad" was not enabled. That was no surprise, given that Zep Hill, its owner, was involved in illegal activities and would probably be too paranoid to have any of his devices to be traceable or somehow tied to a cloud service.

After twenty minutes of fiddling with the iPad, Charlie was down to just a few more files to check. He put his cursor over one named "Z list" and opened it. Here, he'd finally found Zep's list of johns.

Charlie steeled himself and proceeded to peruse the list of Zep's johns.

He quickly looked for the fake name he used when calling Zep. Finding it, he breathed a sigh of relief after seeing that nothing beyond basic contact information for Ron Wendell, and the girls this client had procured, was typed next to the name.

Next, he looked for his real name on the alphabetized list. He blew out another breath of relief. Nobody named Charlie Casey was on the list.

He smiled with relief.

But his relief quickly faded as he glanced to his right and spotted the laptop he'd taken from Bixie's apartment, last night. The laptop was something he was avoiding opening. He'd put it off by busying himself with his other immediate tasks. The laptop, Charlie knew, would be filled with personal data of the female life he had snuffed out.

Returning his gaze to the Zep's iPad screen, Charlie went to click out of the "Z list" file but stopped himself after catching sight of a name on the list—Sal Maginn. Almost disbelieving his own eyes, Charlie leaned into the screen to study the name more closely. After glimpsing the address and contact information for Maginn, Charlie backed his head away from the screen, while continuing to eye the name.

Letting go of the mouse, he hit the mouse pad with his fist. He looked down and away from the computer screen, then spotted his phone and grabbed it. He dialed a number he knew by memory. It was a man that Charlie, out of respect, purposely never made him part of his phone's contact list. He waited for an answer. But, after a minute, only Sal Maginn's voice message went off. Charlie left a message for him to call him, immediately regretting that he used his own cell phone to call his Sal.

Charlie put the phone down, and his eyes landed back on Bixie's laptop. He went to reach for it but stopped when he heard the ring of his phone.

He looked at the screen and answered it with, "How are you, Sal?"

"Same old shit, Charlie." It was the familiar voice of Sal Maginn coming out of the receiver, and it continued with, "How the hell are you?"

Under any other circumstance, Charlie would be glad to shoot the breeze with Sal. But today's call was not made for social purposes.

"Sal, I need to see you," Charlie said.

A few seconds went by before Sal answered with, "When?"

Charlie noticed that Sal had dropped his cheery voice. Sal was one of the last people on earth that knew Charlie well enough to know when something was not right with him. At the moment, Charlie took comfort in that but felt his chest tighten as he reminded himself about the trouble that he may have unwittingly brought to his old friend's doorstep.

"Sal, can I drive over tonight?"

"Sure, kid." Then, apparently trying to lighten things up, Sal added, "And, bring your trunks, Charlie. I have a hot tub party going."

Forty-five minutes after ringing off from Sal Maginn, Charlie was awaiting the signal change at the intersection of Sunset Boulevard and Pacific Coast Highway. Glancing over PCH, to his right he saw the lights of Gladstones. It was the restaurant that Sal and he enjoyed many times. He remembered drinking beers on its outdoor patio, while enjoying the view and sound of the ocean waves below. But the days under those patio umbrellas seemed like decades ago. Though Charlie knew it was only a few years back.

The signal arrow turned green, and Charlie turned right onto PCH. Navigating the curving highway, he found himself sneaking looks to his left where he was treated to sparkles of moonlight hitting the waters of the Santa Monica Bay. He had a thirty-minute drive before he'd be at Sal's house.

Pushing a CD of music into its player, he mentally tried to escape into the sounds of jazz as his headlights lit up the road ahead and pieces of hills to his right.

But later, as the jazz CD was finishing its final piece, a thought hit Charlie. He quieted the music and pulled off the highway and into a side street. He was about 10 minutes from Sal's house.

He grabbed one of the burner phones he'd brought along and dialed Sal's number. After a few rings, Sal's voice came into his receiver.

"Charlie? Are you lost?"

Behind Sal's voice, Charlie could hear loud music, giggling, and splashing water.

"No. I'm close to your place." Charlie paused. "Sal, how'd you know it was me who was calling? I'm calling from a burner phone for precaution."

Suddenly, the background noises Charlie was hearing from Sal's side of the call were fading fast, then nearly gone completely. He heard a door close. Sal must have moved to his small study, Charlie figured. The man always treated him with importance. Charlie felt a few seconds of comfort in knowing he had Sal not only as a friend but an uncle-like figure.

But Charlie's feelings of regret quickly returned as he reminded himself why he was paying Sal a visit. He'd found Sal Maginn's name on Zep's client list that he'd found on the pimp's iPad.

Sal finally answered him.

"I knew it had to be you, Charlie. Nobody calls me much since I've retired."

Charlie thought he detected a hint of loneliness in Sal's voice. A sadness came over him. He should've been seeing his friend more often, and now it might not be possible in the future. Before he could speak, Sal voice came back on the line.

"And what's up with using a burner phone, tonight. Are you in trouble?"

"Maybe," Charlie said. "And Sal, that's why I'm calling. I shouldn't have asked to come over. It will put you at risk."

"What are you talking about, kid?"

"I may be hot. Heck, Sal I may have a tail on me now for all I know. I wasn't thinking straight about coming to visit you. Let me just tell you over the phone—"

Sal interrupted him with a laugh.

"I'm insulted."

"Why?" Charlie said, surprised to find himself laughing.

"For you to think that I'm some disloyal chump. And, that I'd keep you from showing your mug around here because you're drawing heat from the cops or somebody worse. Charlie, after saving my life back in Atlanta, I owe you my life."

"Sal, Atlanta was twenty years ago."

"I don't give a flying fuck how long ago it was. I'm a free man because you didn't run away when you could've. If it weren't for you, I would've been taking my shits on cold steel toilets and exercising in cement-encased yards. And, that's if I was lucky to live." Sal lowered his voice. "Charlie, you risked the same fate by coming back into that house full of gunfire to get my wounded ass out. Nobody in this business would've done that. Even for a friend."

"You would've, Sal."

Charlie thought he heard a snivel come over the phone lines. Sal cleared his throat.

"Now I am mad, Charlie. You've got me emotional. I'm hanging up and you're gonna get your ass over here."

Ringing off, Charlie put the phone aside and rested his hand on the stick shift. He found himself thinking back to a turning point in his life, at the age of 10. It was the day his father had deserted him and his mother.

His mother told him that his father just needed to work more and had to live elsewhere to do so. She told Charlie that his father would be by to see them, often. He knew she believed it, but he remembered sensing otherwise. Looking out his side car window, he recalled reaching his teen years and realizing he was right—his father never would be coming by to visit.

Charlie shifted his eyes to his rear-view mirror. As he caught sight of a few cars on PCH whizzing past the side street he was idling on, he realized it had been a while since he'd thought about losing his father's presence. But it was flooding back to him tonight.

As a kid, he'd learned to deal with his father's desertion, in his own way. It wasn't by talking about it. No. He recalled his main coping tool—a pencil.

Charlie figured he must've been thirteen when he began drawing as a coping mechanism. At first, he drew pictures of what he thought his father would look like if he'd ever see him again. Soon though, his artistic efforts of escapism turned to drawings of mountains, fields, rivers, and other natural scenery.

But the simple canvases he created never replaced the loss of his father. His drawings only dimmed his pain.

Now looking over the dash, with his hand resting on the vibrating stick shift, Charlie recalled how one day he sketched an outline of a brain. He let himself imagine this drawing to be his own brain. With his pencil, he parceled off a small section of it. This piece of mental acreage would be reserved for the few people he loved and trusted, people he could count on.

Charlie knew he had changed the day he drew that brain outline. He'd never trust anyone again. That is, unless he'd given them the key to his own fenced-off area of mental sanctuary. His father would never be let into this mental space. The man had forfeited his right to Charlie's trust, forever. His mother, his best friend Tab Smith, and eventually his girlfriend Laura Hadley would be given keys.

Remembering all this now, he shifted into gear and realized it'd been decades since he'd given any thought about the parcel of mental space he'd drawn out, all those years ago. But while hitting the gas pedal and making a U-turn, Charlie realized he had, some years back, subconsciously added another name to the list of the trusted few who had a key to his protected mental garden. It was Sal Maginn, whose house he now resumed his drive towards.

CHAPTER 18

With his car idling at an intersection, Harris felt both tired and hyper. Tired from getting up before 5:00 a.m., and hyper from what he woke up to—a multiple murder case.

The signal turned green, and he made a left onto Sunset, then a quick right into the parking lot of the Coffee Bean & Tea Leaf.

After parking the car, Harris got out and looked around for a red car. Spotting it, he shut his car door and shook his head, as he began to walk across the parking lot toward the shop door. Once inside, he ordered a triple espresso.

While waiting for his drink, Harris scanned the room for his meet-up. He spotted him, seated at a table tucked into a corner, with a tall, iced tea.

Harris waited until the black man looked up from his tablet device and caught his eyes. The man's face quickly disappeared under his baseball cap, returning his focus to his tablet screen while taking a sip from his iced tea.

The baseball cap was protecting not only the man's face but a huge amount of afro hair, a lot of which had escaped out of the hat. Harris also noticed the man's legs were in a state of perpetual movement. And all the bling the man was wearing seemed to be bouncing around with tiny sparkles of light hitting all the pieces at various intervals.

"Triple espresso," was shouted out from behind the barista bar.

Grabbing his triple shot, Harris grabbed the creamer. While adding cream to his espresso and moving only his eyes, he did another once over around the room. Nobody had paid any attention to the drink being called out to him. He also noticed that half the tables were empty. And the taken tables, other than where his meet-up was seated, were taken up by the usual specialty-coffee shop rats—wannabe screenwriter types and out-of-work internet news junkies, all with their frozen faces locked on a glowing screen of some sort. *What kind of zombie world have we created?* Harris wondered as he took a sip from his paper cup. Nobody looked at anyone in public places, anymore. But that was good for his meeting here.

He walked over to the leg shaker's table and sat down across from him. The man looked up from under his baseball cap at him again but quickly looked away and began eyeing the room as if he were looking for someone.

Harris folded his hands over the notepad he'd brought in with him, studying the man who always looked like he was going to jump up and run away.

"Don't worry Tommy," Harris said. "I've looked around the room. Besides, for a paranoid confidential informant you don't really take much precautions."

Tommy shot his eyes back to him and said, "How's that?"

"You drove here in that candy-apple red muscle car of yours." Harris looked him up and down and continued with, "You're also a shaking jewelry stand."

The legs of Tommy stilled, and he said, "Detective—"

Harris cut him off with, "Did you know Zep Hill?"

Tommy showed a surprised look and blurted out, "Why would you ask that?"

"He's a pimp."

Now showing even more surprise on his face, Tommy said, "So?"

Harris looked exasperated and said, "You're a pimp. And, pimps tend to know other pimps."

Tommy backed away a bit and held his tablet like a deck of cards in front of him.

"I'm a former pimp," he said. "And I have to stay away from pimping, remember? That's the deal I made with you cops."

Boring into him, Harris said, "Tommy, that's only half the deal."

After pausing for a sip of tea, Tommy responded with, "I know. Playing a rat is the other half."

Tommy looked out the window, onto the parade of cars whizzing by on Sunset Boulevard. He took a breath and looked back at Harris who was eyeing him.

"You think I had something to do with those killings?"

Harris studied the CI for a second. He brought his cup up to his mouth to take a hit of his drink, but not before saying, "So, Tommy. You've heard the news."

Putting his tablet down on the table, Tommy pointed to its screen and said, "That's what I've just been reading about. I knew something was up when you wanted to see me. So, I searched the local news and found out about Zep and the others getting wacked. And, now Detective, you think I had some connection to these killings?"

Harris shook his head and said, "I am just asking if you knew Zep Hill."

Tommy pushed the tablet away from himself.

"Look, Detective, I probably only met Zep once or twice. Maybe at a party or something." Tilting his head, he added, "This was when I was pimping, of course. But, I didn't run with him even back in the day. Nor, did we ever bump into each other's territories."

After making some notes on his pad, Harris looked back up and said, "Do you know who would want to kill Zep or a prostitute that was under his charge named Bixie Brown?"

"No," he said, smiling. "And, I've never heard of Bixie Brown until I read the news about Zep just now. And, just an FYI Detective, Bixie was probably just her hooker name."

Harris blurted out, "Her actual name was Bixie Brown. Nothing else. We checked it."

Tommy shook his shoulders, saying, "Like I said, I've never heard of her before hearing the news."

Finishing his espresso, Harris said, "Any local pimps ever threaten to kill you or anybody you know?"

Tommy smacked his lips together after swallowing some iced tea and replied, "Nope."

Putting down his pen, Harris looked away from the table. He took a breath and looked back at Tommy.

"Tommy, you're sure not offering much information. I have a fucking triple murder on my hands that involves a pimp and a prostitute. That's the business you were in. Or, for all I know, you are still in. Tommy, we let you out of your cage because we thought your eyes and ears were more valuable to the LAPD on the outside." Harris paused and added, "Maybe I'd better take you back to the cage, today."

Blowing out a breath, Tommy said, "Detective Harris, I'm telling you all that I know."

Ignoring his last comment, Harris said, "I want to ask you about your client list."

Tommy said, "You mean my list of johns when I was pimping?"

"Yes." Pointing at him, Harris continued with, "Now I want you to think about this before you answer, Tommy. Was there anybody, any client, that stood out as unusual?"

Leaning back in his chair, Tommy looked at his iced tea for several seconds. He grabbed it and took a long sip and swallowed.

"I always tried to check out the people I offered my services to," he said. "You don't want any vice squad guys as clients."

It was now Harris who swallowed. It steamed him whenever a criminal talked about their operation as one would a legitimate business. But he remained silent.

"And Detective, I usually succeeded in finding a bit about each and every client," Tommy paused. "But there was this one dude who was unusual. He was secretive. A type of guy you get curious about."

Harris lowered his head.

"How was this dude unusual?"

Tommy smiled.

"Detective, this dude never asked for any particular girl...or I should say any particular lady. This guy always referred to any hooker as a lady, not a girl or woman."

Looking sideways, Harris said, "So you're saying what made this client unusual was that he showed respect to your prostitutes?"

"Yeah. And that certainly stood out. But I wasn't thinking of that." Tommy looked around and then back at Harris. "I'm just saying this secretive dude didn't have any preferences when calling for one of my girls."

Harris picked up his pen back up without thinking, as Tommy continued to talk.

"See Detective, most johns would request a particular person or a specific type of woman—Mexican, Asian, white, black, old, young, or whatever. Past those initial descriptions, any client demands can, of course, get kinky." Tommy tilted his head. "But, this secretive cat always just asked for a lady. That was it. Nothing special."

Nodding, Harris began to jot down some notes. He was feeling the rumblings of a hunch. It was boiling up from inside his brain bank that held decades of investigation experience deposits. He paid more attention to his hunches with each passing year, as they were bearing fruit with increasing frequency.

He looked back up at Tommy.

"You also mentioned he was secretive."

Tommy nodded.

"This dude would always be at some hotel and tell me to send over a lady."

The undefinable hunch about this client of Tommy's was continuing to grip Harris, as he continued to listen.

Tommy took another sip of his drink and continued.

"I even paid a couple of hotel clerks here and there to find out the name this dude used to check in. But, it never matched the name he used when he called me. And, he always paid for his rooms in cash. Never a credit card."

By now, the hunch Harris was feeling had passed into the realm of a conscious thought. Harris found himself thinking again about how much risk last night's killer of Bixie took to kill her pimp, Zep Hill. The killer took further risk in going to Zep's house to steal his hard drive. As Harris told Garcia, his partner, these steps proved the killer used prostitutes and had dealings with Zep, in particular.

Those steps also told Harris the killer was a guy who took no chances on his identity being revealed.

By weaving his hunch into the facts of last night and his own assumptions, Harris had developed a theory. The secretive dude that Tommy was telling him about might be a triple killer.

"Do you know what he looked like?" Harris said.

Tommy slowly shook his head.

"Detective, I never laid eyes on him. A few times, I stalked the hotel where he had me send over a girl. But, I never spotted him. My girls would tell me the dude was a tall, thin, middle-aged guy." Tommy smiled. "They also said he was a big tipper."

Not wanting to stop the flow of information coming his way, Harris just nodded while wondering how much of the tips Tommy demanded back from the ladies. Holding his pen with his mouth open, Harris asked his next question.

"Who were the ladies that met with this secretive client?"

Tommy looked away with a snort and a chuckle. But his face went blank after looking back at Harris's cold stare.

"I don't remember," Tommy said. "And, as you know, I destroyed all my records after I was tipped off that I was about to be busted. But, even if I could recall what girls serviced this dude and I was, by some miracle, able to track them down they wouldn't be able to help you. Most of the girls are too loaded up on meth or Vicodin or worse to remember much about a guy or guys they took care of last night. Let alone remembering some dude from months or years back."

With his eyes and pen moving along his notepad, Harris said, "Anything else about this mysterious client?"

"Detective, this dude just had a vibe about him. I'd say he had some kind of charisma, even if I only spoke to him over the phone." Letting go a chuckle, Tommy added, "Funny thing, I didn't even suspect he might be vice. For all I know, maybe he was undercover."

Stopping his pen, but keeping his eyes on the notepad, Harris said, "Tommy, I take it you don't know this guy's name?"

"Well, he always gave his name as Tim. But, I knew that wasn't his real name."

Harris looked up to see that Tommy had grown serious as he continued talking.

"One night he, the secretive dude, called. I knew it was him by the sound of his voice. And, I could tell something was not right with him. He was drunk or wasted or something. Anyway, as usual, he told me to send a lady over to some hotel room he was at." Tommy paused. "But this time he didn't use the name Tim."

Losing consciousness of the ambient noise of the coffee shop, Harris cut in with, "What name did he use?"

Tommy showed him a wide smile and said, "I'll never forget it, since it's the name of my favorite uncle—Charlie."

Ten minutes after Tommy left the Coffee Bean, Harris stepped out of the shop. He stopped a few feet from the shop door and lit up a cigarette. While distinguishing the match with a few shakes of his hand, he heard a commotion. He looked left and dropped the match without thinking.

Harris saw an attractive middle-aged woman with a purse slung over her shoulder in a business dress. She was headed towards him and the coffee shop's entrance, which was directly behind him. And she was frantically waving a hand at some gangly-looking man following along beside her. It was obvious to Harris, the greasy-haired pest following her was an unwelcomed presence.

Harris could see the woman was walking too fast for her high heels while trying to get free from the man who was telling her how pretty she looked. Before Harris could intervene, the woman fell forward onto the parking lot pavement. She and her purse spilled onto the asphalt, right in front of him.

The gangly man that had been pestering the woman stooped down to help her. But Harris interrupted his efforts.

"Don't touch her."

The thin man looked up through his stringy hair at Harris and went still. The man almost fell backwards as he attempted to get up on his bare feet while backing away. He scampered away as Harris tossed his cigarette away and crouched down next to the fallen woman.

As the woman began to push herself up from the gritty pavement, Harris made a few awkward attempts to help her up. Not daring to lay a finger on her, he began making more silly attempts to help with the purse and its strap that had fallen off her shoulder. But he didn't manage to touch that, either.

The only thing Harris touched, and that was by circumstance only, were slices of the woman's long silvery hair. In the commotion, it seemed to be everywhere between him and her. Also hitting him was the woman's shampoo fragrance or perfume. Harris couldn't tell where all the enjoyable girly scents were coming from.

When Harris caught sight of her eyes, she had them locked onto his now-exposed holstered gun, inside his suit jacket.

"Oh, um…I'm a detective," he said as he rose in tandem with the woman.

When she looked up at him, it was his time to freeze. Her face was so naturally beautiful he never noticed he was staring at her with his mouth open. Now it was her words that put him at ease.

"Detective, your timing is perfect."

She broke into a smile.

Harris was lost in the moment and thought he saw a sparkle in her eyes.

"Thank you," he said, patting down his tie.

As she began to brush herself off, Harris felt a surge of feelings invading him. It was a romantic cloud overcoming his being. These were clouds he had not seen in his mental skies for years.

The woman readjusted the strap of her purse on her shoulder. Next, she brushed her hands together to rid them from the grim of the pavement.

Harris said, "I'll go in and get you some napkins."

She stopped him from moving by pulling out some napkins from her purse.

"Thanks, but I have plenty on me."

A few seconds passed as the woman cleaned her hands with some napkins. As she was finishing, she looked back up at Harris. She squinted from the sun hitting her eyes. Harris was nearly a foot taller.

"Am I allowed to ask detectives their names?"

Harris nodded.

"It's Detective Daniel…" he began but quickly caught himself. "Sorry. My name is Daniel Harris."

Tilting her head with her eyebrows raised, she smiled and said, "It doesn't sound like you say your name very frequently, outside of your profession."

Harris looked away for a second, then looked back down at her.

"That's true."

She nodded slowly while still looking up at him.

"My name is Laura. Can I buy you a cup of coffee?"

Harris sighed.

"I can't at the moment, miss."

"Please, it's Laura…Laura Hadley."

Harris hesitated and said, "Laura, can I take a rain check.? I will call you sometime soon."

He could not believe what had come out of his own mouth.

"Sounds good, Daniel," she said, reaching into her purse and pulling out a business card.

He took her card. And suddenly had a feeling of happy disbelief. A mini date had apparently been produced, out of nowhere.

Harris already felt different. He now had a slice of life, outside of his job.

Driving out of the parking lot of the Coffee Bean, Harris made a stop just before leaving and turning onto Sunset. Checking his rearview mirror, he caught a glimpse of the woman with long flowing hair he now had a future coffee date with. Shooting a look over at his passenger seat, he read the business card she'd given him just a few minutes ago. He liked the sight of her name—Laura Hadley—in print.

Looking back up at his rearview mirror, he resumed watching Laura walking to her car. She was holding a cup of coffee with her purse slung over her slender shoulder. He liked her deliberate and confident walk. Harris found himself lost in the moment, watching her as she climbed into a black BMW.

As her door closed, Harris thought of the color of her eyes, which he'd noticed even in the sunlight of the parking lot. He knew hazel eyes can frequently appear to shift in color from brown to green or green to brown. But Laura's appeared only a sparkling green.

Harris told himself to forget about Laura's classiness and good looks. He knew this whole thing would mean nothing. She'd only offered him a cup of coffee as a way of thanking him for getting rid of her straggly and pestering admirer. He caught himself feeling stupid for thinking anything else of the chance encounter and Laura's friendly offer.

As he squeezed his car onto a busy Sunset Boulevard though, Harris found a small part of himself holding out hope. Maybe this Laura Hadley, with her offer of coffee, had meant something more than just a gesture of thanks. And if so, he realized what he'd just done—he'd put her off due to an investigation.

And even though this current case involves a triple murder, he could hear his ex-wife now—*It's always a pressing case with you Daniel— one murder or three— you put me, and even yourself, aside for all of them.*

He knew his ex-wife was right.

Worse still, he knew his ex was correct in telling him their marriage was doomed from the start. When Daniel met her, he was an LAPD beat cop, soon to be a detective. In marrying him, she'd always tell her friends that she'd married a man who was already married. She would explain herself with a phrase that he'd heard her repeat numerous times—*The day Daniel signed up with the LAPD, he had walked down the aisle of his first marriage.*

CHAPTER 19

Hearing the clicking of his left-turn signal over the hum of his moving Porsche, Charlie turned off PCH. As he drove along Broad Beach Road, he saw the lights of houses on his left. To his right, his headlights caught pieces of parked cars.

A quarter mile down, he passed Sal Maginn's driveway. He noticed parking on the right side of the street near Sal's place was at a premium tonight. Not that it mattered. For tonight he preferred that his car be parked a block or so away. Since last night's events, Charlie felt like he was carrying some contagious virus. He didn't want to infect his friend's home with it, any more than necessary.

Charlie continued driving down the street and parked. Exiting the car, the smell of the nearby ocean hit him along with the faint sounds of crashing waves, just past the row of beachside houses.

As he began to walk toward Sal's place, he thought about when the two had met some 23 years ago. He was 30-years old and Sal was 52 when a mob-contractor, who knew both of them, paired them for a rush hit job.

From the moment the contractor introduced them, Charlie liked Sal. Though they only worked a few times together after that first killing job, they became almost inseparable as friends.

But since Sal had retired a few years ago to the beach house, they'd seen less of each other.

Managing a smile as he walked, Charlie remembered thinking he knew a lot about his chosen profession after being just 4 years into it. But then he met Sal. And Charlie began to learn the true ropes of the killing trade from him. Both, from working together on a few jobs and the long shop talks they'd have over beers.

Reaching Sal's place, he stopped at the foot of the short driveway leading to a couple of varnished wood garage doors. Looking up and around the mansion, he caught some slices of its glass, steel and concrete, all lit up by exterior lights. Realizing it had been months since he'd stood here, Charlie wondered to himself about how time just escapes into thin air.

A minute later, he was knocking on Sal's door while hearing the faint sounds of female laughter. Despite that, he knew Sal would answer the door himself. The man always told Charlie he considered it rude to have a guest of any home be greeted by another guest, a possible stranger.

The door opened and a grinning Sal was looking at him. "Charlie, I didn't think it was you since you usually text me to open the guest garage," he said. "Where'd you park?"

"Down the road," Charlie said with a wave of his hand.

"Well, fuck you too." Sal said with a slight smile. "And come in. You're looking good, kid."

Charlie stepped into the foyer and smiled while saying, "You're still taller and still stronger."

"You failed to mention I'm still bald." Sal chuckled, as he began to turn away, and added, "And kid, that won't ever change."

Charlie followed Sal a few paces into the living room, stepping onto its cherry wood flooring. Pausing, Charlie tilted his head while looking around the expansive split-level space. He was surprised to find funky-looking paintings of objects made up of bright colors hanging on the white walls. Looking up to the high ceiling, he noticed an array of recessed lights. A lot was new.

"This is nice," he said.

Sal scratched the back of his neck while taking in his own home interior.

"Oh, yes. I had the house changed since you were last here. The crazy interior designer I hired said this house should have the look of chic modernism combined with stylish comfort. I didn't know what the fuck she was talking about, but I hired her since she had a huge set of knockers."

Still scanning the room, Charlie nodded. He looked past the living room and through its tall glass walls, and onto a patio completely encircled by parts of the house. There, he saw a few topless girls inside a steaming hot tub paying no attention to Sal or him. He pointed toward the girls.

"I thought you said nobody calls you since you retired."

Sal looked toward the patio.

"Those girls are only here because I let them occasionally crash at my house and use my credit cards. And, I can tell you they use the cards more often than the house." Sal shook his head, then looked back at Charlie. "If you're on the run, as you say, don't worry about these girls memorizing your face. They're paid to be looked at, not to look back. Especially at any guests I have. Kid, let me introduce them to you."

Charlie stood still. And Sal took note, pausing a few seconds while eyeing his visiting friend.

"Let me grab a couple of beers," Sal said, apparently remembering Charlie was not exactly on a social call. "Then we can chat privately on the back patio."

Ten minutes later, Charlie was seated in a cushioned patio chair with a couple of beers on the table in front of him. He was on the ocean-facing back deck of Sal's house. The girls in the hot tub were separated by a slice of wall, their giggles no longer heard over the sounds of the ocean.

As Sal was adjusting a couple of patio heaters, Charlie looked down and to his left. He stared at the sand that was just a few feet away, below the edge of the wooden deck.

Somehow the sand triggered teenage memories for Charlie. Memories of when he and Tab Smith would occasionally spend summer nights sleeping on the sands of Newport Beach. They'd have brought only their bikes, sleeping bags, and whatever spare change they managed to scrounge around to put in their pockets.

Looking up and out to the dark ocean, Charlie managed a small smile from the good memories. Focusing on the tiny whitecaps rolling onto the shore some fifty yards away, he wondered why people's lives get so fucked up in adulthood.

Sal's voice broke his thoughts.

"Something must be on your mind. You haven't touched your beer." Sal took a seat across from him and continued with, "Talk to me."

Charlie eyed him. "I came here to warn you about something...something that's my fault."

Sal went to protest but Charlie held up his hand and continued.

"I knocked off a pimp named Zep Hill last night."

Turning away, Sal seemed to Charlie to be searching his memory for that name.

"And Sal, I got a hold of his client list." Charlie took a breath. "Your name is on it."

Holding his beer, Sal said nothing as Charlie held his eyes and continued.

"Luckily, I believe I have the only client list of Zep Hill's that exists."

Sal swallowed a swig of beer.

"Charlie, don't worry yourself that the cops might be coming to my door and questioning me about this pimp's murder. Which I assume you're implying." He wiped his mouth and said, "Kid, they're more than welcome to come by."

Charlie's face dropped forward, with his eyes remaining fixed on his friend.

"Sal, if the cops come by it won't be a simple meet and greet. This pimp's killing—"

Sal cut him off with, "Charlie, I've planned my retirement well. I've set up many legitimate businesses over the years. Hell, I'm embarrassed at how much income taxes I pay. So, I could give a fuck if the cops come over asking me questions about renting chicks. Or, if they start fishing around to see how I've come to live so well."

Charlie just held his stare.

"Besides Charlie. People like you and me are always in danger. And, I know I am an old guy. I guess I've grown used to the possibility of the past catching up with me."

Charlie nods and gets up to go, but before he can say his goodbyes Sal's voice stops him.

"You should, too."

Charlie halted and eyed his friend who remained seated.

After a few seconds past, Sal said, "You're in danger right now kid, but you have to learn to live with that in our line of work."

Sal motioned for him to retake his seat and Charlie did so. A few seconds of time were filled by the sounds of the ocean.

"Charlie, I don't recall the name of Zep Hill from whenever the hell I called the guy for a girl or two or three. I don't keep track of the names of the pimps I use. There are too many of them." Sal smiled, but quickly dropped it. "But it hit me a minute ago that I'd heard the name of Zep Hill while flipping TV channels this evening."

Charlie froze for a few seconds and said, "Sal, I'm in a real mess."

Sal pursed his lips and said, "I want to know what happened."

Charlie grabbed hold of his beer but didn't lift the bottle off the table. He seemed to be holding onto the bottle for dear life. Looking at Sal, he proceeded to tell him what took place last night.

Twenty minutes later, Charlie was just finishing up telling Sal about last night's trifecta of murders concerning the cartel money launderer Alejandro Vargas, the prostitute Bixie Brown, and the pimp Zep Hill.

After he concluded, Sal threw his head to one side.

"Kid, these things were always an occupational risk. Complications should be expected. After all, killing people can get messy."

Charlie swallowed and looked away. He didn't like hearing the word that described his profession—killing. It only served to remind him who he was—a paid killing machine. He looked back at Sal.

"Do you ever wonder how guys like us ended up as we did?" He said.

"I don't understand."

Charlie hesitated.

"We're killers, Sal." Looking down, Charlie clarified his question with, "What made us possible?"

Sal smiled and said, "Now you're going psychology on me, kid."

But Charlie could see Sal growing serious, which surprised him. He waited till Sal spoke.

"What made us possible?" Sal said, repeating the question. "Speaking for myself, it's me that made me the devil I am."

Titling back in his chair, Sal took hold of his beer in his lap.

"Charlie, I was put through the Catholic school system, which my fellow classmates and I called the salt mines. Every one of us kids in there hated it. We hated the uniforms, the boring church ceremonies, and all the other fucking rituals. Most of all, we hated the terrifying nuns that ran the asylum. They'd hit us on our hands with their rulers if we looked at them wrong." He laughed. "I'm seventy-five and I still get jolted whenever I see a nun."

Sal shook his head and after a quick swig of beer he continued.

"But one thing those ruler-yielding nuns taught me was that a sin puts a black spot on your soul. The day I learned that in 2nd grade, I started counting all the black spots on my soul." He smiled and said, "Sure, the nuns told us kids we could clear those little spots off our souls by confessing them. But, I never confessed but a token amount of my sins in that darkened confessional box the nuns took us to every Wednesday."

Sal gazed at the ocean waters, then back his guest.

"You see, Charlie, I never wanted those black spots off my soul. No. Instead, I bragged to my classmates about how many I had kept. By 4th or 5th grade, I had so many black spots littering my soul that I'd lost track of the count."

Charlie smiled but stayed quiet.

"My point is, kid, I've always been an evil person. And the black spots on my soul are my own markers. Nobody else is to blame. The Gods and the Devils will make me pay for those someday."

Sal lifted his beer but put it back down without a sip.

"But Charlie, I also have black holes on my soul from where pieces of it have been removed by others." He paused. "And, they paid for these black holes. I made sure of that by knocking all of those devils off, one-by-one. They're all in hell now, where I'll soon be joining them."

Relaxing his face, Charlie said, "I'm not so sure about that."

Sal's face lit up.

"That's what I like about you, Charlie. You're always on the side of your friends. But kid, I've got no excuse for the path I've chosen in life. I had it easy from the start, with two loving parents. And, a loyal Labrador to boot. You, on the other hand, had a bad break with your father deserting you and your mother." Sal shook his head. "And he never returned."

A loud wave crashed along the shore, and Charlie looked in its direction. As the sound of the receding wave died down, Sal grabbed his attention back.

"Kid," he said, cocking his head sideways. "I haven't seen you like this. Last night must have really hit you hard."

Lifting his head while eyeing Sal, he said, "It's not just last night."

Sal threw back another swig, and then put his beer down on the table.

"If you're not happy—"

"Are you?" Charlie said, cutting him off.

Grinning, Sal answered.

"I'm a fucking hitman. And unless you're in the army, if you kill for a living you're not going to be happy. I made a lot of bad money for killing a lot of bad guys. Call it a deal with the Devil." He paused and with a shrug added, "But I have my house, my credit-card bought blondes, and my toys. And despite my advanced age, I should have a few good years left to enjoy them."

A small breeze passed over the deck.

Sal lowered his voice and said, "Kid, if you're not happy, you should get out of the business. You've got more than enough green paper socked away."

"I'm going to get out. And, that means moving away." Turning right, he looked at the back of Sal's house and said, "Malibu would've been a nice place to retire to. But, that's not possible for me."

Wincing, Sal said, "The cartels?"

Charlie nodded.

"Yes," he said. "They'll be hunting me down."

Sal spread his hands open.

"That's the problem with the foreign drug outfits. They're a trap. Sure, they pay big, but then they've got you in their web." Sal took a slow sip his beer and said, "That's one of the many reasons I stuck to freelancing for private parties."

Charlie watched Sal under with the glow of a heat lamp behind him.

Exhaling Charlie said, "I may not be calling you anymore."

Sal cocked his head but kept quiet.

"Like I said, I'm moving away, Sal. Communicating with you electronically when both the good guys and bad guys are looking for me would put you in danger."

"Fuck that shit talk, kid."

Sal went to say something more, but Charlie held up a hand. Another loud wave crashed and slowly its sounds faded away. Charlie stood, but Sal remained seated and looked up at him.

"Watch yourself, Charlie," he said, pausing for a few seconds. "Those cartels don't have any lambs inside them…only lions, tigers, and bears."

After Sal's front door closed behind him, Charlie felt the comfort of his friend's home leave him. By the time he reached his car, it had been replaced with all the disastrous events of the last 24 hours. The killing of Bixie was a constant cloud following him.

As Charlie started his car, a further dread overtook him. His dinner meeting with Laredo was fast approaching. The drug cartel employer had told Charlie that he wanted the meeting "to test your attitude." Laredo's way of testing his attitude was to give Charlie another killing assignment. And that was the last thing Charlie needed, now.

Thirty minutes after Charlie Casey had driven away from Sal's beach house, he was inside a convenient store. He didn't know he was being carefully watched through the store's glass walls. The man watching him was inside a car, out in the store's parking lot. He was idling behind Charlie's Porsche.

The man watched Charlie's head moving above some retail racks, then stop. Given that it was half past 1:00 in the morning, the man figured Charlie was at the coffee dispensers preparing a hot drink. A quick look around the lot, the man found it empty.

It was time to move.

Leaving his vehicle, the man went to the back of Charlie's car and reached under it. He quickly found a slice of metal and placed a magnetic GPS device on it. He gently tugged at the device, reassuring himself it was securely attached.

Seconds later, the man was back in his car and speeding out of the parking lot. Turning onto PCH, he drove for fifteen minutes before hearing the ping of an anticipated text message on his phone. It was from Artie Abalian. Slowing down some, he read the text and nodded. It was a confirmation that Charlie's Toyota Corolla, inside his home garage, had been wired with a GPS. The text also stated that the battery-powered GPS, the man had installed on the Porsche just minutes ago, would be replaced with a wired-in device within a day.

Wherever Charlie drove, either in his Porsche or his Corolla, he was now being tracked.

DAY 3

CHAPTER 20

Det. Alex Garcia placed the large coffee down in front of Det. Daniel Harris.

"Alex, you could have picked a quieter coffee joint," Harris said, obviously referring to the loud rap music blasting above them from ceiling speakers. "It's six a.m."

Harris took a sip of his coffee and looked like he bit down on a lemon slice. Reacting, Garcia remembered he forgot to put cream in Harris's coffee.

"Daniel, I forgot to put cream in your coffee."

Garcia went to get up for cream, but Harris stopped him.

"Forget it, Alex. Just tell me what you got."

Garcia pushed aside his own coffee and looked down at his notebook.

"I'll start with the ballistics. Rob Johnson said he looked at the bullets. Other than to confirm that Vargas, Bixie Brown, and the dog were hit with a rifle and Zep Hill from a handgun, he had nothing more to add. Of course, he said he can't possibly complete any official testing this early in the game."

Nodding, Harris said, "Keep on it. We want to know immediately if the killer acts again. Tell Johnson we don't want to wait for official confirmations. We want his immediate suspicions if any ballistics line up with our triple killer's guns."

Garcia was noting it. But paused his writing. And eyed Harris.

"I'll keep in touch with Johnson. But Daniel, don't take this wrong, why don't you contact Johnson?" Garcia smiled and added, "I would think a senior detective has more pull than a rookie, as you call me."

Harris shrugged.

"Johnson don't like me."

"I'll bet he thinks you're pushy."

Harris brushed off the comment with a wave of a hand.

Alex smiled again.

"Daniel, nobody in the department seems to like you."

Harris's response was to take another swig of his obviously bitter tasting coffee and change the subject.

"Alex, any luck with any pimps?"

Garcia shook his head.

"I met with two pimps and talked to three others by phone. Nothing at all." Garcia paused. "Daniel, did your confidential informant have any information or names?"

Harris displayed unusual hesitation.

"My CI had nothing on Zep Hill or Bixie Brown." Pausing, Harris added, "But when my CI was an active pimp, he had a client that was different."

Garcia's eyebrows shot up.

"Different?"

"Yeah. Different."

Garcia waited for Harris to continue.

"The CI told me that this particular client, when requesting a prostitute, always referred to them in a respectful manner. Like calling them a lady, instead of just a girl." Harris looked down. "And the client was extraordinarily cautious. He'd used multiple names that were obviously fake. But, then my CI found out this guy's real name by a fluke. But only his first name. And, no other information on him."

Now Garcia took a sip of his coffee. And broke the few seconds of silence.

"Well, Daniel. What was the CI's unusual client's first name?"

"It was Charlie." Harris looked up and eyed Garcia. "And I have a strange hunch about this Charlie. Our triple killer took a lot of risk cleaning up his pimp tracks by killing Zep Hill. That sounds like my informant's mysterious client."

Charlie pulled up to the curb. He was a block away from the steak house on La Cienega Boulevard where he was to meet Laredo. The two had a dinner appointment, but he was early.

As Charlie cut the engine, he had a strange feeling he couldn't shake since leaving his home. Someone might have followed him. But, then again, just yesterday Laredo had told Charlie he knew where he lived. Maybe the cartel leader was fearing Charlie disappearing.

So maybe Laredo put a tail on him. Charlie half smiled. He had, just a few hours ago, worked on some details about leaving the country, for good.

Charlie knew coming to this dinner tonight might be some kind of setup by Laredo and his cartel cohorts to take him out.

But skipping tonight's dinner was not an option that Charlie found tempting at the moment. He had unfinished business concerning his long-deceased best friend, Tab Smith. And he sensed that he still owed Bixie Brown something more than just killing her beastly pimp. Charlie wanted to make sure there were no other human animals, like Zep Hill, alive that did Bixie wrong and may have played a part in her turning to a life of street walking.

Charlie exited his car.

Fifteen minutes later, Charlie sat at a corner booth in the dark steak house. He was awaiting the man he'd been working for the past twenty years. A man he still only knew by a single name.

Charlie's chest sunk as he caught sight of the Mexican national walking towards his booth. After all these years, there was no losing the fear of Laredo. The portly man could pass as any Texas or Mexico border town padre.

But Laredo's plump figure was only half his physical story. To Charlie, the man had the face of any one of the many bulls that he'd witnessed being stabbed at the bullfights in the Plaza de Toros México. Charlie attended such disagreeable spectacles only when Laredo would designate them for business meet ups in the cartel enforcer's home base of Mexico. The symbolism of the gory bull killing events was not lost on him. For Charlie knew the display of the bull being jabbed to death was Laredo's way of continually reminding him that *you are my bull, and this is what will happen to you if you cross me.*

When Charlie first met Laredo, the man's hair was as black and shiny as a crow's coat. Now it was streaked with gray and a bit thinner. Charlie knew that beneath that curly mix of hair was the mind of a devil. The man from Mexico had never shown Charlie a single redeeming quality. Laredo was all business. And his work was that of evil.

As Laredo slipped into the booth, a waiter placed menus down. But before Charlie opened his, Laredo pointed at a menu item and announced to the waiter, "We'll both have this. And a potato with everything on it." The cartel man handed back the menus while specifying the choice of beer he wanted brought to the table.

After thirty minutes of near silence, Laredo had pushed his plate away and grabbed hold of his second bottle of beer. He addressed Charlie.

"Charlie, I don't like to repeat my words. But, as I told you yesterday, you fucked up in the hills of Hollywood. The Alejandro Vargas hit was a bad thing."

Charlie decided not to defend himself. Laredo took a swig of beer and continued.

"Look. I have a new job. It involves two names—Bennie Densmore and Scott Nelson."

Taking one of the few sips of his own beer he'd taken tonight, Charlie hoped his shock didn't show. This was a troubling request, on a few levels. Bennie was a part of Charlie's circle of colleagues. Maybe Laredo was shutting down Charlie's operation and killing off all the people in it. If so, Charlie knew the last one killed would be himself. Killing Bennie and Scott would be akin to getting his own grave readied.

Charlie put his beer down and eyed Laredo.

"I didn't know you did business with Bennie Densmore."

Laredo offered a smile and said, "We knew you did."

Charlie looked away and then back at Laredo. "Who's the other guy…Scott Nelson?"

"You're losing your edge, Charlie." Laredo feigned disappointment. "I would have thought you'd be aware of not only Bennie's business life, but his personal life."

Laredo took another swig of his beer. He grew serious.

"Charlie, Scott Nelson is the boyfriend of Bennie's. And this Scott has been selling you and others down the river. He's an intelligence analyst inside the LAPD." Laredo raised his chin. "We need to shut his fucking mouth up. Bennie and Scott both must be handled within a month. They know too much. And, since they are part of your operation, they are your responsibility."

Charlie threw his hands open. "I don't know where Bennie or his boyfriend live."

"Finding them Charlie is part of your pay. We know they live together. But, we haven't been able to get their address."

Charlie tilted his head.

"Laredo, Bennie is an expert at finding people. I can assure you he knows how to hide. So, it could take longer than a month."

Laredo shook his head while maintaining eye contact.

"Some people are going to die within a month." Laredo finished his beer and added, "I hope it's only Bennie and Scott."

Charlie managed a nod.

Pushing his empty beer bottle aside, Laredo produced an envelope and said, "There's one other item."

Laredo slid the envelope across the table to him. Charlie looked at it and hesitated. Using his fingers, he slid it closer to himself but did not open it. He looked up at Laredo for an explanation.

"Charlie, someone wants a favor." Pointing toward the envelope, Laredo added, "I have nothing to do with the business inside that. But, I'm told, it too is time sensitive."

Laredo threw cash onto the tip tray and took his leave. Charlie stayed a few moments, giving the cartel man time to get out of the establishment and drive away.

Ten minutes later, Charlie was back in his car holding the envelope Laredo had given him. He went to flip on the interior light but stopped himself. If one of Laredo's men was going to shoot him, Charlie didn't want to make it easy. Besides, there was enough light entering his car from the street. He opened the envelope. It was from a friend of Charlie's. One he had known since childhood. His name was Bruce William.

Charlie had been unable to communicate with Bruce for the last 5 years. That was when Bruce had begun his current prison sentence. Both Charlie and Bruce knew the gig. They couldn't associate with each other during Bruce's incarceration. Doing so would only hurt both men. Bruce would be jeopardizing his parole date if he continued to associate with any shady characters from his crime days. And Charlie would be risking exposing his hidden life by bringing himself out of the shadows for law enforcement to see.

To Charlie, Bruce was closer to a brother than a friend. They both had grown up together since early adolescence—attending the same schools and playing on the same sports teams. They also both belonged to the Deadbeat Club. Bruce's violent father had left him and his mother when he was in grammar school.

Charlie was aware that Bruce had worked with Laredo in his drug dealing operations. So a note from Bruce coming from Laredo was not a complete surprise. What was a surprise was Laredo doing Bruce the favor. The cartel enforcer never did a favor for anyone. But Charlie brushed aside such thoughts and read Bruce's note.

The note spoke of Bruce's father having returned to Southern California and currently living at the Sampson Century Motel in LA. After decades of being gone since leaving his wife and kids, Chad William was pestering Bruce's mother for money. She rarely complied, which prompted William to beat her. His mother would never press charges.

Bruce explained in the note that his own 11-year-old son was living at the home and witnessing the abuse. Charlie understood Bruce's message, though it wasn't spelled out explicitly.

Before starting the car, Charlie looked around the side street of West Hollywood where he'd parked. He couldn't shake the feeling he was being watched.

Charlie's intuition was correct. He'd been followed the moment he had left his home tonight. And he'd been watched as he left the steak house and walked to his car.

As Charlie started his Porsche, the man that had been watching him shifted his own car into drive. The man looked at his phone screen tracking Charlie's movements via GPS. The man would not lose Charlie.

CHAPTER 21

After returning home from his dinner with Laredo, Charlie found himself restless. And for good reason.

Charlie had been ordered by Laredo to take out Bennie Densmore and Scott Nelson. And the note from his friend, Bruce William, added another name to his to-kill list. Moreover, there was an ongoing manhunt in Los Angeles for a triple killer. And though the police may not yet know it, he himself was the target.

For Charlie, all this produced an internal pressure build up. One that he couldn't ever remember feeling. He decided to step out to his backyard. It was a physical place that always relaxed him.

Within a minute or two, Charlie was at the far edge of his backyard lawn. He never put up a fence or any bushes for barriers that would block his view of Los Angeles and the canyon behind his property.

Charlie almost allowed himself a smile as he stood looking down into the dark space of the canyon, below. He took a deep breath and picked up the scent of the spring smells the canyon gave off. They were therapeutic for almost any ailment he suffered.

But soon a question broke his peaceful moments—*What made me possible?*

He quickly cleared his mind of it only after making a deal with the troubling question—he promised himself he'd find an answer to it.

The question had been formulating in his subconscious for some weeks. It had lately been breaking into his conscious mind. And whenever he prepared to make a kill, the thought was an inconvenience at best and a fatal distraction at worst. Yet the question wasn't going away. He wondered if there was a trigger in humans that caused a defined change in them. Perhaps he had hit upon a trigger of sorts. He didn't know, but something was up deep inside of him. That he did know.

Charlie turned back away from the Canyon and looked down at his grass lawn, softly lit by some of his house lights. Many times he'd slept out under the stars, here on his grass. He'd just throw down an old foam pad and sleeping bag he'd kept since high school. It always brought back memories of the few backpack trips he and Tab Smith would take during their senior year of high school. One of them would manage to find a car that was dependable enough to nearly guarantee them making it to a trailhead of one of the local mountains.

But Tab and camping out and hiking were all part of Charlie's past. Nearly all of his old friends were gone—either dead or just vanished when Charlie himself chose to disappear from his former world. And Charlie knew his old world, and former self, were never coming back.

Charlie headed back into the house. It was time to face Bixie Brown's laptop that he'd taken from her apartment after killing her pimp, Zep.

Minutes later, Charlie nearly had to steady himself to grab hold of Bixie's laptop. It was a reminder to himself that he was a killer of a female. And he'd be one forever.

He flipped open the laptop.

Charlie wanted to learn about Bixie's life. He no longer cared if there was anything on the device that could tie him to her now-dead pimp, Zep Hill. Instead, Charlie figured he owed it to Bixie to learn about her life. Still, he would check to make sure nothing tying his friend Sal Maginn to Bixie was on the device.

He thought of Bixie, not as a whore but as an innocent lamb. One he'd slaughtered and one he had to pay his respects to. His way of showing his respects to her was to find out who she was and what made her turn to walking the streets for pay.

After booting up Bixie's laptop, Charlie proceeded to search its contents of folders, files, and emails.

Concerning Sal possibly having been one of Bixie's clients, Charlie was relieved to find nothing inside the laptop files to indicate such. In fact, there was nothing about Bixie's street work in any of her files or emails.

Charlie's next search through the laptop was for personal reasons. He hoped the data would paint a picture of Bixie Brown's personal life.

He was not disappointed.

Charlie did find a personal journal typed by Bixie. The document chronicled nearly a lifetime of pain. Bixie's tales of her emotional struggles started when she was 8-years old. That is when her "daddy," Sam Brown, was murdered. After this event, nothing much was pretty about Bixie's life, save for her face. For the rest of her childhood, Bixie was either beaten by her stepfather, Skip Riggers or simply ignored. Her mother, Mindy Brown, was not much better. At best, she'd been an apathetic mother.

After landing in prostitution on the tough streets of Hollywood, Charlie read many of Bixie's emails pleading to her mother and stepfather to allow her to come home. Bixie expressed a desperate need to get off the LA boulevards. But despite how dire her electronic SOS messages were, her pleadings went unanswered. Charlie saw that after a few months, Bixie had stopped emailing any of her family, all together. They'd cast her aside, as an unwanted black spot on the family soul.

As Charlie closed Bixie's laptop, a shame came over him about his past use of prostitutes.

Charlie at first used prostitutes for a simple release of sexual build up. He was too shy to fully enjoy a lady's company when he knew that she was there simply for the money. Even when he sensed the girl had sympathy for him or, God forbid, actually liked his company, he would remind himself of the phoniness of the whole arrangement.

After a few years of paying for hookers, he soon became more comfortable with such fake encounters. With this anesthetized comfort came a boldness. Charlie's newly found what-the-fuck attitude allowed him to order up his whimsical desires. In short, he'd become a professional john.

But one thing he never was able to shake off was the humiliating feeling after the act was done. He despised the drive home from each hooker encounter. His only self-allowed comfort was from the knowledge that he had no choice. Given his profession of killing, socializing to any degree outside of business was just too risky. Any steady female friend was out of the question.

Charlie approached his use of prostitutes with caution. He never requested from Zep Hill any girl he paid for, twice. With one encounter, a prostitute could easily forget her john. But with two or more meetups, she might remember Charlie and that would not be okay. Charlie was a man who wanted to be forgotten.

But now, after reading Bixie's sad tale of life, Charlie knew he was done with using prostitutes. And Charlie also realized something in him needed feeding—a hunger to make right with Bixie's soul.

Charlie wasn't taking committing murder outside of his profession lightly. But he knew a lot of murders were committed over such petty things as a parking spot or romantic jealousy. He would be murdering over something much bigger—righting some long-ago wrongs against a helpless little girl named Bixie.

DAY 4

CHAPTER 22

Charlie sat at his dining room table. He had finally woken with some decent sleep. Maybe the sleep came because his mind seemed to have settled on some things.

For a switch had flipped inside of him. Charlie now knew he had to quit his current life. It was no longer working, if in fact it ever had.

But as he gazed out his sliding glass door and onto his back patio, lit by the mid-morning sun, Charlie realized that he'd come to a fork in the road on his escape route to a new life. One road led to redemption. The other road led to revenge.

He pursed his lips.

Redemption was for popular-fiction novels and G-rated movies. And he was not inside either one of those. No. He would seek revenge.

But Charlie also would partially seek some redemption.

Charlie knew his biggest sin, thus far in his life, was the killing of Bixie, a non-criminal. Bixie's laptop had told him all about her being beaten and mentally abused by her monstrous stepfather, Skip Riggers.

To gain a tiny sliver of redemption from shooting Bixie dead, Charlie would kill Skip Riggers. He made this decision last night.

And, this morning, he'd decided to perform an act of revenge. He now knew it was time for his long-ago silent promise to his best friend from childhood and on, Tab Smith. Nearly from the moment Charlie found Tab dead from suicide, he had declared Tab's father, Clarence Smith, a dead man.

For Charlie knew his other close friend, Sal Maginn, was right about some folks taking pieces of your soul from you. Sal was right to hunt those thieves of his soul material down and to kill them. Now, Charlie thought it was time to hunt down the thief of Tab Smith's soul material. He would kill Clarence Smith.

But before Charlie could take care of either Skip Riggers or Clarence Smith, he had a timely good deed that needed to be done. Per his note from another childhood friend, Bruce William, Chad William was an immediate danger to others and so had become a prioritized target.

Charlie found the mid-morning sun continuing to rise as his thoughts returned to his reading of Bixie's journal of horrors, last night. The journal had brought him back to the question that had been haunting him for months—*What made me possible?* He suddenly realized Bixie's life story was what ultimately brought the answer to him. It was anger that made Bixie walk the streets. And it was anger that made Charlie a killer.

And Charlie now knew what made all of his Deadbeat Club friends end up on the bad side of life—anger. The club was supposed to be about having fun with the idea of being a kid of a deadbeat dad. But, at 53-years of age, Charlie now saw the club in a far darker way. It wasn't about fun. The club was about anger, either buried or out in the open. And Charlie now knew that anger is what made him possible.

Charlie stood up and walked to the sliding glass door and opened it. Taking in some fresh air, he began to think about the final act in closing out his current life. It would be an act of escape. Afterwards, he would create a new life.

But he still had the problem of Bennie Densmore and Scott Nelson. Laredo had ordered the two to be taken care of.

Charlie would continue to mull what had to be done with Bennie and Scott. Besides, he still didn't know where the two lived. And he still needed the services that Bennie offered him.

Stepping out onto his sunny patio, Charlie seemed content with the immediate work ahead of him. Once his targets had all been hit, he would vanish from the country. He would live out his life quietly on some faraway land. Perhaps a desert, a forest, or a sandy beach.

For once, Charlie had a future that wasn't going to involve killing. And that was calming.

While looking up and taking in some more sunlight, Charlie's phone chirped. He saw that it was Bennie Densmore calling. Bennie was just the man Charlie needed to talk to.

CHAPTER 23

Det. Daniel Harris decided his ex-wife had been right about him. She'd been his "second wife" as she would always say. His "first wife" was his work. And each case he worked became his next "wife," as his ex had always pointed out to anyone who would listen.

And though Harris's current case was a triple murder involving a money launderer, his prostitute, and her pimp, Harris made a date. Laura Hadley would be the first time he saw any female in a romantic way since his divorce.

Harris made a point to be early for the dinner date. So after a quick smoke that would have to last him through his date, he had arrived at the fish house a full 20 minutes before the 8:00 p.m. prearranged time. But walking in, a "hello" greeted him from somewhere. He looked to his right, and a smile was now greeting him. Both the "hello" greeting and the smile came from Laura Hadley, who stood up and offered an outstretched hand up at him. As he reached out to shake Laura's hand, he concentrated on a not-too-firm but not-too-limp grip. But once he touched her hand, he didn't much think about any grip rules. Laura's soft hand had jumbled his thinking.

Harris let go of Laura's hand and indicated that he would check on their reservation. He was expecting her to sit back down in her lobby chair. Instead, she moved to his side and followed him to the host post. He liked it.

Harris and Laura stopped touching their dinner plates. And Harris had never noticed the food. Laura's face of beauty and flowing hair intimated him too much to even half relax. And her calm demeanor made Harris clam up, still more. Finally, he was able to relax a bit as her easy-going small talk had a soothing effect on him.

After their plates were cleared away, Laura had hot tea and Harris a coffee. The talk turned serious. Laura had some questions about Harris's background.

"So, Daniel. You're divorced?'

"Yes. It was finalized two years ago."

"Any kids?"

Harris shook his head.

"No."

Harris found Laura studying him.

"Can I ask what happened?"

Harris sighed.

"My detective work got in the way." Daniel shrugged. "The divorce is all on me."

Laura showed him a gentle look. He continued.

"That's why I'm here, now with you, Laura. I made a decision after our parking lot meet-and-greet. And that was to make a date with you, despite the current case I'm working. And, it's a pressing case."

Laura nodded and said, "If I may say so, it will make you a better detective if you have a personal life."

Now Harris nodded.

"I've come to realize that." Harris was so focused on Laura he hadn't touched his coffee. "But that's not why I asked you to dinner. And so quickly after meeting you."

Laura turned her head and lifted an eyebrow.

"No?"

Harris looked down and then back up, at her.

"No."

Laura let go of her teacup. She threw her hands open and asked, "Then, why the rush to have dinner with me? For all I know, you're handling that triple murder case that's all over the news."

"I am."

Laura froze.

"Daniel, you could've put our date off. I would have understood that you can't put off a triple murder case like that."

"I haven't put the case off. My choice, tonight, was just not to put you off."

Laura looked confused and said, "But again, why the rush for our dinner?"

Harris hesitated.

"Because Laura. I sensed you were worth it. And, tonight, I found out I was right."

Laura's head backed away slowly. She smiled.

"Daniel. I think I just fell in like, with you."

Before Harris walked Laura to her car, he had learned a thing or two about her. He had learned that she had never married. She had hinted there had been issues from her upbringing that had stopped her from marrying anyone.

Before Laura had closed her car door, she had offered Harris a hug. And a "thanks" for a wonderful dinner. She had also surprised him by asking him to come to her 35th high school reunion coming up, next weekend. Harris accepted the invite.

DAY 5

CHAPTER 24

Charlie didn't feel like himself. Starting tonight, he was going to be hitting a string of personal targets. And he'd never killed, other than as a hired gun. But he had to push any interfering thoughts, aside. He was determined to finish the tasks he'd laid out for himself. Only then, would he allow himself to leave the country for refuge and retirement from killing.

The address of Charlie's target tonight was a motel room. The address of which his friend, Bruce William, had spelled out in his note that he'd passed along via Laredo.

The room was part of the Sampson Century Motel. Located in south-central Los Angeles, the motel catered to monthly renters who were usually transient in nature.

The target had been living at the Sampson for several months. Charlie knew the general location of the motel. It was in a crime and gang ridden neighborhood, which might make things less risky for the job. Charlie had always believed that cops didn't much like patrolling or answering emergency calls in such high-crime neighborhoods. Still, as he drove to the motel, he caught himself keeping one eye on his rearview mirror. He knew that something as minor as a flickering tail light could change a criminal's life, forever.

Charlie wished he had the time to get a one-time throwaway car from Lew Holt for tonight and his other upcoming jobs. Still, he was glad that Lew had recently checked out his Toyota that he was driving tonight, for anything that needed fixing.

Besides watching out for curious traffic cops, Charlie still had a feeling someone had been following him, recently. Perhaps Laredo had put a tail on him. Anything was possible since his fuck up, a few nights back, with the Alejandro Vargas hit. Charlie kept this in mind as he continued along Century Boulevard.

Coming up to a red light, he heard a ping on his phone. Looking over at the phone lying on the passenger seat, he saw a text from Artie Abalian. He leaned over a bit and read the text without touching the phone. The trustworthy craftsman was letting him know the door of room 255 of the Sampson was unlocked and the room unoccupied.

Charlie nodded to himself. He made a mental note to himself to give the supersized Armenian a few extra thousand. And he made a mental note to, again, thank Sal for putting him in touch with the can-do locksmith, all those years ago.

The scene was set for another perfect killing.

But again, Charlie couldn't muster up any of the professional pride he usually felt when all was set for the kill task. No. He concluded several months ago that those days were over.

Besides, Charlie had long ago let go of the notion of a perfect killing. He now held that a perfect hit was only possible for psychopaths. All other killers had to pay up for their misdeeds. The debt would be owed to the mental demons of guilt.

Staring up at the red light, Charlie realized his career path had made him despise the color red. It was the color of what he spilled for a paycheck.

The light turned green, and he hit the gas. He tried to comfort himself with the thought that he'd soon be leaving the country. But his luck would have to hold. There were two threats to his leaving—the LAPD and a devil named Laredo.

Charlie knew that motels in seedy areas, renting to such human shits of society as his target tonight, could be run rather loosely. Managers of such establishments tended not to want to see, hear, or know much about any of the activity of its daily or monthly room renters. Such hotels were also used to having cars coming and going at all hours of the night. Many of those cars wouldn't have been listed on any check-in forms of its guests.

So Charlie wasn't worried about his Toyota drawing any unwanted attention while it was parked inside the lot of the Sampson Century Motel, tonight. Still, standing inside room 255 he spied from one of several torn slices of the window curtains to check on his car. He wanted to make sure his car was still in the lot and in one piece. All good. His thoughts turned back to his target.

Chad William was a preferred type of kill target. Charlie always enjoyed the added advantage of knowing or, better still, having seen the person that he was targeting for a kill. With William, he would enjoy both advantages. But they were greatly reduced since he hadn't seen or talked to the man in decades.

Charlie took another one of his many peeks, of the last two hours, through the motel room curtains. Suddenly, he spotted a man. He recognized the walk and Popeye figure of the man. This man was heading toward the staircase which leads to the second floor where Charlie was, inside room 255.

Only Charlie's eyes moved as he watched the man nearly stumble as he reached the second floor. Popeye was drunk tonight. And his unhealthy-looking body didn't offer evidence that he'd been eating much spinach these last few decades.

But Charlie knew Chad William was no Popeye. No. The cartoon character never beat Olive Oly, his lady. William, now coming toward the room Charlie was inside of, was beating his ex-lady.

Chad William was the deadbeat dad of Bruce William, the last surviving member, besides Charlie, of the Deadbeat Club. Taking care of Chad fit into Charlie's newfound purpose in his life—personal revenge hits. Killing William tonight, would right one of the wrongs that made Charlie and Bruce and their fellow Deadbeat Club members become what they became, as adults.

Chad had been showing up lately at his ex-wife's house for some warm food and whatever beer money he could physically shake from her. Calling the cops was not an option Mary William considered, since Chad had threatened to kill their grandson she was caring for, if she ever did.

Charlie moved away from the curtains.

Less than a half minute later, Charlie was sitting on the closed commode inside the bathroom of Chad William's motel room. He'd waited patiently for over two hours for the sound he was now hearing. It was the sound of the room door being unlocked. He had barely heard it over the soft roar of the running water coming from the empty shower, next to him.

As the room door opened, Charlie heard the traffic sounds of the nearby boulevard rush into the motel room. But after hearing the door shut, he once again was hearing the running shower water. But now, he could also hear some shoes moving along the well-worn carpet in the bedroom of the room.

Still seated on the closed commode, Charlie looked down at his phone on the floor in front of him. Its screen was displaying the feed of a dropcam he'd earlier placed on the small nightstand next to the motel room's bed. Via the camera feed, Charlie saw Chad William freeze in place, as the man took in the unfamiliar scenery splayed across the floor of his unkempt room.

Charlie watched as William fell for the bait he'd set. Being a man himself, Charlie couldn't blame him. He knew William's male sexual nature would trump any caution when deciding whether to follow the clothing items lying on the floor.

And that's what happened.

Continuing to watch from his phone screen, Charlie saw William walk around the zig-zag trail created by black high-heel shoes, black fishnet stockings, and a red dress. The items lead him to the noise of the running shower. And finally, to the entrance of the bathroom.

Now, Charlie was watching for the second time in less than a minute a frozen Chad William but no longer from the phone screen. William was now straight in front of him and no longer wearing the smile he had on when he came into view at the bathroom doorway. William had quickly dropped his smile when he found himself a couple feet from a stranger sitting on the toilet. A stranger who had a weapon pointed at him.

Holding the gun with its suppressor attached to it, Charlie read Chad William's dancing eyes. Through them, Charlie could see that William was trying to sort out what was happening, here. Charlie also sensed William was trying hard to clear the current alcohol clouds out of his head.

William shook his head a bit. The desperate looking man appeared to be trying to think about how to get out of the mess he was now facing.

Panic was apparently setting in, as William wet his lips. The man traded looks between Charlie and the gun he was holding and the shower curtains, hiding the cold running water.

For a split second, Charlie wondered whether Chad William knew this was all tied to the physical beatings he was giving his ex-wife. They were happening almost daily, from what Bruce had told Charlie. A push one day and a punch another. If Bruce's mother was lucky, William would let her off with a simple batch of screams. And all in front of his grandkid, Bruce's son.

But Charlie didn't have the time to wonder beyond a few seconds. The job of killing left precious time for analyzing the target's mindset.

Charlie pulled the trigger.

With Chad William falling to the floor, the beatings of Bruce William's mother had come to an end. And the home of Bruce's son was now a better place to raise a kid.

DAY 6

The morning after the Chad William motel hit, Charlie woke up with a remembrance that he was facing an additional problem. The name of this additional problem was Bennie Densmore.

Bennie had called Charlie just yesterday morning with an unusual request. The computer hacker asked Charlie to meet him. They had met in the past, but it was always for business purposes and always at Charlie's request. For Bennie did jobs for Charlie, never the reverse.

So a meetup request coming from Bennie told Charlie that the hacker had something up his sleeve. And it had to involve money. Since Charlie still needed the services Bennie offered, he had to play along.

And so tonight, the two men would have dinner.

Charlie was walking up to the host stand when he spotted Bennie. The computer hacker was waving at him from one of the front patio tables. Charlie walked over and sat down, opposite Bennie who offered him a nod and said, "Thanks for coming."

It'd been a few years since Charlie had seen Bennie. He noticed the slight and irritating grin the man wore was still there. And Bennie was now completely bald and had put on many pounds of flesh.

The noise surrounding their table was much higher than their own voices. The patio section of the fish restaurant was adjacent to a busy pedestrian sidewalk. And the sidewalk fronted the traffic infested Sunset Boulevard in West Hollywood.

But with all this white noise and activity going on, Charlie noted that Bennie was focused on the small leather bag Charlie had slung over his right shoulder. It seemed to make Bennie squirm, a little. Charlie removed the sling bag and placed it on the ground next to his chair. He looped the strap of the bag around his right foot, as a precaution against forgetting the bag.

As Bennie dug into his battered fish and chips, Charlie turned to look at the sidewalk foot traffic. He watched as several twenty-something, scantily dressed, giggly girls walked by. The sounds of high heels hitting the sidewalk could somehow be heard above all the surrounding white noise. The clubbing crowd was roaring for action on this Southern California cool spring night. The young ladies reminded Charlie of how life was passing him by, all due to his chosen profession.

And while alcohol was keeping the younger club crowd walking the Sunset Strip warm, the tableside heat lamps were warming Charlie and Bennie.

After Bennie washed a big bite of fish down with his iced tea, he spoke up. "Aren't you gonna eat, Charlie?"

Charlie responded by taking a stab at his sole and followed that with a gulp of his own iced tea.

With their meals finished, and small talk dying out, Bennie turned to business.

"Charlie, about an hour ago, I sent you a zip file. It contains all the info you requested on Skip Riggers and Mindy Brown. Bixie's stepfather and mother."

Charlie grew tense and irritated. Tense from hearing Bennie say Bixie's name, aloud. Irritated because Bennie was doing it for effect. But Charlie kept his cool.

"I got it."

Bennie then produced an envelope and pushed it across the table to Charlie.

"And here's the updated passport you requested."

Charlie grabbed the envelope and said, "That was quick."

"Well, my guy had your previous one from a couple years back. He simply updated it."

A few seconds passed. Bennie eyed Charlie.

"You must be planning to leave the country."

Ignoring the comment, Charlie reached down and placed the envelope, holding the passport, into the front pocket of his leather bag.

Bennie wouldn't let it go.

"Leaving the country would be understandable." Bennie offered a sliver of a smile. "I mean, with what's all over the news."

Again, Charlie didn't take the bait. Bennie got serious.

"We've been doing business for several years, Charlie. I'd like to think that I've made you rich. And, frankly—"

Charlie cut him off with, "We're squared up, Bennie. I wired that payment overseas last night."

Bennie nodded. "Yes, I received that."

Charlie raised his eyebrows. "Then what's this about?"

Continuing his line of thought, Bennie said, "Charlie, a few days ago I researched your background. Your business accomplishments are impressive. I also figure your kind of work must pay well, given the risks."

Charlie didn't move or react with words. Bennie's voice picked back up.

"I've kept my mouth shut over the years." Bennie sighed. "So, I think you owe me a big payment."

Charlie, again, said nothing. And Bennie was forced to continue.

"Call it a long-term employment bonus." Bennie lifted his pudgy face. "It's only fair, Charlie."

Charlie looked down.

"I can't do that, Bennie." Looking back up at the hacker, Charlie added, "Not without some insurance."

"Insurance?" Bennie said.

Reaching down, Charlie grabbed his leather bag. He looked around and found the happy-go-lucky restaurant patrons were not paying any attention to Bennie or him. So he brought the bag up to the table and opened it for Bennie to see its contents.

Bennie's eyes went wide.

"What's that, Charlie?"

Lowering his voice, Charlie answered.

"It's two bundles of hundreds."

Wetting his lips, Bennie was eyeing the bag's contents when he said, "In my past life, I was a bank teller. That's two hundred thousand dollars."

Charlie closed the leather bag. "Would that qualify as a big bonus?"

"Of course."

"It's yours, Bennie. But, again, I need insurance."

Bennie was still eyeing the bag when he said, "What kind of insurance?"

"An address."

"Whose address?"

"Yours."

Bennie finally looked up from the bag. Charlie continued.

"These bundles are yours, tonight. But, I will only give them to you at your house." Bennie went to protest as Charlie finished his thought with, "You know what I've done. So, I need to know where you live. This will be my insurance policy that your money demands will end here."

Bennie swallowed.

"Charlie, I do indeed know what you've done. You have me a little concerned." Bennie offered him a nervous laugh. "You're not gonna kill me tonight, are you?"

"No." A second went by. Charlie said, "I will follow you to your house."

Letting out a long breath of air he seemed to be holding, Bennie now lowered his voice and said, "Charlie, you're the only killer whose word I trust."

DAY 7

CHAPTER 26

Charlie sat in his Corolla. He was parked on a side street that enabled him to comfortably view the front of a decades-old tiny chapel. The building had faded white paint that had chipped in a lot of places.

The chapel was hosting Bixie Brown's service, today. And since the funeral home and chapel was relatively close to Bixie's Fairfax Avenue apartment, it made it doubly difficult for Charlie to handle, emotionally. After all, he knew he was responsible for this ceremony.

The funeral had just concluded. Charlie was relieved to find no press reporters or photographers watching as the mourners spilled out of the chapel. There were only a handful. And he quickly picked out the two people he was here to find.

Charlie spotted Bixie's stepfather Skip Riggers and her mother, Mindy Brown. He knew what they looked like from the photos he'd seen both on Bixie's computer and more recent ones Bennie Densmore had grabbed off social media sites.

The hatred Charlie felt for Bixie's stepfather Skip Riggers, after reading Bixie's journal on her laptop, had just doubled upon seeing the man in person. Riggers could pass for a beardless Santa Claus, one with short white hair and a deep purple drinker's nose.

Charlie wouldn't bother getting his emotions all tangled up against Mindy Brown, Bixie's mother. She was a true she-devil of a mother if there ever was one. But for Charlie, he'd leave Mindy to worry forever about her own fate. He was only personally interested in Skip Riggers. Namely, putting an end to his life. This was due to the beatings and emotional damage Skip had brought to Bixie, as a child. All of Skip's abuse had begun after her father, Sam Brown, was murdered. And all of Bixie's pain caused by Skip and Mindy was documented in her journal.

So Charlie had Bennie do some digging on Skip and Mindy. Bennie had informed Charlie that Sam Brown's murder remained unsolved. Bixie's stepfather and mother were investigated for the murder of Sam Brown. According to court documents filed by the local DA handling the murder investigation, Skip and Mindy had a financial motive to kill Brown. Sam Brown was a union worker and had a life insurance policy attached to his employment. Upon his death, Mindy received a substantial life insurance payout. Ultimately, the couple was never charged for Brown's death.

But the police were not the only ones suspicious of Skip and Mindy's involvement in Sam Brown's murder. Charlie had learned through Bixie's journal that she had suspicions that the two had killed her father. A father that Bixie missed daily. A father that whenever Bixie spoke about missing him or referred to him as "my real daddy," Skip would hit her. All the while, Mindy would turn a blind eye to the physical and mental punishments Skip would bestow on her daughter.

Such thoughts were flashing in Charlie's mind as he continued to watch Skip and Mindy chat with mourners of Bixie's. He thought about why the pair had flown to LA, from their home in Wisconsin, to hold a service for Bixie. One motivation for the trip was obvious to Charlie. He assumed a few, near and distant, relatives cared enough to pay their respects to Bixie. So a funeral service was necessary. Skip and Mindy didn't want to risk their family's wrath by not putting on a complete service.

And no doubt, by holding Bixie's service in LA, Skip and Mindy wanted to remind everyone that Bixie ran away from them. And she perished due to choosing a life of drugs and prostitution. The stepfather and mother wanted no blame in any part of Bixie's sad ending.

But for Skip and Mindy, holding a funeral for Bixie, all for the sake of appearances, was not their only motive to fly out to Los Angeles.

Just yesterday, Bennie pointed Charlie to a news piece he'd uncovered. The news item solved the riddle, for Charlie, as to the real motive of Skip and Mindy expensing a trip from Wisconsin to LA. It had not much to do with Bixie's funeral.

Charlie found, from the short news article sent by Bennie, that Skip and Mindy had filed a wrongful death claim against the estate of Alejandro Vargas. The couple was suing the now-dead cartel money launderer, on behalf of their Bixie's estate. Skip and Mindy's legal team held Vargas and his criminal life responsible for the death of Bixie.

But Charlie put all this aside, for the moment. His immediate attention was repaying Bixie Brown the unpayable debt he owed her for taking her life. And dealing with Skip Riggers was all part of Charlie's debt payment to Bixie.

And dealing with Skip began with Charlie starting his car. With his car idling, he watched Skip and Mindy offer a final hug to a mourner at Bixie's service, just before they climbed into what appeared to be a blue rental car. Skip was driving.

Charlie waited until Skip's car had pulled out of the chapel's lot. He then tailed Skip and Mindy's car, putting a comfortable distance between him and them.

Less than an hour later, Charlie saw the couple pull into a pricey looking beachfront hotel on The Strand in Hermosa Beach. Skip and Mindy had turned Bixie's funeral trip into a mini vacation of sorts.

Charlie pulled over. He had a view of the couple as they parked in the hotel lot. He watched them get out of their car. Mindy headed toward the hotel, but Skip was making a trip to a trash bin. He was carrying some object. Charlie instinctively brought up his binocs and zeroed in on Skip, as the man reached the bin.

As Charlie watched, Skip opened a container and tossed a pile of dusty material into the bin. Skip was careful not to allow the cloud of dust hit him. He then trashed the container. Charlie realized that Skip had just tossed out Bixie's ashes.

Before bringing down the binocs, Charlie turned them on Mindy. He caught her in a shaded area, where she had witnessed what Skip had just done with her daughter's ashes and urn. Bringing down the binocs, Charlie had no doubt Skip and Mindy would be making up a fairytale-like story about where they had spread Bixie's ashes.

As he watched Skip and Mindy enter the hotel lobby, Charlie placed a call to Artie Abalian. Besides being a security alarms and locks consultant, Charlie had occasionally used the always-willing Armenian for special tasks. And he had one for Artie, today. It would be to watch the movements of Skip and Mindy.

CHAPTER 27

Harris heard the chirp of his cell. He saw the name of the caller on its screen. Maybe the detective assigned to assist him on the murder spree that began in the Hollywood Hills, had some pertinent news on the case.

Putting out his cigarette, Harris answered the call.

"Alex. What do you have for me?"

"Something from Rob Johnson in ballistics," Garcia answered. "I'd asked Johnson to tell us immediately if he had any suspicions that any ballistics, new or old, line up with either the rifle or handgun used by our triple killer. As you had instructed."

Garcia paused for a split second.

Harris got up from his desk chair, the only chair he had inside his condo. He found himself bracing for news of another murder victim. A fourth victim, if he trusted his math at this moment.

"Go on, Alex," he said as he looked out of the lone window his room offered.

Garcia cleared his throat.

"Johnson said he thinks the bullet from a killing at an LA motel a couple nights back matches the handgun bullet from the pimp Zep Hill's killing."

Harris exhaled and asked, "What motel?"

"The Sampson Century Motel. It's a few miles from LAX, on Century."

Harris sensed Garcia was going to add more details.

"The name of the victim is Chad William. He was renting a room by the month, at the motel. William has been employed, off and on. He has a domestic violence conviction, but that was years ago." A pause. "Our killer has now shot a money launderer, a hooker, a pimp, and now a motel dweller."

"Alex, do they have a motive for the William's killing?"

Now it was Garcia who exhaled.

"No. The William's killing does not line up with the others. There's nothing connecting Chad William to Vargas, Brown, or Hill. At least not on the surface."

Turning away from the window, Harris ended the call. He had a feeling there'd be more killings before a motive for the William murder could be developed.

It was just past 11 p.m. Charlie was keeping his eye on a blue sedan. The rental was parked inside the lot of a seedy motel on Figueroa Street. It was the car he'd seen Skip Riggers and Mindy Brown in, earlier in the day. They'd driven the car away from Bixie's funeral and to their beachfront hotel.

Charlie had employed Artie Abalian to watch the blue sedan and report back should he see it move from the couple's hotel lot. It had. And Abalian had followed it. He informed Charlie that a man was driving the car, and he was alone. The description of the driver Abalian gave to Charlie fit the looks of Skip.

The dependable Armenian had tailed the rental car to Figueroa, where he watched the driver pull over and pick up an obvious female street walker. The man had then driven a short distance, checking into the motel with his prostitute.

Thirty minutes later, Charlie was parked on Figueroa Street. He was now directly across from the motel where the man, who Charlie had now assumed was Skip, was at. Charlie had driven here to pick up the tail of Skip, taking over from the Armenian.

The way Charlie figured it, Skip Riggers, an out of towner, had simply done a google search on where to find prostitutes near LAX. He pictured Skip putting his wife Mindy to bed after a few glasses of wine, before slipping out to do his dirty deeds.

Skip Riggers didn't stay long at the Figueroa motel.

It was a few minutes after midnight when Charlie watched Skip getting into his rental, alone. Charlie started his Toyota and began to follow Skip's car. The drive was short, as Charlie saw Skip turn off Figueroa, onto a side street and park. Skip exited the car. The man walked around the corner to a bar with a neon sign that was flicking what seemed to be the last of its electric life.

As Charlie watched Skip disappear into the bar, he exhaled. Skip's night cap would give Charlie only a short time to devise a plan to end the life of Bixie's former childhood abuser.

Forty-five minutes later, Charlie was sitting down inside a darkened doorway. He was just 10 feet away from a curb, facing the right-front side of Skip's blue rental. The car was now tilting towards its front right tire. A tire Charlie had let the air out of some 30 minutes ago.

Near Charlie's legs, that were hanging out of the doorway, were two empty beer cans he managed to find.

Charlie watched Skip Riggers come around the corner. The man only gave Charlie's legs a passing glance. A drunk bum crashed out on the side street of a dive bar was nothing that would bring much attention to anyone in South Los Angeles. To Skip, Charlie appeared to be nothing more than one such bum.

That was Skip Riggers's first mistake. His second was to fall for the flat tire setup.

Skip noticed his tilting car and walked over to the front right side of his rental. He crouched down next to the curb to examine the flat tire. That is when Charlie, at eye level with the man, addressed him.

"Stay down where you are."

Skip jerked around to face Charlie. He then threw his head back. A reaction from seeing a gun pointed at him.

"Don't move," Charlie said. After studying the man in his sights, he continued. "Are you Skip Riggers?"

"Yes."

Bixie's stepfather tried to size up the expressionless face of his captor. "If this is about money, I can give you my wallet."

Charlie barely shook his head.

"I don't want your wallet."

Skip wet his lips and swallowed. This was not good news. He now became even more focused on the gun that was facing him. Things weren't adding up. And, as his eyes adjusted to the low light level of his surroundings, he found that his well-dressed tormentor did not look anything like a typical street thug. Most disturbing to Skip, was the calm demeanor of the man pointing the gun at him.

With a now dry throat, Skip tried to take a stab at clarifying the predicament he was in.

"Then what is this about?"

Charlie rewarded him with clarity.

"Bixie."

A look of surprise came over Skip's face.

Charlie fired off two muzzled shots.

Skip Riggers collapsed into a more pronounced ball-shape figure than he already was. He would never get up again.

Charlie completed a partial payment he owed to Bixie Brown.

DAY 8

Charlie awoke the next morning in a business state of mind. His mind wouldn't allow him to relax until his immediate tasks were completed and he was out of the country. He only had one personal target left—Clarence Smith.

Professionally, Charlie had the computer hacker, and now blackmailer, Bennie Densmore and his lover, LAPD analyst Scott Nelson, to deal with. These targets were to be hit, per Laredo's demand.

As Charlie cleared his morning meal off his dining room table, the chirp from his phone was not a welcomed interruption. Especially as he eyed the phone's screen. It spelled out the name of the caller—Laredo.

Charlie braced and answered. The cartel boss got right to his question.

"It's been a week, Charlie. Have you dealt with those two we spoke about?"

Charlie was glad that he had some progress to offer, on that front.

"I have their address."

Laredo ignored the comment.

"When are Bennie and Scott going to be taken care of?"

Charlie could only muster a response he knew to be weak. "Soon. We spoke of it taking at least a month."

Exhaling, Laredo said, "Soon is not soon enough. And, we did not speak about it taking a month or more. You did."

"These things take planning."

Laredo lowered his voice. "What is the address?"

Charlie did not like this question.

"Bennie rents a house in West Hollywood. It's a few blocks south of Sunset."

"I asked for the address."

Charlie knew he had no choice but to give him the street address of Bennie. He had only gained it from Bennie the other night, after following the hacker home after their dinner. Charlie spelled out the address and waited for Laredo's next move.

"Charlie, I'm going to allow you a little more time. But, if you don't act on these two guys in a timely manner, your life will be on the line." The cartel man let that sink in. "And, remember Charlie, we do know where you live."

Laredo clicked off.

Placing the phone down, Charlie wondered about Laredo's request for Bennie's address. It was not a normal request. Maybe it was just a pressure tactic. No matter, time was now a precious commodity. Still, Charlie wouldn't put off dealing with Tab Smith's father. No. Clarence Smith would be next up on Charlie's target list. If the LAPD caught up with Charlie it wouldn't matter much, so long as he'd avenged the death of his best friend, Tab.

After Clarence, Charlie would deal with Bennie and Scott. Luckily, Charlie had, for years, been planning out the death of Clarence. It was only a matter of implementing his detailed plan.

And now was the time.

Det. Daniel Harris turned on his laptop and logged onto an LAPD database. He was back at the desk, tucked into the corner of the only bedroom, inside his Westwood condo. Since his divorce, this was his home workspace.

Still, he preferred his cramped domestic setup to his ultra-modern cubicle inside what he still called the new, yet decade-old, LAPD headquarters. He still missed the hustle and bustle ambience of the old Parker Center, even if his desk there was part of a jammed squad room. The headquarters of today was too sterile for his taste.

And just as Harris gained access to the database, he took advantage of one of the fringe benefits of working at home—he lit up a smoke.

Thirty minutes and three extinguished cigarettes later, Harris logged off the LAPD database.

He had been reading the murder book of Chad William, who had been shot with the same gun used to kill Bixie Brown's pimp, Zep Hill.

But Harris had also researched more than the physical aspects of Chad William's killing. He was looking for a motive, which may point to a suspect.

He checked Chad William's crime background. And other than the domestic violence conviction Garcia had told him about, Harris found that William had been in trouble for failing to pay child support. That legal trouble, like the domestic violence charge, was years ago.

Recently though, the detective handling the case had reported that William's ex-wife had been hassled by the man for money. And he had pushed her around whenever she refused.

Harris did find one last thing of interest concerning Chad William. The man had a son. His name was Bruce William. And when Harris drilled down into Bruce's crime background, he found that he was 5 years into a 10-year sentence. His crime was drug dealing. Bruce was serving his time in Soledad, California.

Harris pushed off his small desk and stood up. Taking in his bedroom, he vowed to begin a home improvement program. It'd start with the multiple half-empty coffee cups on his nightstand.

But his thoughts quickly returned to the killer he was hunting. Harris found some thoughts coming to his mind.

Chad William. What connected him to the killer? The pimp, the prostitute, the money launderer. Those 3 killings could be explained. But what, if anything, connected Chad William to the killing spree that began at the Hollywood Hills house?

Turning off his laptop, Harris had another thought.

Maybe Chad William's murder had nothing to do with the killings related to the Hollywood Hills house. Perhaps the killer had a separate motive for killing Chad William. Maybe the killer was on 2 separate tracks of motives.

Harris collapsed his laptop. Looking around his cramped quarters, he seemed to be searching for some guiding summation about the killer he was hunting.

A conclusion came to him. The killer was purposeful. This was no serial killer, murdering for thrills or at random. No. Harris reminded himself that he was dealing with a professional killer. And pros don't just kill for the heck of it. They kill for money.

Still, Harris told himself to focus on a motive or motives that went beyond financial gain. Something was telling him this.

He would now try to turn off his spinning mind for a few hours of mid-day sleep. But he wasn't hopeful.

Just prior to fading into sleep, a final thought came to Harris. It was the same summation he told Garcia about the killer.

This guy's different.

The sleep Harris got was thin and short. A single ring ended it.

On the second ring, with his head spinning, Harris sat up on the edge of the bed. He sank so deep into the edge of the bed that he felt like he was in a chair. He went to blame the sinking on the old mattress that his divorce settlement let him keep. But he knew the true cause. So he silently vowed once again to lose a chunk of his bulky frame.

He looked at his ringing phone screen and managed to tap the green button to answer it.

"Alex. What do you have?"

"I don't think this is anything related to our killer. But, I just got word that Bixie Brown's stepfather, Skip Riggers, has been fatally shot. It happened last night. Sometime past midnight."

Harris was now mad that he had earlier cleared the last of the half-empty coffee cups off his nightstand. He was forced to settle for the half-empty glass of water he found there, to soothe his groggy throat. Det. Alex Garcia's voice came back into his ear.

"Riggers had exited a bar near LAX on Figueroa when he was shot. He was alone."

Harris said, "What's the story."

"Daniel, it appears to be a routine attempted robbery turned fatal."

Clearing his throat, Harris said, "I recall Bixie's parents living out of state."

"Correct. Skip Riggers and Bixie Brown's mother, Mindy Brown, had flown here to give Bixie a local funeral." Garcia let out a breath. "All of this came from Headquarters. That's all I know."

Harris said, "You said this all came from Headquarters."

Garcia's voice coming out of the phone flattened.

"Daniel, some people at Headquarters don't like to deal with you. And—"

Cutting him off, Harris said, "So, you didn't get the news from Rob Johnson?"

"No, Daniel. I haven't heard from ballistics concerning Riggers." Garcia paused. "It's probably a low priority for Johnson. Given that it seems to be just an attempted robbery, gone south."

Harris took a sip of water and paused before speaking into the phone again.

"Alex said *attempted* robbery. Why? Nothing was taken?"

"It appears that nothing was taken from Riggers. Perhaps, a witness or passerby interrupted the crime. Thus, causing the would-be robbery to panic. And, flee before he or she could grab Rigger's wallet."

Putting down the glass of water, Harris said, "Where was Mindy Brown at the time?"

"Back at the hotel room where she and Riggers were staying."

Harris got up from the bed.

"Alex. Push Johnson to look at the ballistics. Even if it's just an unofficial reading."

Garcia came back with a question.

"You don't think Riggers's killing is related to our Hollywood Hills killer?"

With this question, Harris gripped the phone tighter. His gaze frozen at his bedroom wall. Instead of answering Garcia, he ordered him to do one more task.

"Set up a meeting with Mindy Brown and me. It can be at the hotel where she is staying."

Garcia's voice in the receiver broke his thoughts. "What do we want from Mindy?"

Sitting down on the edge of his bed, Harris answered.

"A lot, if the ballistics on the Skip Riggers shooting line up with our killer."

DAY 9

Charlie continued to feel an internal time clock ticking. He was driving to the LA home of Clarence Smith for the purpose of righting a long-ago wrong. Entering the home of Smith would be simple. All thanks to the skill set of Artie.

For Charlie, the drive to Compton was also causing an extra dose of internal anger to build. It reminded him how Clarence Smith, after splitting with Tab's mother, had moved nearly an hour away. At 5-years old, Tab was left in the dust by his father who only visited him a few times after that.

Getting off the freeway, Charlie was now close to Clarence Smith's house. And with each passing mile, he was closer to completing the last of the targets on his personal hit list.

It was always an eventuality that Charlie would seek justice for Tab Smith's death. A death that Charlie knew was something other than what it was labeled by the Coroner's office.

And though the wrong deeds of Tab Smith's father may have been done long ago, their results were still fresh in Charlie's mind. The bad deeds done by Clarence Smith had cost Charlie his best friend. And what remained of his own deteriorating self, Charlie knew he'd never feel complete again. His soul was not the same without Tab's presence.

Making the turn onto the street where Clarence Smith lived, Charlie's thoughts were not on the job he soon would be doing. Instead, he found himself thinking of train tracks and pennies.

Charlie remembered how Tab and him, as kids, would somehow make it down to San Clemente beach a few times during the summer. They were young enough to be too terrified to join the teenage bodysurfers riding the waves. But they were old enough to know how to produce smashed pennies by laying them down on the train tracks that ran alongside the sandy beaches.

Unconsciously smiling, Charlie recalled how excited Tab and him would be once the noontime train had passed. They'd leave their beach towels and run back to the tracks to collect the pennies they had laid on the tracks. The coins would now be smashed, earning them each neighborhood bragging tokens.

As Charlie parked his car, his mind stopped on a particular beach memory. After collecting another round of smashed coins one day, Charlie offered up a new idea to his best friend. He suggested to Tab that they should try to sneak onto the train. Maybe they could do so, at the San Clemente train station when nobody was looking.

But Tab told Charlie that he'd never ride a train. It would be years before Charlie would find out why.

Shortly before Tab died, he had finally explained to Charlie why he never rode a train. The reason was that at an early age, Tab had come to realize his own father favored playing with his model trains over playing with him.

Sitting in his quiet car, Charlie felt a renewed sense of disgust overcome him. Tab had meant less to Clarence than one of his collectable passenger cars.

Clarence Smith walked into his living room which doubled as his hobby room. There was never any actual need for the room to have a dual purpose. No visitors, invited or not, ever came to pay him a visit.

He swallowed as he sat the cold and wet beer bottle down on the tiny side table, next to his model train controls.

Using his raggedy blue jeans, he wiped the moisture off his hand. He faced the train controls.

And though he had to pee, he lit up the controls and began to maneuver them. He smiled as the train began to move.

It was Friday night and Clarence was feeling good, having just walked in after returning home from his mechanic shift a few minutes ago. No pee urge was gonna delay him from feeding his train addiction.

Clarence watched the observation car round a curve and disappear into the mouth of a tunnel, along the tracks. His eyes shot to the other end of the tunnel. A few seconds passed before his locomotive and its five passenger cars emerged from it.

Another turn along the tracks, and the train began a steep climb up a hill. The hill was beautified with green trees and multiple-colored shrubbery. Clarence's smile remained because he was on the train, per his imagination.

Whenever he ran his elaborate model trains, Clarence imagined himself as a passenger and always sitting inside the last car. Indeed, he pictured himself in the observation car looking out of its curved glass panel. He was there, inside his favorite car, when the train shot through any of the three basswood tunnels he had so meticulously constructed by hand. When the train rounded one of the turns on the track or climbed one of its steep mountains, he was there to experience it, all inside his mind.

Ironically, Clarence had never been on a real train in his life. He had a fear of them for as long as he could remember. His model set allowed him to enjoy train rides, free of the entanglement of fear.

Apart from his trains, Clarence was a man who hated everybody and everything. Nobody was or had been immune to his bitterness, not even his son. His thing about his kid was that he looked and acted like the devil herself—Clarence's ex-wife.

The logic of Clarence's hatred of everyone and anything would be difficult to sort out. Sure, he was black and had grown up poor in a white Texas neighborhood. But Clarence hated all people—white, black, yellow—and all other races. His fellow black co-workers knew to keep their distance from him. Same with his Hispanic or white co-workers. If he were tall and handsome instead of looking like an overweight toad, he'd still hate his looks.

Clarence did like one thing—his home. It was only because it housed his trains and offered sanctuary from the outside mess of his hated world. Otherwise, he'd hate the dingy two-bedroom with peeling-painted walls and filthy carpet for reminding him of his lot in life, at age 72. Any of his spare money he had left over from his monthly paycheck went to trains. The much-needed home improvements were a low priority. Clarence lived in a pigsty of his own creation. Yet, if needed, he'd find a way to blame others even though he slept in a bed of his own making.

He hated his nickname. "Frogman" was given to him by some friends of his father's when Clarence was just ten years old. The older men were familiar with the Clarence "Frogman" Henry song, "Ain't Got No Home." These men teased little Clarence, saying that, besides looking like a frog, his gravel voice sounded like one, just like the singer's.

This teasing had cast a pall over Clarence, one that followed him throughout his life. As long as he could remember, he'd thought of himself as a frog—one living in a fishbowl with all of humanity mocking him.

Only his "tracks," as he referred to his train setup, gave him an escape from the burden of hatred he carried around. Without his tracks, he'd be lost inside his fishbowl. For his tracks kept not only the small trains that travel on them moving forward, they also propelled him along to face his next dreaded day.

How Clarence would manage without his trains, he couldn't begin to imagine.

Decades ago, with his divorce from Tab's mother, he'd given up more than his fair share of what little marital assets him and his then-wife Kathy held. All for the purpose of keeping his tracks. And he never forgave his ex-wife for using the threat of taking half of his trains away, in their divorce, to extract more out of their settlement.

But the horrified thoughts of his long-ago split were nowhere near his consciousness as he slowed the train down as it approached the tiny train station. He was proud of the station. It was one he'd spent the better part of a vacation week creating, some years ago.

With the train now stopped at the station platform, Clarence indulged his imagination again. He pictured himself exiting the train and walking over to the café he'd recently added onto the station. There, he'd enjoy a cup of steaming coffee and a sweet roll.

What joys Clarence's imagination brought him.

Soon, using the throttle controller, he got the train moving away from the platform. But noticing the tiny restroom signs of the station, as the train moved beyond it, only served to remind him of how bad he had to piss.

But a piss could wait a little longer, still. Since, in his mind, he was now back inside the observation car. And with it rounding another curve, his excitement was building as he watched the train head toward the longest, and his favorite, of all the tunnels he built over his tracks.

Within a few seconds, the tunnel had swallowed the entire train. Clarence's eyes shot to the tunnel's exit in anticipation of the train zooming out.

But then he heard a thud. This was followed by a whining, high pitched sound. The train had become stuck inside the tunnel.

Clarence's jaw dropped.

The room became eerily still, save for the continuing whining sound of the train as it tried to move ahead of whatever was blocking its way forward.

Looking down at the controls in his hand, Clarence frowned at them as if they were to blame.

Handling the controls, he tried something simple to get the train moving through the tunnel, again—he reversed the train out of the tunnel, some inches. And then, he guided it back inside. But the train stopped again, with another thud, inside the tunnel.

Clarence looked sideways as a new sound rang out from inside the tunnel.

This new sound was some piece of a song that was intermittently repeating. He couldn't quite make out the words of the singer, but the sound was vaguely familiar.

This is all strange, he thought.

Since Clarence lived alone, he couldn't think of any reasonable explanation for the blockage in the tracks, complete with this song clip, other than some act of sabotage. A feeling of fear began to build in him as the singer's voice continued to intermittingly compete with the whining sound of the train.

He let out a breath and told himself there must be a simple explanation, but he sensed otherwise. With the controls, he backed the train out of the tunnel again and paused the train's position.

This left the room with only the intermittent sound coming from inside the tunnel. He turned his head, to focus his hearing on the sound. Clarence froze. He now recognized the song that the clip was taken from. It was a song he never wanted to hear again—"Ain't Got No Home."

Somebody must be playing some kind of sick practical joke, Clarence told himself. If so, he failed to find the humor in it. But there was nobody in his life to play such a cruel joke on him. Being a loner, only added to the eeriness of his situation. *Who could have done this?* He wondered. The answer, as to who was playing with his train set and his mind, was only a few feet away from him.

Standing inside the darkened hallway, Charlie Casey was watching Clarence, from 10 feet away. Charlie was holding a cell phone.

To further concentrate on what was happening, Clarence cut the power of the controls. The song clips continued to play.

Clarence walked a few feet to the problem tunnel. Stooping down, he looked inside it. Whatever the device was that was giving off the music, it was too far beyond a curve in the tunnel to see it. However, he could now see the object had lit up the inside of the tunnel.

With hesitation, he stuck his left hand inside the tunnel with less than an inch of total wiggle room around his hand. A foot and a half into the tunnel, just as it curved, he managed to grab onto something that felt like a phone. He went to pull at it, but it was stuck on the tracks. Giving it another yank, he freed the object as it continued to intermittingly sound off with the haunting clips of the hated song. Finally, Clarence was holding the object. It was a phone, one that was taunting him with its ringtone.

As Clarence looked at the menacing phone's screen, his eyes widened, and his head lurched forward. The caller's name was someone who couldn't possibly be calling.

Clarence swallowed and whispered the name, "Tab."

Now, there could be no mistaking, Clarence knew some kind of horrible joke was being played on him. First, the phone was playing a ringtone that was mocking him with a clip of the very song his hated nickname derived from. And now, the caller ID was showing the name of his only son, who was long dead. *Who the hell would be playing this trick on him*?

To stop the phone's terrifying ringtone, Clarence tapped the red circle on the screen, ending the sound that was haunting him. His action also made the name on the screen—Tab—disappear.

He was so preoccupied with the phone it never hit him that someone had to have entered his home today while he was gone. No. All Clarence could think about was the ringtone that was mocking him and the name on the phone screen doing it—Tab.

With the room still, Clarence stared at the phone. He now had a decision to make—should he call back the number that just called? His mind froze, but his heart sped up. Fear and indecision gripped him.

Finding the recent-calls list on the phone's screen, he put his finger on the one and only call showing in the column. It carried the name, Tab. He stared at it for a few seconds.

"Fuck it," he said aloud and pressed on the screen to return the call.

Staring at the screen, he watched a few digital seconds pass in silence. Then, he jerked his head up as the sound of the tormenting ringtone returned to the room. But this time, the sound was coming from directly behind him. It sounded like it was coming from another phone.

Clarence's heart was beating so loud that it sounded to him that a drumbeat had been added to the repeating song clip that was playing. He turned his pounding chest around, toward the sound. His head jerked back, as he faced a man looking down at him from several feet away. The stranger was holding a phone. It was still chirping out the disturbing ringtone.

Charlie was eyeing him.

After a few more clips of the ringtone, Clarence watched the stranger press somewhere on his phone, mercifully ending the horrifying audio.

A few seconds of silence passed. Clarence's frog-like voice broke it.

"Is that the phone I just dialed?"

"Yes," Charlie said.

Wetting his lips, Clarence said, "Is your name Tab?"

"No."

The man's apathetic vibe made Clarence unable to calm himself down. What could this stranger want? He swallowed and asked his next question.

"Who are you, then?"

"A friend of Tab's."

"My son?"

"Yes."

Clarence looked down. He'd heard the man's voice before, but where? Putting his mental clues together, Clarence figured the stranger was one of Tab's childhood friends. He steeled himself and studied the man's physical traits for a few seconds in hopes of identifying who he was, but he couldn't place him. It'd been three decades since Tab's death, and many more years since he had even seen Tab. Any of Tab's childhood friends were a memory box of Clarence's that was empty.

Looking back up, Clarence shifted his focus to trying to guess where this was all headed. He held his stare at the man for a few seconds before finally speaking.

"I get the song clip, but what's the rest of this game about...and who are you?"

Charlie pocketed his phone and said, "What about the song clip do you think you get, Mr. Smith?"

Clarence tightened his lips. The *Mr. Smith* was unnerving.

"First, who are you?"

"This is my game." Charlie paused without expression, then added, "I make the rules here."

Backing up an inch, and with his mouth closed, Clarence was stunned into silence. He was not liking this man's game.

"Now, once again Mr. Smith, what about the song clip do you think you get?"

Clarence somehow managed to mentally recapture the dialog, answering with, "The phone's ringtone. It's from the song that my nickname comes from."

Charlie shook his head.

"The song has to do with your son."

"Well, what's that got to do with Tab?"

Charlie grew serious.

"It concerns Tab's unexpected passing."

"His suicide?"

Shaking his head again, but now slower, Charlie said, "No. His murder."

Clarence bit down on his teeth as Charlie continued.

"You see, I was the one who found Tab hanging in that apartment bedroom."

Clarence's jaw dropped. "You're Charlie Casey."

Ignoring the comment, Charlie continued.

"And after I had found Tab in that bedroom, I told his mother almost everything I saw." He paused. "But I never told her what I heard. Especially since it had to do with the man who killed him."

Clarence's chin shot into his throat.

"And just who killed my son?"

Charlie's eyes narrowed.

"You."

Raising his voice, Clarence said, "And how do you figure that?"

"You broke his heart by abandoning him. Deep down, Tab was always crying out to you, but you never heard him because you weren't listening. I figure that's why he chose to go out listening to that old 45." Charlie looked down and back up at Clarence. "I'll never forget the sound of the needle bumping up against the end of the record."

Charlie exhaled and continued.

"I certainly didn't want Tab's mother to know about the record. Why make her suffer beyond physical facts about Tab's death? So, I picked up the needle and grabbed the record. I have it framed at my house as a reminder of the son you took from her. And, the friend you took from me. The record gives me inspiration to perform my job, particularly the one I'm about to do."

Clarence gently put the phone down on the train table. He eyed Charlie and spoke slowly.

"This is all a lot to absorb." Clarence stomach was churning. "What job are you about to do?"

There was no expression on Charlie's face when he answered with, "Kill you."

Clarence didn't know how Charlie had suddenly produced a gun. But its presence caused him to suffer an immediate reaction. The man felt something warming his now-shaking legs. He looked down and saw a few dark circles spreading on his faded blue jeans. Clarence looked up at Charlie, half embarrassed, just as the first of three bullets hit his chest.

Crashing to the floor, Clarence Smith no longer had to pee.

Back in his car, Charlie felt a relief now that Clarence Smith was no longer enjoying his train set. He now considered Tab's death to be avenged. And while Tab could now rest in peace, Charlie knew he couldn't. At least not yet.

For now, he would bury, once again, his emotions surrounding Tab. He wanted to have his thoughts on his best friend resurface at a better time.

DAY 10

CHAPTER 31

Harris was walking into the entrance of the hotel where Mindy Brown, the mother of Bixie Brown, was staying. Skip Riggers, Bixie's stepfather, had been staying with Mindy, before being shot dead.

Per Harris's request, Alex Garcia had set up a meeting between Harris and Mindy today. It was to be in her hotel room.

Five feet past the hotel entrance doors, Harris noticed the smell of the Hermosa Beach waters had dissipated. The noise of the beach volleyball games fronting the hotel had been replaced by elevator music.

Entering the lounge, Harris spotted Garcia sitting in one of the many pastel-colored sofa chairs. He walked up to him.

"Let's go up to Mindy's room."

Garcia stood up.

"Daniel, I thought you were meeting Mindy alone."

Harris shrugged.

"I thought about it. Mindy might open up to you. You're easy going, young, thin, and nice looking."

Garcia showed him an expressionless face and said, "You're big and intimidating. Mindy will think she, legally, *has* to tell you the truth."

Harris noted that this was the first time Garcia didn't just take an order from him and follow it. He also realized what Garcia said made sense.

Barely nodding his head, Harris responded.

"What room is she in?"

Before Garcia could answer his phone lit up.

"It's Johnson in ballistics," Garcia said, before answering.

Just listening to Garcia's side of the phone call, told Harris all he needed to know. The killer that shot Bixie and the other 3 victims was now responsible for the shooting of Skip Riggers.

Ten minutes later, Harris was inside Mindy's hotel room. He'd just sat down at a small round table the room offered. Mindy was opposite him, backlit with the sun rays coming in from the ocean view room window.

"I was sorry to hear about your daughter and husband. I'm Detective Daniel Harris of the LAPD. I lead the murder probe of your daughter. I had tried to reach you on the phone a few times, briefly after Bixie's death. I didn't hear back. I assumed you wanted some time alone."

Mindy offered no response. So Harris continued.

"And, probably I will lead the investigation of the shooting death of your husband." Harris paused. "Mrs. Brown, the killer of your daughter, is the killer of your husband."

Looking away from him, Mindy remained silent.

"Mrs. Brown, we have reason to believe the killer of Bixie took her laptop and phone. And, I have to assume he has looked through these devices."

Harris let that sink in. But it was obvious that Mindy Brown did not wish to talk about anything he had brought up.

After letting several seconds pass, the only noise heard in the room was the sound of the A/C kicking off. Harris now figured he had nothing to lose. He let out a breath and asked Mindy the question he came here to get an answer to.

"Mrs. Brown. Would there be anything on Bixie's laptop or phone that would make a man angry with Skip Riggers?"

Mindy looked back at him.

"Detective, I'm scared that I'm next."

Thirty minutes later, Harris was exiting the hotel elevator that had landed him on the lobby floor.

He walked over to Garcia and informed him of what Mindy Brown had told him in her hotel room. When he finished, Harris took a drink of the bottled water he'd grabbed from a hotel guest refreshment table.

After taking a sip of his own water, Garcia reacted to the information Harris had provided.

"Let's see, Daniel. Skip Riggers tormented Bixie, his stepdaughter. Mindy Brown admits she was complacent. The killer presumably finds all this domestic horror on Bixie's laptop. And, he is upset about it. So, taking revenge for Bixie, he shoots Skip Riggers dead."

Garcia shook his head and continued.

"Daniel, you somehow predicted all this. You even knew to have Johnson immediately look at the ballistics on the Skip Riggers shooting." Garcia eyed Harris. "What's your secret?"

Harris looked away.

"Alex, if you are chasing a frequently acting killer, you have to make some assumptions just to stay a few steps behind him. You soon get to know his modus operandi. Only then, can you hope to finally get a step or two ahead of him."

Garcia grew still. "What is the killer's M.O.?"

When Harris answered, he seemed to be talking to himself.

"He kills only bad guys."

Harris stood up and walked toward the doors of the hotel. Garcia followed him. When the doors split open, the men walked out. They were hit by the sunshine and beach scene. The men walked in silence until they reached their cars.

Before they split up, Harris gave an order to Garcia.

"I promised Mindy that we'd put a police detail at her hotel room door."

Squinting while looking up at Harris, Garcia responded.

"Got it." Pausing, Garcia said, "Do you think our killer will go after Mindy Brown?"

"No." Harris thought for a split second. "I don't think he's that type of guy."

DAY 11

CHAPTER 32

Harris realized this would be the first high school reunion he had attended. And it wasn't even his own school. Not even his high school football team buddies could talk him into going to one of his own. Harris simply had no interest. Truth be told, he was too shy to mingle among his former classmates. Still, he was happy that Laura had invited him to hers.

Laura had told Harris she had attended only her 30th. And enjoyed it more than she thought she would. Now she was excited to attend another, just five years later.

As he squeezed into his car to begin his drive over to Laura's apartment, he could feel the tightness of his polo shirt. The tight fit, and where he was heading tonight, reminded Harris of the 100-plus pounds he'd put on since leaving high school.

Two hours later, Harris and Laura arrived at the hotel where the reunion was being held. It was now 8:30 pm.

After pulling into a parking slot, Harris shut the car off. As the car grew quiet, he turned to Laura.

"Nervous?"

She twisted towards him and smiled. He suddenly grew shy. And wondered how he was this close to such a pretty face.

"No, I'm not nervous," she answered. Laura dropped her smile and turned away, looking out over the car hood.

Harris kept his eyes on her, as she continued.

"It seems the people you really want to see at a reunion are always the type that would never come to one." She paused. "But, they may also be the ones you are most afraid to see. Funny how that is."

Laura returned her eyes to Harris.

"Thanks for coming with me, Daniel. I might be nervous if you weren't taking me."

An hour into the reunion, a *Boston* song had just faded out over the speakers. A split-second break in both the music and the annoying DJ.

Laura smiled at Harris.

"Daniel, I need to use the powder room."

Harris nodded. As Laura got up from her chair, he stood up.

"You're a perfect gentleman," she said. "I haven't seen a man stand up for a lady in years. Let alone me. You're a keeper."

He smiled.

Harris watched Laura walk away. She was stunning in her blue draped front dress. He stood still, enjoying the noise of her heels fading away. The clicking sound her shoes made somehow sounded classy.

Now was the time to check his phone. He knew nothing urgent had happened on the murder spree, since Garcia hadn't called. Still, the case gripping LA was on his mind.

After his phone messages told him there was nothing pressing on the murder case, he still fought the urge to think about it. Harris reminded himself he now had two lives. One normal life, one working.

This newly added normal self, he knew happened when he met Laura. And he was determined to keep it.

One thing that hadn't changed since meeting Laura, was his smoking habit. As such, he stepped outside.

A half a minute later, he lit up a cigarette. He was standing, taking in the deserted scene of a small side patio, off the ballroom floor. Looking down at the mesh patio table next to him, he spotted a reunion program. These booklets had been handed out, at the door, to all attendees. His own unopened copy was back at the table he shared with Laura.

Harris reached down and grabbed the program. Between a hit on his smoke, he opened it and found a listing of names of Laura's classmates. The detective side of him prompted him to peruse the list. He was about to take another drag on his cigarette when he paused. A name on the list stuck out to him. One he had come across, just last night. The smoking break was over.

He shook his head. There was no use in denying it. A work mindset was creeping in. The name he had spotted in the program was to blame.

Harris was glad he had made it back to their table before Laura.

Looking down at their barely touched drinks, he lifted his head to see Laura sitting back down across from him. She smiled at him, but she looked pale.

Laura slipped over to the chair next to him. He liked it. And it was easier to be heard over the blaring music.

She leaned into Harris.

"While in the powder room, I heard that a classmate's father was…," She looked around before adding, "murdered recently."

Now Harris knew the reason for Laura's sudden paleness. "Are you okay?"

"Just a little shaken up."

Nodding, Harris waited a few seconds and then asked, "Was his name Chad William?"

Laura's eyes went wide.

"You mean Bruce's father?"

"If the Bruce you are talking about is in jail, then it is your classmate's father," Harris said.

Laura covered her mouth.

"Yes, Daniel. I know Bruce William is serving time." She went still. "So, Chad William was murdered?"

"I'm afraid so. And, it was recent."

Laura shook her head. She eyed Harris.

"How did you know Bruce was a classmate of mine?"

Harris said, "While taking a cigarette break, I found Bruce William's name on the program. I didn't know if your classmate was Chad's son. I do now."

Taking in the news, Laura said, "This is strange. The classmate's father I just heard about was Clarence Smith. He was the father of Tab Smith."

Mentally noting the name of Clarence Smith, Harris said, "Two fathers of classmates being murdered recently is indeed strange."

"Yes." Laura shot a look at Daniel and added, "But that is not why it is so strange, for me."

Harris said, "You must have known these two fathers."

"No, I didn't." She lowered her voice. "And neither did their sons. At least not very well."

Harris stayed quiet as she explained herself.

"You see, Daniel. After high school, I found out about a club. It was made up of six teenagers. All had fathers that they hardly ever saw. Hence the name of the club—The Deadbeat Club."

For Harris, the noise of the reunion seemed to shift into background, as Laura continued.

"It was not a happy group of teens. No. These teens hated their fathers. And, blamed much of their own problems on them. They'd come to hate any bad fathers."

She took a sip from her drink and continued as if talking to herself.

"Bruce William and Tab Smith, the son of Clarence Smith, were members of this club. And now, I find out their fathers are both murdered. And, close together."

"Laura, that is an even stranger coincidence." Harris held her eyes and said, "Is Tab Smith here tonight?"

Shaking her head, Laura answered.

"No. Tab passed away, years ago. And, I should say, that Chad William and Clarence Smith were the last deadbeat fathers. In fact, not only are all the dads all gone now, nearly all of the Deadbeat Club members have passed away. Besides Bruce, there is only one other club member still alive. Or I should say, might be alive."

Harris saw that she was tearing up. He offered her a napkin. She dried her eyes with it and resumed talking.

"As I was saying, Bruce William may be the only surviving club member." A few seconds passed and she said, "There is one more member left, but no one has heard from him in many years."

Harris said, "This seems tough for you."

After composing herself, she explained.

"Remember Daniel, that I told you that it seems the people you really want to see at a reunion never seem to show up." She cleared her throat. "Well, I was referring to the club member, that I just referred to, who hasn't been seen in many years."

Harris said, "This club member...he must have meant something to you."

"He was my boyfriend. I broke it off." She smiled and put a hand on one of Daniel's hands. "But that's in the past."

"I'm okay with this, Laura." He paused. "We all have a past."

CHAPTER 33

Charlie had no idea that his high school reunion was in full swing, just an hour away from his home. But his past life was just that—past.

He was sitting in his darkened backyard on a rickety chair he didn't remember ever buying. Charlie shifted in the chair to get physically comfortable. Getting mentally comfortable was proving to be more challenging.

Tonight, he was suffering from another murder hangover. It had been a couple days since he'd dealt with Clarence Smith. But the Skip Riggers, Chad William, and Smith killings were all personal hits. Charlie had never done those types of killings before. Even with his paid killing gigs, in the last few years, it had taken him longer to mentally recover from them.

Getting up from the lopsided chair, Charlie remembered having a feeling of relief after each killing job. That post-kill relief hadn't come to him in several years. Again, he told himself, change would have to come.

Looking up at the dark space of the sky, Charlie took a breath. Letting it go, he focused on his next problem—Bennie Densmore and Scott Nelson. His cartel employer, Laredo, had instructed him to kill them both. Charlie knew the two live-in romance partners represented personal risks. Bennie was blackmailing him, and Scott, he figured, would sing like a canary if he was brought in for questioning.

Heading back inside his house, Charlie knew the time had come for him to deal with Bennie and Scott.

It was past 2 a.m. when Harris pulled away from Laura's apartment, after dropping her off from the class reunion. He knew he wouldn't be able to sleep. His mind was spinning from a story that Laura had told, back at the reunion. He had a hunch it might relate to the killer he was chasing down.

By 3 a.m., Harris was inside his sterile cubicle at LAPD headquarters, in front of his computer screen. In minutes, he was reading the murder book on Clarence Smith. And thanking his lucky stars that Smith had moved into LA County years ago.

He read that Smith was killed via gunshots, just two nights ago. Between sips of machine dispensed coffee, Harris recognized a familiar pattern from the killing. A 9mm gun was the murder weapon and nothing was taken from Smith's house, where he was shot. The killing seemed to be a personal vendetta, according to the report. Just like Skip Riggers. And just like Chad William.

Harris put down his coffee and picked up a pen. He shifted his chair to be positioned to write on the yellow notepad on his desk. Across the top of the page, he wrote down the names Chad William, Skip Riggers, and Clarence Smith.

Looking at the names, he thought back on what Laura had told him about the Deadbeat Club. William and Smith were fathers of club members.

Harris also mentally noted what Mindy Brown had told him about Skip Riggers.

On the yellow pad, under each of the names Chad William and Clarence Smith, Harris wrote "Bad Father." Under the name of Skip Riggers, he wrote "Bad Stepfather." Harris put the pen down but kept his eyes on the notepad. He looked at the three names and the titles he'd given them.

Harris knew the killer he was searching for, had shot both William and Riggers. And jumping ahead of any ballistics report, the facts pointed Harris to assuming Clarence Smith was another victim of the same shooter. In addition, at the reunion, Laura had explained a connection between William and Smith. With all that in mind, Harris looked again at his written notes.

He turned his head and froze.

Harris had a new thought. One that connected two drifting hunches. The hunches were not on the yellow pad, they were in his mind. And these hunches had names associated with them, but one was unknown.

The known name had come from a former pimp and current LAPD confidential informant named Tommy. He thought back on what Tommy had told him about a mysterious client of his, back when he was pimping. Tommy had recalled a particular phone call with the secretive john. One in which the john had let his first name slip. Tommy had remembered the name, since it was the name of his favorite uncle—Charlie.

The unknown name was a past boyfriend of Laura's that she had mentioned, back at the reunion. Laura said nobody had seen or heard from this person in years. Growing up, this person had been a member of the Deadbeat Club. Laura had informed him that the club was made up of teens who not only hated their own absentee fathers but hated all absentee fathers.

Harris thought of two things he'd assumed or knew about the killer—he uses prostitutes and had killed a bad father, in Chad William, and a bad stepfather, in Skip Riggers. But now, with Clarence Smith's murder, Harris was thinking the killer may have struck another bad father.

Rubbing his chin, Harris knew Tommy's mystery client, named Charlie, used prostitutes. And Laura's long-vanished ex-boyfriend had a bad father and hated all bad fathers.

Leaning back in his chair, Harris had a thought—*What if Tommy's mysterious client and Laura's vanished ex-boyfriend were both the same man.* If they were the same man, Harris realized he'd have a suspect. To find out, Harris would have to get the name of Laura's ex-boyfriend. For his suspect theory to hold up, Harris knew Laura's ex-boyfriend's name had to start with Charlie.

Harris twisted his chair, causing his left arm to tip over his empty paper coffee cup. Ignoring his sloppiness, he grabbed his phone. Its screen brought his mind back to what time it was—5 a.m. A call to Laura would have to wait a few hours. It was too early to wake her.

He called Garcia, waking him up to instruct him to ask Rob Johnson to run the ballistics on the Clarence Smith shooting.

DAY 12

CHAPTER 34

Several hours after being woken up at 5 a.m., Det. Alex Garcia had called Harris to relay the word on the ballistics. The 9mm pistol used on the Clarence Smith shooting was the same gun used by the killer of Chad William, Skip Riggers, and Zep Hill.

Harris considered the Zep Hill shooting to be directly related to the Hollywood Hills murders of Bixie Brown and Alejandro Vargas. Whereas with William, Riggers, and, now, Clarence Smith, Harris categorized these as personal, vindictive hits of the same Hollywood Hills killer. A killer he hoped he'd be able to finally identify. All with the help of the lady he was dating, Laura Hadley.

Pulling into the parking lot, Harris braced himself for a difficult chat. He was at a Starbucks to meet Laura. She'd agreed to meet with him at midmorning, He needed to ask her for a name. A name of a person that meant a lot to her. A name that could upset her, as he noted from last night's reunion. He didn't want to bring any of this business into her apartment. So he asked Laura to meet for coffee.

To add to this, Harris was conscious that any meeting with Laura was not just a normal business meet up. Just knowing he was soon going to see her again in minutes, despite leaving her off at her apartment several hours ago, made him feel different. Yes, something was turning in his soul. And he felt good about it.

Ten minutes after parking his car in the Starbuck's lot, Harris was seated across from Laura. He had coffee in front of him, while she was sipping hot herbal tea. And with each sip she took, he noticed the red lipstick she left on the white plastic top of her cup. It was a split second of enjoyment for Harris, who was here hoping to crack open the murder case he was on.

After apologizing to Laura for having to ask her for some information that might make her uncomfortable, Harris spoke.

"Laura, last night you mentioned a Deadbeat Club. You said there were only two surviving members. One was Bruce William. And, the other," Harris lowered his voice and continued with, "was a former boyfriend of yours, who nobody has heard from in years."

Laura interrupted with, "Decades actually."

Harris nodded. Then continued with a question.

"This former boyfriend…what is his name?"

Laura's eyes watered up.

"Sorry, Daniel. It's still difficult after all these years."

Harris took hold of one of Laura's hands. She squeezed the hand and released it. Reaching into her purse, hanging on her chair, she soon produced a pen and a small piece of paper.

She sniffled and said, "It's easier if I write it down."

With a shaking hand, Laura jotted down something on the paper. She eyed Harris as she handed it to him and said, "That's his name."

Taking hold of the piece of paper, he kept his eyes on Laura. Harris showed her a small smile and held it for a few seconds. Finally, he looked down and read the name—*Charlie Casey*.

Twenty minutes later, Laura had given Harris all she knew about Charlie Casey. This included his birthdate and a general description of what he looked like, when she last saw him. She had no pictures of Charlie to offer Harris. She had tossed them out years ago, in a moment of despair.

Harris had one final question.

"Besides you, Laura. Who else was close to Charlie?"

Laura took a sip of her tea, then answered.

"When I met Charlie, I soon found out there were only three people he trusted. His own mother was one. Tab Smith, his best friend, was another." She looked down and continued. "Both passed away in the same year."

Harris interjected with, "How long ago was this?"

"Thirty years ago. Tab, Charlie, and me were all twenty-three, at the time."

Laura looked out the window they were seated next to. She didn't seem to be focusing on anything. When she continued talking, it was if she was talking to herself.

"Tab took his own life." She paused. "Charlie always blamed Tab's father for it. He'd once told me he had proof that Tab's father was to blame. But, Charlie never fully explained himself."

Laura looked back at Harris with a blank face and continued talking.

"Charlie changed after that. With his mother's passing and Tab's death, within such a short time, I think Charlie's happiness ended." Laura smiled. "And on top of all this, I broke up with him shortly thereafter."

She took a sip of her tea and stared down at the table. Her voice lowered.

"Funny thing about Charlie, he must've been chased by half the girls at our high school. Yet, he wasn't even all that good looking." She looked at Harris wearing a forced smile. "I'm sorry, Daniel. I don't know why I'm telling you all this."

Now Harris leaned forward.

"Charlie was a big part of your life. I understand that." Harris leaned back and half smiled. "Besides, I'm the one who asked about him."

With that, Laura seemed to snap out of a trance.

"Yes, you did Daniel." Laura perked up. "So, who else, besides me, was close to Charlie? That is, besides his mother and Tab Smith? Well, there was one other person Charlie trusted. It was Bruce William."

"The one in prison?" Harris said.

"Yes. And, the one whose father you told me was murdered recently."

After he waved Laura goodbye, as she drove away, Harris put a smoke in his mouth and jumped into his Crown Victoria. He was leaving Starbucks with a heavy heart, since he knew Laura had been emotionally shaken discussing her former boyfriend.

Harris was also leaving the coffee house with the name of a suspect. Although Charlie Casey was no sure thing.

With Charlie, Harris told himself, he was either going on a wild goose chase to a dead end, or he had his killer. Harris believed the later—Charlie was the man that started a murder spree that begun in the Hollywood Hills.

Turning onto Fairfax, Harris had now narrowed his murder-spree investigation down to one goal—find Charlie Casey.

Harris would search all the police databases at his disposal for Charlie Casey. But he knew the killer he was hunting was a veteran professional hitman. And if Charlie was that kind of killer, Harris knew there would be no actionable intelligence on him in any of the databases that LAPD afforded him.

He quickly concluded there was only one way to track down Charlie. It would be with the help of a man Charlie grew up with and trusted.

With that goal in mind, Harris got Alex Garcia on the phone. He instructed the young detective to get him the contact information for Bruce William's attorney and the prosecutor who sent William to prison. He also told Garcia to begin lining up a jail visitation appointment with Bruce William, who was serving time up north in Soledad.

THREE DAYS LATER: DAY 15

Three days and a 6-hour drive from LA later, Harris was sitting alone in a room. The dull gray painted concrete walls displayed gang inscriptions. The air smelled of aged body odor. The epoxy-coated floor completed the institutional esthetics. Harris always believed if he could take anybody contemplating becoming a criminal and place them inside any interview room of any prison, half or more would change course.

He had arrived at Soledad State Prison to meet Bruce William. Harris wanted William's help in tracking down the man's childhood friend, Charlie Casey. He knew it was never easy to get a career criminal's help in finding a missing criminal or a suspected one. But, after doing some research on Bruce, Harris thought he had a good bargaining chip to offer the inmate in exchange for his assistance.

Sitting kitty-corner at the only table in the room, Harris was reviewing his notes when one of the doors opened. A couple of prison guards escorted a slender man in an orange jumpsuit with a mess of graying brown hair into the room. Harris knew, from booking photos, that the man in the orange jumpsuit was Bruce William, the 54-year-old convicted drug dealer and son of recent murder victim Chad William.

Harris watched the guards remove the handcuffs that William had on and pointed him to a chair, to the left of where Harris was seated.

Eyeing William's droopy face as he sat down a few feet from him, Harris studied the man. Bruce William gave off a matter-of-fact vibe.

The two men offered each other a facial greeting of sorts. Then Harris leaned forward and folded his hands on the table.

"Mr. William, as you know, this conversation has all been cleared with the DA's office and your attorney. Perhaps, you have considered this deal we wish to offer you."

Bruce straightened up in his chair, wearing the flat expression he walked in with.

"Detective, you can call me Bruce. And, the only thing my attorney told me was that he approved this chat, today. I don't know about any deal. My lawyer just said to listen to what you have to say."

Harris spread his hands apart and said, "Your attorney told me that you had heard the news about your father. And, I wish to say I'm sorry about your father."

Putting up a hand, Bruce said, "Don't be. The man meant nothing to me."

Harris paused, then said, "What do you know about it?"

"You mean my father's death?" Bruce shrugged. "Just that he was murdered in some rundown hotel near LAX."

Harris stayed silent.

Bruce cocked his head and looked up at the camera, in the upper corner of the room, apparently eyeing it since there was nothing else to eye.

"Look Detective, giving me your personal condolences about my father can't be why you pulled me out of my cell."

Harris shook his head.

"No. I wanted to tell you we know who shot your father."

"So, who's the guy who did me the favor?"

Harris eyed Bruce and said, "Charlie."

Bruce didn't give off any physical reaction to hearing this name. Nor did his voice change when he spoke.

"I only know one Charlie."

Now Harris grew still and said, "Charlie Casey killed your father. I'm telling you, Bruce, something the public doesn't know."

Bruce looked down at the table then back up.

"Obviously, somehow you found out I know Charlie. But, I haven't spoken to him in years, and I haven't seen him in decades. And anything to do with my father being shot, just doesn't concern me."

Det. Harris lowered his voice and said, "Does seeing your son concern you?"

Bruce froze.

"What's this all about, Detective?"

Harris leaned back.

"You have a friend—Charlie Casey. A lifelong friend, from what I understand." Harris let that sink in. "Besides your father, Charlie has killed multiple people in the last couple of weeks. I'm sure you've heard about the killing spree."

Bruce kept quiet. Harris continued.

"We both know that Charlie is out of control. And, he needs to be stopped."

Bruce lifted his 10 fingers off the table and said, "Again, Detective Harris, what does this have to do with me?"

Harris leaned into Bruce.

"Look, I know you have a son. And, you're in jail with 5 years left on a 10-year sentence. So, you have a problem. You need to see your son, but you're inside four walls of concrete." Harris folded his hands. "Well, Bruce, I have a problem too. My problem is I need to find Charlie Casey. Let's face it, I am the only one that can get you to your son. And, you're the only one that can get me to Charlie Casey. I want to make both happen."

A pause. Bruce broke it.

"Go on."

Harris offered a small smile.

"Bruce, we can spring you out of here. You can go see your son. Play football, basketball, or whatever with him. Your prison sentence would not only be greatly reduced, but immediately suspended for the time being."

Bruce kept quiet. Harris lifted his head.

"We just ask that you find Charlie Casey."

Using only his eyes, Bruce looked up at Harris. "Detective, you're assuming I can find Charlie."

Harris threw his hands apart.

"Even if you make an honest attempt to find Charlie, I can ask the DA and all to reduce your sentence. Possibly to time served."

Bruce looked down and paused for a moment. He looked up and spoke. "I can't wear a wire. To get to Charlie, I'd have to meet with a lot of, what you guys would call, bad actors. Some of them, I too would call bad actors." Bruce paused. "And, I can't have any kind of tracking chips imbedded in me or whatever. I also can't report on who I meet while looking for Charlie."

Harris frowned. "You're asking a lot."

Shaking his head, Bruce said, "Not if I want to live to see my son again. A mole in my circles gets himself killed."

With his eyes studying Bruce, Harris paused. But he knew what his response was going to be. He had no choice but to allow Bruce William to walk, on his own conditions, out of jail. Charlie Casey was killing at a fast pace. Harris had to take a chance with the drug dealer who could possibly find Charlie. It'd be a long shot at best, even if Harris could trust Bruce to hold up his part of the bargain.

Harris took a breath.

"Okay, Bruce. Deal."

DAY 16

Harris walked into the Canter's Deli. He quickly spotted Alex Garcia, who was waving at him from the same table that they both sat at the last time they were here.

Twenty minutes later, their sandwich plates were dropped off at their table by their waitress. By the time they'd eaten, and their plates were cleared from their table, Harris had fully caught Garcia up on the latest developments. This included his visit to Soledad to cut the deal with Bruce William.

After Harris finished his briefing, Garcia had a question.

"Daniel, do you trust Bruce William to actually look for Charlie Casey?"

Ignoring the question, Harris eyed Garcia.

"We know where Bruce is going to be living, at least while he is supposed to be tracking down Casey for us. Alex, I need you to follow him wherever he goes." Harris paused. "I know this sort of thing would take five guys normally. But, if we do this the normal way, William will soon figure out he's been tailed."

A smile crossed Garcia's face.

"So, you don't trust the drug dealer?"

Harris picked up the check and said, "I'd just like him followed."

TWO DAYS LATER: DAY 18

CHAPTER 37

A Saturday night full of bright stars. And Bennie Densmore was high on life. Just last week, he was able to squeeze Charlie for a couple of bundles of hundred-dollar bills. The computer hacker also had a new promising client. And his lover Scott Nelson was seated next to him. Both of them were soaking up the warm and bubbling waters of Bennie's sunken patio hot tub.

Bennie's right hand was playing with Scott's head of jet black curly hair, all shiny from a generous dollop of mousse. His left hand was holding a wine glass filled with red liquid enjoyment. The happy pair had their backs facing the sliding-glass patio door, of which the lights of the living room were splashing out onto the otherwise darkened patio. Coupled with the underwater lights of the hot tub, all this display of lighting made for a perfectly relaxing setting. So much so, that Bennie was even able to put money-making thoughts aside for the moment and enjoy the shared view the two had of the flora creations that Scott had labored so hard to grow.

But the couple's nighttime romantic paradise of flowery views and mood-setting lighting was suddenly spoiled by a dark presence—a shadow.

This shadow began to overtake them, from behind. It was splitting the light emanating from the living room. Bennie became aware of the shadow. He watched as it formed into the shape of a human figure. The shadow quickly overtook his and Scott's own shadows and the entire length of the hot tub.

Then the shadow stopped. Bennie noticed things grew quiet.

He withdrew his hand from Scott's head and then laid his wine glass down on the wooden lip of the hot tub. Too afraid to turn around to see who the shadow belonged to, he looked at Scott. His lover had noticed the shadow by now. Bennie watched as Scott shrugged and turned his head around and looked up, to face the owner of the shadow.

Bennie heard a subtle burst of air and the sound of a wine glass shattering. Scott's head had exploded, splaying liquid and particulates over Bennie's face and portions of his upper body that was above the bubbling water. He instinctively rubbed his eyes and refocused.

Then the shadow maker spoke with a male voice.

"Don't talk. Get out of the tub."

Doing as he was told, Bennie stepped out of the hot tub. As he did, he felt the stickiness of blood, body fragments, and patches of hair glued to him with the help of mousse. As he finally faced the intruder, who was dressed in black from head to toe and pointing a pistol at him, Bennie was surprised to find himself feeling humiliation, not fear, as he stood dripping in blood-soaked water. He felt the killer laughing at him just like his fellow students often did on the school playgrounds. Finally, the intruder gave him his next order.

"Come inside."

Out of habit, Bennie reached towards the towel rack. The mistake nearly proved fatal. As the gunman shook his head, Bennie withdrew his outstretched arm. The intruder, using the gun, waved Bennie towards the sliding-glass door and into the house.

Just as he began heading into the house, Bennie could see, from the corner of his eye, his neighbor's upstairs bedroom window. He caught a glimpse of a dark outline of a human frantically fidgeting around with something. For once, Bennie was hoping his nosey neighbor had been spying down on his back patio activities. Bennie was praying that this neighbor had witnessed the hot-tub horror show. Or, at the very least, had heard the shattering of Scott's wine glass and was now calling the cops. This was the hacker's only lifeline.

As Bennie stepped into the living room, the intruder followed behind him.

"A few more steps," the gunman said. "Now, turn around."

Bennie faced the gunman, who was pointing the gun at him. He realized that being allowed to look at him, even if the man's ski mask only exposed his eyes and nose, did not bode well for his own life expectancy. Awaiting further instructions, Bennie tried to figure out who the gunman might be. He quickly received an answer.

"I work for your new client, Laredo." He lifted the gun up a bit. "And, I need to ask a question."

Bennie had sensed that Laredo was dangerous. But the money he was offering for future projects was too good to turn away. He should've been more cautious. His thoughts quickly returned to considering his chances that his neighbor had called 911. He continued to hear the gunman out.

"Since you last spoke to Laredo, is there anything new you have done for another client of yours—Charlie Casey?"

Eager to please the man, Bennie told the gunman about updating Charlie's fake passport. He left out the business of how he extorted bundles of hundreds from the hitman. Even facing death, the hacker couldn't part with such a big chuck of currency.

Bennie thought the gunman seemed satisfied with the passport story. The visiting killer had one more question.

"Where in this house are the computers?"

Bennie tilted his head toward the hallway. Then froze, realizing any movement he made, without being told first, might be a deadly mistake. He answered his captor.

"First door on the right. It's my home office. And the first door on the left. That's…that was Scott's work room."

The gunman nodded and pushed the gun out, further.

With two finger movements from the gunman, Bennie Densmore went from being an illicit computer hacker to a coroner's investigation.

As Charlie was making his way to the West Hollywood home of Bennie Densmore and Scott Nelson, he didn't notice that his Porsche was being followed. The man following him had been tailing or monitoring his movements since Charlie had left the Malibu beach house of his best friend, a couple weeks back.

Charlie was paying a surprise visit to Bennie and Scott. With all the things going on, he just thought it best to not make unnecessary appointments. In Charlie's world, everyone seemed interconnected these days.

As Charlie drove past new and old apartment buildings, he knew Bennie and Scott would never know just how close they came to death tonight. If it hadn't been for his choice to walk away from the business of killing, Charlie would've killed them both tonight. For he knew once someone blackmailed you they never stopped.

Charlie slowed down as he neared his destination street. He wondered to himself if this visit was a waste of time. It was long odds that Bennie and Scott would take his advice to leave Los Angeles, perhaps the country, immediately and go hide out for a long while. If the couple left, besides saving their own lives, it would buy Charlie time with Laredo who had ordered him to kill the pair.

Charlie made a left onto Bennie's street. With the left turn, his plans for tonight changed.

Police lights of all kinds were flashing a few houses ahead of him. As Charlie eased off the gas, he could see all police activity was surrounding Bennie's house. There were bystanders across the street and to the sides of the house, roped off by yellow crime scene tape. Charlie decided to keep his car moving.

As he was waved past Bennie's home by a police officer directing traffic, Charlie got a peek at the crime scene. He saw a body bag, resembling an elongated water balloon, on a gurney bumping along Bennie's front lawn. The payload was heading towards a coroner's van.

Driving past the death house scene, Charlie didn't bother to turn on the radio to check the news. He knew that death had, after all, come to Bennie and Scott tonight. It could have been Laredo's doing, but Charlie couldn't assume that. As a professional hacker, Bennie had more than a couple of dangerous clients. Maybe Bennie had tried to squeeze a "long-term employment bonus" out of the wrong client.

Leaving the neighborhood, and back on a main boulevard, Charlie quickly had decided not to say anything to Laredo. He'd gamble on Bennie's killer not being one of Laredo's hired guns. Charlie had been under pressure from Laredo to take out Bennie and Scott. So, Charlie would hope that Laredo would assume he was the guy who finished off the couple.

But while he sped by the busy weekend sidewalks of West Hollywood, Charlie knew he had been avoiding a concern that might affect his own mortality. For if indeed it was a Laredo associate who was responsible for the deadly works back at Bennie's place, Charlie knew his own life was in imminent danger. He just might be the last part of Laredo's clean up concerning the Hollywood Hills disaster.

As he approached a stop light, Charlie decided he'd plug ahead with his plans for the next couple days. For the task of leaving the country, would soon be accomplished.

The signal light turned green, and Charlie headed towards home. The man following him made a right turn and stopped tailing him, for he knew where Charlie was headed—home.

CHAPTER 38

After taking a short drive to unwind from the deadly scene back at Bennie and Scott's house, Charlie pulled into his garage and exited his car. Walking around the car, he came to his house door and unlocked it just as the garage-door-triggered light went out. He opened his house door and stepped into the laundry room but didn't bother with the light switch, on his right. Instead, he utilized the light source of the moonlight reaching him from his kitchen windows. He walked through the small room and into his kitchen area.

Walking into a darkened home, Charlie always felt vulnerable. He guessed it was another consequence of growing up without a father. As a middle-aged kid, he'd only have his mother with him whenever they'd return home at night from some outing. If someone had jumped out of the dark, inside their home, he knew it'd be left up to him to defend the two of them. There was no all-powerful dad to get behind or in front of them.

But tonight, Charlie felt no fear as he stood and took in the peacefulness of the moonlight bouncing off the Saltillo tile flooring of his kitchen. Allowing himself to be temporarily swallowed up by the semidarkness felt restful. The mental chatter of his current mess-filled world died down, if only by a notch and if only for a few seconds. He wondered why he hadn't allowed himself more moments like this in his life. A life that was now more than halfway over.

Charlie turned toward a light switch on his left. Before flipping the switch up, he sensed a noise. It was coming from the blackness of the living room he was looking into from an open entryway.

Then he heard a voice.

"Don't move, Charlie."

As instructed by the male-sounding voice, coming from his darkened living room, Charlie didn't move. Squinting, Charlie began to see the outline of a male silhouette take shape. In his right peripheral view, a human shape was forming. The person was seated on his living-room sofa couch.

"You killed my father," the voice continued.

The voice now sounded vaguely familiar, but Charlie couldn't place it. Then a room light went on, as the voice spoke again.

"Turn to your right. Slowly."

After doing as instructed, Charlie let out a breath as recognition set in of who the voice belonged to. It was Bruce William, his longtime friend and fellow onetime member of the now defunct Deadbeat Club they had helped form in high school.

Bruce dropped his effort at disguising his voice.

"Charlie, I always wanted to see if I could've killed a professional killer."

"How'd you get in here?"

Bruce lowered his head a bit and said, "You don't wire your house. And, while my specialty has been drug dealing, before I got busted, I had started a side gig—burglarizing homes. I was just too embarrassed to tell you or anyone else, since I've always hated thieves."

Bruce dropped the gun and continued.

"But Charlie, after five years in the can, I'm out of the bad-guy business."

Charlie took a few steps into his living room where Bruce was seated. Bruce's gun was now lying on the table in front of him. Charlie looked at the friend he hadn't seen in years.

"It's good to see you, Bruce." He stared at Bruce for a few seconds and said, "Do you want a beer?"

A minute later, Charlie and Bruce were seated across from one another at the dining room table. Charlie slid a beer over to Bruce. He then twisted the top off one he'd brought for himself.

After taking a quick swig of his beer, Bruce eyed Charlie and said, "So, Laredo gave you my note."

While swallowing a gulp of beer, Charlie nodded.

Bruce pointed at him.

"I owe you. And, my son, though he's too little to know it, owes you." Bruce looked away and said, "I couldn't let my kid grow up with that monster as his grandfather. He beat me and my mother before deserting us. Then, while I've been in prison, he came back to beat my mom on a regular basis. All in front of my kid."

Charlie sat still. A few seconds of silence passed. Bruce continued.

"The cops are on to you, Charlie."

Resting his beer on the table, Charlie didn't react.

"Charlie, they offered to reduce my legal troubles if I help find you. I'll have to make something up when I meet with the detectives in a few days." Bruce shook his head and smiled. "Maybe it was my white lie about not having seen you in decades, but the pigs don't fully trust me. I had to shake off a cop tailing me while driving here."

Charlie let out a breath and said, "In a few days, you can let the cop follow you here and give me up. Or at least my address. That should be enough to square you with them."

Bruce grew serious. "How's that?"

"I'm leaving the country."

With his lips crumpled, Bruce said, "Charlie, you're my last connection to our club. Everyone's gone now."

A few seconds went by, before Bruce continued.

"Where you headed?"

"Mexico."

"Mexico?" Bruce cocked his head. "Laredo sending you down there on   business?" Charlie shook his head. "No. I'm going to Zamora for something personal. There's a guy named Jorge I have to find."

Smiling, Bruce said, "And when you find this Jorge are you going to kill him?"

Charlie was taken aback by the comment. But then he realized he deserved the question. He shook it off in a split second, hoping someday his past would not follow him. Washing a hand over his head, he answered.

"No. I'm done with that life." He paused. "Bruce, I'm going to Mexico to tell the man that he's got a daughter that needs to see him."

Bruce took a slow sip of beer while staring down at the table. Putting the beer down, he smacked his lips.

"I have a son that needs to see me. And, he needs to see me on a regular basis. That's why I ain't moving loads for no cartels, anymore." He looked up at Charlie. "What's your reason for going straight after all these years?"

Charlie held his friend's eyes while rubbing his index finger along his chin for some seconds.

"My life. It's been wrong."

Pursing his lips while nodding, Bruce stared at Charlie for a long while and said, "After Zamora, where are you going?" "I haven't decided."

Throwing his palms open, Bruce said, "What are you gonna do with yourself?"

With a shrug, Charlie said, "Put my life on the table. Some pieces of it I will keep, but most of it I'm gonna toss out. What remains of it, I'm going to use as a base to build a new life."

Charlie paused before continuing.

"You're going straight Bruce, and you once worked for Laredo. And, unlike me, you're not going to be disappearing." Charlie eyed Bruce. "Laredo don't like people quitting on him."

Bruce raised his eyebrows and said, "For my son, I'll have to take my chances. Besides, I did Laredo a favor when I was on the inside—I didn't sing. That's why he did me the favor of passing my note to you. So, I think I'll be okay."

Charlie nodded.

Wetting his lips, Bruce said, "My mom and son can live in peace. And, it's all because of you. I can never pay you back, Charlie, for what you did for them and me."

"Yes, you can."

Charlie then asked Bruce to take over the task of delivering flowers to his mother's grave. He told Bruce to buy the flowers at Valdez's Roses. Further, he explained the system of the yellow roses count. Lastly, Charlie asked his friend to read some poetry over her grave, every so often.

Bruce agreed to all. He told Charlie he wouldn't be doing it only for him, but for Charlie's mother, Anne.

After thanking Bruce for this favor, Charlie said, "Do you need any money?"

Bruce shook his head. "No. I'm good."

Charlie showed him a smile and said, "You are good."

After a couple hours of catching up, Charlie saw Bruce out the door of his home. A few minutes later, Charlie was laying his head down on his pillow to try to get some sleep. He had several things to do before he left the country. He wouldn't leave the country without doing two of them.

Charlie wanted to pay one last visit to his mother's grave. But before he did, he needed to take a ride on a train.

DAY 19

It was just past 6:00 a.m., and Charlie was inside the hallway of his home. He was eyeing the framed vinyl 45 RPM record. The same record he'd used numerous times to build up his anger. But this time, he wasn't using it for work. For Charlie was not going to be killing again. No. This time, he was looking at the record to celebrate the freeing of his best friend's spirit. Tab Smith's spirit no longer had anything to do with the song. He could now rest in peace. And his spirit was now free to enjoy a train ride.

Charlie lifted the frame off the wall. A square of white beige was visible where it had hung. The record itself would now represent Tab's spirit.

Minutes later, Charlie was backing out of his driveway. Lying on the passenger seat of the car was the framed record. After changing gears, Charlie couldn't help but smile. Tab and him were going for a train ride today.

A couple hours later, Charlie was parking his Porsche. He'd arrived at the Amtrak train station near the San Clemente Pier. Thirty minutes later, he was seated on a train headed for downtown Los Angeles. Charlie had purchased two round-trip tickets. One seat himself and one seat for the framed record. Charlie believed that Tab was finally going on a train ride, something he never had allowed himself to enjoy when he was alive.

It was mid-afternoon when Charlie stepped off the train. He was back in San Clemente. His head turned to look back at the train tracks. They were on the same track lines that he and Tab, as kids, had smashed pennies on. Charlie shook his head while almost disbelieving that those beach memories were made decades ago. *Where did the time go*, he wondered.

Holding the framed record by his side, Charlie looked down on it. The emotional weight of the record had left him. Tab's spirit was no longer tied to it. Charlie looked up and remembered a store he poked around in a few decades ago. Maybe it was still in business. He started towards his car.

Just a few blocks away, inside San Clemente's downtown shopping area, he parked his car on Avenida Del Mar. He grabbed the framed record and exited his car. A half minute later, among the many quaint shops and eateries, he spotted the vintage record store. He soon was entering its doors.

Walking up to the checkout counter, Charlie put the framed record down. The store clerk behind the counter was a young female with multitudes of tattoos, facial piercings, and hair colors. She seemed to Charlie to be more intent on her gum chewing than helping him. Charlie addressed her.

"I'd like to give this record to the store."

Between smacks of gum, the clerk answered. "Do you want store credit or cash?"

Shaking his head, Charlie said, "Neither."

"Do you want the frame back?"

"No."

Staring down at the framed record, the clerk stopped her gum chewing. After a few seconds, she looked up and eyed Charlie.

"Why are you giving this away?"

Charlie looked down at the record. "It belonged to a friend of mine. He let me use it. But, neither of us have any use for it anymore."

Driving from San Clemente, Charlie made it to his mother's grave just before sunset. Standing before it, he laid down the bouquet of 30 yellow roses. But a single flower had caught his attention. It was a tiny red rose. The rose was inches away from his mother's gravestone. It was taped to a gift card sized envelope. The card was pinned to the ground by some tiny colored toothpicks. A small pen was clipped to it.

Charlie reached down and untethered the card and rose. After removing the pen, he flipped the card over and saw one handwritten word—*Charlie*. His chest heaved. Charlie thought he recognized the handwriting.

He opened the card and read the message. A shock of fear overtook him. He would finally have to face the cloud he'd been trying to ignore for the last 3-odd decades of his life.

Managing a swallow, his eyes reached the writing at the bottom of the card. It offered a date, a time, and a place. The month and day of the date was one Charlie remembered each year. The place was spelled out in words, not by an address. At the bottom of the card, only a first name was used to sign it.

Unconsciously Charlie looked around, then placed the card back into the envelope. Using the pen, he wrote an *H* on the envelope. He put the card, the rose, and the pen back where he found them.

With the card's RSVP instruction completed, Charlie had an appointment for tomorrow tonight.

DAY 20

CHAPTER 40

It was just past 8:00 p.m. when Charlie pulled up to a house and parked. He was on time for his appointment. Twisting his neck left, he took in the street he hadn't seen in decades. On this night, it was lit up by the glowing street-light globes. And the street was quiet, save for a faraway dog with a faint and persistent bark. He almost smiled. After all the years growing up in Tustin, he never appreciated its boringness. But he also knew the last thing a kid would value was a boring city.

Turning his neck to the right, he looked at the house he hadn't been inside of for decades. While it brought back the good memories of picking up Laura Hadley for a night out, he knew it held bad memories for her.

For it was the house where Laura's father had taken off from, just after Laura's 10th birthday cake had been cut. The shock and timing of it had left Laura, still a kid, to blame herself.

Charlie knew Laura's father eventually returned to the home, just before the passing of Laura's mother. But by then, Laura was an adult and out of the house. Charlie remembered she had vowed never to return to the home. The pain of her father leaving left a devastating imprint on the house.

Seeing there were some lights on in the house, Charlie looked for signs of activity. None. And even though he had this night planned out, he grew nervous at what he was about to do. It'd be the last task he'd mandated himself to do before escaping the police and Laredo, by leaving the country.

He let out a breath.

Out of habit, Charlie reached back to retrieve his gun case. He stopped himself after remembering he wasn't going to need it tonight. No. The only tools he'd bring inside the house to face the person he was planning to meet would be his own words.

He slipped out of the car.

Walking up the driveway, a different memory of Laura and him flashed in front of his mind with each step. Finally, he arrived at the front door and realized this house call was not a good idea. As he turned away to walk back to his car, the front door opened. He turned around.

Laura Hadley stood a few feet from him.

After three full decades of not seeing her, the first thing that hit Charlie was how striking she still looked. Her hair was still long and thick, but it was now a glistening silver with only a few remaining streaks of her natural brunette.

He didn't move.

After a few long seconds, he watched her turn her head and look out at his car. He caught a look of bewilderment on her face and let go half a breath, relieved not to see any fear in her expressions.

"A Porsche?" She said.

All his carefully rehearsed plans had now vanished from his mind. He still couldn't physically manage himself and couldn't muster any words. It was still her move.

Laura looked away from his car and back at him, still wearing a quizzical look. He watched her look him up and down.

"Long sleeve shirt, dress jeans, and leather shoes." With a smile, she eyed him and added, "You always were a good dresser, Charlie."

Hearing her say his name moved him into a mood he hadn't felt in years. For a split second, he felt like he was picking Laura up for a date. It was decades ago when he last heard her say his name.

Charlie kept his eyes on hers, hoping he wasn't imagining a look of warmth in them. Before he could say anything back to her, she continued.

"Come inside."

A few seconds later, he was standing in the living room opposite her. The two stood about five feet apart. A warmth, he still thought, was coming off her.

Some silence past. Laura broke it.

"Thanks, for the RSVP."

She glanced down at the card Charlie had read, just yesterday. It was on a nearby coffee table.

"Charlie, I was so happy when I saw the 'H' on the envelope this morning. And, sorry about the spy craft. But, I had to make sure it was you who read my card." She let go a breath. "Silly me, I was half afraid that you might have forgotten my last name."

He eyed her and said, "That's not possible."

Holding his eyes, she smiled. She tilted her head down while keeping her eyes locked on his.

"Charlie, I'm sorry I had to lay the card on your mother's grave."

He shrugged while smiling.

"My mom can always use another rose. And, I knew you had no other means to reach me, Laura."

Now, hearing himself call her by her name for the first time in years shook him. He continued talking.

"And Laura, *Happy Birthday*. It's been a long time."

Laura nodded as they sat down, each taking a separate sofa piece. She composed herself while looking down.

"Charlie, I came here tonight for two purposes. One, was to reclaim this childhood home of mine. And, I wanted to do it on my birthday. I told my father that if he had any hope of reconciling with me, he'd do as I say and let me stay here alone, tonight. And, since arriving a few hours ago, I realized I needed to come back here. I needed to start focusing on the good times I had here. I'm going to let the bad times that I had here, go."

Laura looked back up at Charlie.

"Tonight, is the first time I visited this home since I moved out in my late teens. We were dating then." These last words caused Laura to pause before continuing. "My therapist thought it'd be good idea to come here. So, here I am."

Charlie continued to listen.

"The second reason I came here was to meet you. I wanted to make a request to you, Charlie. And, it's hard to verbalize."

Laura's pleading expression prompted a response from Charlie.

"I am done with…with what has been happening."

Charlie saw relief wash over Laura's face. He looked down, then back up at her.

"I came here because of your note." He paused. "Laura, I also came here to see you before I go away. I'm leaving the country, for good."

Laura bit down on her bottom lip.

"Charlie, you shouldn't have waited thirty years to see me." She looked away. "I wanted to track you down, properly, over the years. But, I stopped myself each time. I knew you somehow vanished.

Nobody knew where you were. Or if they did, they weren't telling. I figured that wherever you'd gone or whatever had become of you, it wasn't good."

"And you'd be right." Charlie pursed his lips. "Why'd you consider trying to find me?"

Looking back at him, she said, "Because I loved you. Because I wanted to tell you I'd gotten help. And, gotten past, as best I can, with my father deserting my mother and me."

Charlie held her eyes, as she continued.

"Our breakup was because of my father, as we'd discussed back then. So, after I worked it all out, I wanted to find you, Charlie…and start, again." Laura tilted her head and looked as if she was going to talk to herself. "But that's not possible anymore."

Feeling a physical jolt hit him, Charlie fought his body's urge to jerk back. He always knew that Laura was going to remain a part of his past, not his future. Still, hearing it verbalized was difficult.

Looking at her, he thought he read the beginning of a smile, not on her face, in her eyes that were now glistening with moisture. He got up.

Leaning forward while looking up at him, Laura said, "I'm glad you came and even more glad to hear what you said tonight about being done."

Lost for words, Charlie managed to offer her a smile, more for her, less for himself. He then turned to go.

CHAPTER 41

As Charlie and Laura were saying their goodbyes, a man was growing nervous.

The nervous man was the same man who'd been keeping tabs on Charlie since his Malibu visit. The man was inside a car, a half block away from the home Laura and Charlie were at.

Guided by the GPS device on Charlie's Porsche, he'd tracked him to the Tustin house he was now watching through a pair of binoculars.

The fact that Charlie had spent more than 20 minutes inside the house made the man antsy. Especially so, given he had no idea that it was the home of Charlie's former girlfriend's father or what was going on inside. All he knew was that Charlie was working a lot of killing jobs, lately. Maybe this was one, or maybe not. He didn't know.

Bringing the binocs down from his eyes, he rested them on his lap. He looked at his phone screen and studied the surrounding streets. This prep work was prompted from his criminal experience which told him to always be aware of your location and possible escape routes.

And if Charlie burst out from the house he was in and took off with high speed, the man wanted to be ready to tail him. Studying the mapping of the nearby streets would go far in allowing him to not just follow Charlie but follow him covertly.

The man rubbed his eyes before bringing the binocs back up to his eyes. *What was Charlie doing in that house?* This question continued to unnerve him.

Finally, he breathed a sigh of relief after spotting Charlie leaving the house.

After watching Charlie getting into his Porsche, he tossed the binocs on the passenger seat and buckled up. Assuming Charlie was headed straight home, it would be time for him to go home, as well.

He saw Charlie pull away from the curb. The man started his car. It was then that he caught sight of a pair of worrisome headlights in his rearview mirror. As a longtime bad guy, the man had developed somewhat of an expertise in spotting the headlights of police vehicles. He thought the lights heading his way, from behind, were from a car often driven by detectives.

His guess proved correct when a black-colored Crown Victoria passed him, as he held still, in his idling car. He shot a look ahead and caught Charlie's Porsche disappearing around a corner, close to the house he'd just left.

Next, he saw the tail lights of the Crown Victoria light up as it slowed to a stop in front of the house Charlie just left. The car then sped up and soon turned the same corner as Charlie had.

"This is bad," the man whispered to himself.

The man allowed himself several precious seconds to think up a plan to help Charlie lose his police tail, one Charlie may not even know he had behind him. The man was glad to have studied the local street routes a few minutes, earlier. This proved a crucial time saver.

The man picked Charlie's car movements back up via the GPS tracking his moves. He saw that the Porsche was heading up a street towards a major boulevard, one that would take several blocks to reach. The man now knew what he had to do. He'd cut off the Crown Victoria detective car that he assumed was still tailing Charlie. And he would do this at a particular intersection. The man would do this just after Charlie crossed through the intersection, on his way toward the major boulevard. This would prevent the police vehicle from following Charlie.

With his plan ready, Sal Maginn shifted into drive, churned his steering wheel and made a U-turn. Straightening out from the U-turn, he smacked his lips. Sal didn't like the odds he gave his own plan of succeeding.

After a few seconds had passed, Sal's doubts of his plan working continued to grow. He concluded it was time to call Charlie and warn him of the police tail.

Turning a corner, Sal reached for his phone with a free hand. Trading looks over the hood with his phone screen, he scrolled down his contacts and quickly found Charlie's name. He went to press the call symbol next to Charlie's number but stopped himself.

Trouble was, he knew what would happen if he called Charlie and told him that he was being followed by a police vehicle. And that he, Sal, would help him lose the tail. Charlie would simply pull over and get himself arrested, rather than risk Sal getting snagged by the police while trying to help him.

Sal realized he'd have to stick with his original, but lousy, plan.

Now with both hands back on the steering wheel and heading to his destination intersection, Sal smiled a sad smile. Charlie was too good of a friend, and he didn't deserve him.

Detective Harris was turning the corner in his Crown Victoria with one hand on the wheel, while tossing out a half-finished cigarette with the other. Blowing out a cloud of smoke, he grabbed his phone. All the while keeping his eyes focused on the tail lights of the Porsche, a good block ahead.

Harris had no clue that the car he was following was being driven by his number one criminal target—Charlie Casey. Yet he was chasing him with the intensity he would've been had he known Charlie was in the Porsche. The reason was simple—this chase involved what he sensed was Laura's personal safety. He'd seen her car parked in the driveway at her father's home, where the Porsche took off from.

Trading looks between the Porsche and his phone screen, he scrolled down his contacts and found Laura's name. Just as he was going to press it the phone chimed, and Laura's name was showing as the caller.

He answered with, "Laura, are you okay?"

"Yes, Daniel," she said. "Why?"

Hearing her soothing and oh-so-normal voice, Harris dropped his shoulders and let out a breath.

Squinting to stay focused on the car ahead of him, he said, "Where are you?"

Laura sighed and said, "I'm still at my father's home."

Harris didn't notice that he'd let off the gas pedal, while his eyes glazed away from their focus on the Porsche. A Porsche that was now disappearing around a corner. Nor did he notice a car coming to a stop at the stop sign to his left.

Lowering his voice, Harris said, "I'm actually nearby. Can I come over?"

As Sal Maginn was coming up on the four-way stop intersection he'd eyed on his GPS screen a minute ago, he saw Charlie's Porsche pass through it. Coming to the stop sign, he looked right and watched the Crown Victoria rolling toward his perspective stop sign. Sal was about to proceed through the intersection and cut his engine mid-way through it, feigning a mechanical problem. This would delay the police vehicle from pursuing Charlie's Porsche.

But before Sal hit the gas, the Crown Victoria surprised him by making a U-turn. Relieved that Charlie was no longer being tailed, Sal decided to follow the Crown Victoria at a safe distance behind. He wanted to make sure the car was not somehow going another route to catch up with Charlie's car, again.

Some minutes later, Sal watched as the police vehicle came to a stop at the same home Charlie had left from, some 10 minutes ago. The Crown Victoria's chase of Charlie's car was over. Sal had no idea why the chase was over, but he didn't care. Charlie was out of trouble. And Sal could see from his GPS tracking screen that his friend was already on the major boulevard and safely out of the area.

Sal breathed a sigh of relief as he passed the parked Crown Victoria.

CHAPTER 42

Harris was now seated inside the home that Charlie Casey had left just minutes ago. Reaching for his cigarette pack, he stopped himself after remembering he was inside the childhood home of his girlfriend.

He looked around. Harris was curious about the home, albeit one that was not so kind to Laura. It was only recently he learned what happened in this house after she'd driven him by it, after another shared dinner last week. Laura had teared up during the drive by. He asked, then, what was going on. And she told him about her 10th birthday. And how her father leaving that night had left her scared.

As she grew older, she told Harris she wasn't able to fully trust any man. But through a few years of counseling, and even tonight's visit to her childhood home on her birthday, she was ready to try her hand at romance, once again.

After she finished, Harris said, "So, you're okay?"

"Yes. But, I have a question." She tilted her head. "Daniel, how did you get here so quickly after we spoke a few minutes ago?"

After a few seconds, Harris looked at Laura, seated across from him. He was wearing a sheepish smile.

Before he could explain himself, Laura said, "I've something to tell you, Daniel."

Daniel held up his hands.

"No. Let me go first," he said. "I've got a confession to make."

She went to protest, but quickly backed down. He gathered himself and spoke.

"Laura, you'd told me that you were coming here…to your father's house tonight to work something out." He lowered his voice. "And my imagination went wild. And, I thought maybe you were placing yourself in some kind of potential harm. It was just a feeling on my part. I got a little worried and hung around the neighborhood."

Laura smiled.

Looking embarrassed, he said, "I guess I went a little overboard."

"No, you didn't," she said. "Daniel, tonight you showed me you cared about me. And, hopefully, it's as much as I care about you. Which is a lot."

Now Harris smiled. Then Laura threw her hands open.

"And by the way, my father wasn't even here tonight. And he's never physically hurt me."

"I didn't know that," he said with a shrug. "But I was also worried about Charlie being out there. And, knowing he is knocking off the bad parents of his friends, I thought maybe he'd do something to your father and specifically tonight. After all, you were more than a friend to Charlie and he knew the significance of your birthday, with respect to your father. And you'd be here and maybe get in the middle of something and get hurt."

He paused while looking up at Laura, who had moist eyes. She nodded as he continued.

"So, Laura, I drove by here tonight and saw your car in the driveway. Then, this Porsche pulls out. And, I gave chase thinking it was Charlie. I called you while I was in pursuit." Harris's hands jerked open. "I was just worried about it. It was a crazy thought."

Laura broke in with, "Why'd you stop following the car?"

"You answered the phone. So, I knew you were not only okay but had probably just a friend or relative over for a visit." Harris shrugged. "Heck, I didn't even see if it was a guy or girl driving the Porsche."

Looking down, then back up with only her eyes, Laura said, "It was a guy in the car."

Harris looked sideways at her and lowered his head, waiting for her to finish.

"Daniel, it was Charlie Casey in that Porsche."

Several minutes later, Harris reached for his phone while looking over at Laura. He offered her a comfort smile. After he dialed Garcia, the detective answered before the first ring had finished.

Harris told Garcia to hold for a second.

Sensitive to Laura's emotions about her visit with Charlie, Harris was about to say something to her. But she waved him off and indicated she had something to attend to in the kitchen. And she took her leave. Still, Harris walked out of the home to talk to Garcia.

Outside, holding the phone to his ear, Harris scanned the neighborhood with his eyes as if looking for something hidden. He was subconsciously on high alert. And his subconscious was also kicking him in the head, reminding him that only a half hour ago he'd been looking at the taillights of the killer he was searching for. But Charlie Casey remained free.

This was all inside Harris's brain, floating and bouncing around as he finally spoke into the phone receiver. He filled Garcia in on what he'd just learned about Charlie, from Laura, including a physical description of him. When he finished, Garcia spoke.

"Daniel, this is a huge break." A pause. "So, who's the goose that gave you this golden egg of information?"

"Not now, and maybe never," Harris shot back.

Garcia responded in a softer voice.

"Okay. What now?"

Harris began to pace the driveway.

"Alex, get an APB out on Charlie Casey. Be sure to note that the name he goes by is fluid. Note that he's planning to leave the country. So, get the airports and private airstrips on alert." He stopped pacing. "And keep the news about this Charlie sighting from the press till six a.m. This will give us six hours to find him before he realizes we know who he is. If we don't catch him before then, we'll have the public's eyes helping us find Charlie Casey and his Porsche. The news reports might get him moving which would make him more likely to make a mistake."

Garcia jumped in with, "It'd also make this Charlie much less likely to chance another killing, knowing he's been ID'd."

"I think he's done with that."

Garcia said, "This Charlie guy is done with killing?"

Harris hemmed and hawed, and said, "I think so."

Looking down at the home's front lawn, Harris could hardly believe his own words. But he couldn't deny his gut feelings. Those feelings told him Charlie was telling Laura the truth when he'd told her he was done with killing.

There were a few seconds of silence, before Garcia said, "Okay."

Harris read his watch—11:30 p.m.

"Alex, I'm going to call good ole Sam and have him draw up a composite of our guy. I should have a sketch of Charlie Casey to you by 2 a.m. Check back in with me after I email it to you."

"Copy, Daniel." Garcia sighed. "It's gonna be a long night."

"Hopefully it'll be a short one," he said. Harris was about to ring off, but Garcia spoke.

"Daniel, what should we nickname this Charlie Casey?"

Harris knew dubbing a wanted suspect with a nickname helped build public awareness.

"The Deadbeat Killer." With that, Daniel rang off and dialed Sam, the sketch artist.

While waiting for Sam to answer, Harris looked across the street. And through a set of thin curtains, he spied the glow of a neighbor's television. He could make out the silhouette of a solitary woman in a chair, backlit by the TV. Harris imagined that same neighbor watching the news that would break, just hours from now, that they had a suspect in the murder spree that had gripped Southern California the last few weeks. The neighbor would learn the suspect was a former Tustin Tiller, a graduate of their local Tustin High School. Harris wondered if the same neighbor would ever find out that Charlie Casey, the killer, had paid a visit across the street from her tonight while she was idly watching TV.

The crackle of Sam's voice in his ear broke his reverie. And it was obvious to Harris he'd woken up his longtime colleague. But he knew the man was used to being called to a crime scene at all hours of the night or day. Sam's work couldn't be put off for convenience. Harris was aware that the accuracy of the image produced by police sketches significantly improves if you can complete it within 24 hours of the witness describing a given suspect.

After Harris gave Sam the address of where he and Laura were at, he ended the call.

Harris knew the composite drawing session would be tough for Laura, though she said she'd be fine. Either way, it had to be done. Luckily, he'd worked with Sam enough to know he was skilled at putting people at ease when they were in his presence for a drawing session. For Sam usually only ever worked with people who were in a state of emotional upheaval, since most were crime victims.

Luckily too, Harris could trust Sam to keep his mouth shut about Laura's identity, should the press ask. The police sketch artist was old school and was good at keeping to his artistry.

Putting his phone back in its holder, Harris realized he was without his pistol. He started for his car to fetch it but stopped himself. Bringing it inside, even under his jacket, might shake Laura up. At the moment, she needed calming.

Besides, as Harris turned and started back towards the entrance of the home, he sensed his gun wouldn't be needed. At least not for defense. He somehow knew that should Charlie unexpectedly return to the house he wouldn't do anything violent on the grounds of Laura's childhood home. Still, Harris kicked himself for letting himself believe this about Charlie. It didn't seem right to concede any humanity to this killer. But life was complicated, he told himself.

Harris waved Sam, the sketch artist, goodbye from the front door. He caught another look at the TV-watching neighbor across the street. She was peeking through her curtains to glimpse the two men. Hopefully, her curiosity of seeing strangers without seeing the owner of the home, Laura's father, would end there. The last thing Harris needed was the local police being called to the house and having to do some explaining.

Checking his watch, he saw that it was 1:30 a.m. It took Sam less than an hour to draw a composite sketch of Charlie Casey, as Laura related the details to him. Shutting the front door and turning to look at Laura, he sensed her mood had picked up since Sam's arrival. Maybe concentrating on helping Sam draw out a sketch of Charlie was a cathartic task. It took her out of the moment, if only for a short bit.

Harris took his seat across from Laura. He gave her the best smile he could offer at this juncture in the hunt for Charlie.

The two sat in silence, looking from side to side, seemingly searching for something that was not going to be found. This went on for what seemed like an eternity to Harris.

Laura's voice broke the ice.

"Look Daniel," she said, throwing her head to one side. "After hearing at the reunion that both Bruce William's and Tab Smith's dads were murdered recently, I knew in my heart Charlie was responsible. Then you came to me requesting his name, and I knew something was up. I got a sense that Charlie may have been involved in more killings."

She paused for a few seconds before continuing.

"Daniel, I would've told you about what I was gonna do tonight. But, I just thought you'd think I was crazy. And, I just needed to speak with Charlie, alone. I really just wanted to tell Charlie not to harm anybody else. There was nothing more—"

"Don't worry, Laura. My only concern is that you're okay."

Laura's voice quivered as she said, "Daniel, I love you. I'm lucky to have found you."

Daniel looked straight at her for a few seconds.

"I'm the lucky one," he said.

CHAPTER 43

Back inside his Crown Victoria, Harris pulled away from the curb of the house. Utilizing his passenger side mirror, he puffed on a smoke as he watched Laura turn from the sidewalk and head back up the driveway of her father's home.

Laura had insisted to Harris that she wanted to spend the night alone, as planned, at her father's house. This, despite all that happened there tonight concerning Charlie.

With respect to Charlie's visit, Laura explained to Harris there was nothing to worry about. She was okay with the visit, and she was further okay with giving him—the top detective chasing Charlie—all the information she could on her former boyfriend. Even helping the sketch artist was, she insisted, therapeutic to her.

As to why Laura wanted to spend the night in a house that was the physical place of her father deserting her, she told Harris the explanation was rather simple. She needed to "reclaim" her childhood home for herself. After all these years, she'd realized that she'd let her father ruin her entire childhood. This included the happy and memorable times she'd spent in her room and home, as a kid. Beginning tonight, she was done with that.

Turning a corner, he lost his rearview mirror view of Laura and the house. Harris was glad that he was able to put his gut-level emotions aside when he'd told Laura he understood her decisions tonight. In reality, he only partially understood what she explained to him about Charlie Casey's visit. Same went for her desire to "reclaim" her childhood home.

Besides, Harris believed a man could only ever hope to partially understand a woman. They were too complicated and mysterious for males. And as for friends, both female and male, who told him *you're too old school in your thinking Daniel*, he always offered only one response—*we'll go fuck yourself*.

It was well past midnight. And Sal Maginn was turning off Sunset Boulevard, in West Hollywood. He pulled into the underground parking lot of a modern high-rise condo building made, it seemed, of only glass and steel on the outside. The lowest current price point of any of the units was north of $2 million. It was a private building where your neighbors in adjacent units are rarely home and all-but never seen.

And Sal, like his neighbors in the building, rarely used his condo. He'd bought it years ago as an emergency hideaway. Such a hideaway was a necessity in the field of high-end professional killing. And though he was retired, Sal maintained it just in case he ever needed to disappear from the cops or worse. Sal wasn't being chased tonight, but after following Charlie he was tired. Too tired to drive back to his main home in Malibu.

Sal parked his car in his assigned spot. He rolled his shoulders to relieve some tension. His friend dodged another bullet. As his car engine shut down, Sal thought back once again to the time Charlie saved his life back in Atlanta.

While he and Charlie were working a kill job together inside of a house, things suddenly turned south. They found themselves running out of the home with gunfire coming from behind. Charlie made it out. Sal didn't. He'd been knocked down by a bullet that had grazed his leg. With a risk of getting shot himself, Charlie went back inside and retrieved Sal.

Sal thought back on a lighter moment of this experience. After Charlie had rescued him, and after their car was miles away from the scene of horrors, Charlie, who was driving, looked over at Sal, who was holding his injured leg and in obvious pain.

"Welcome to Atlanta."

Sal smiled remembering how Charlie's comment made him let go a painful laugh.

CHAPTER 44

As Charlie was winding along Astral Drive towards his house, his mind was twisting and turning with thoughts of Laura. Such was his entire drive home from his visit with her, tonight.

It was just past 1:00 a.m. as he turned onto his driveway while pressing a finger to activate the garage remote. His eyes were watching the garage door slowly opening, but his mind remained on Laura.

Charlie realized he'd gotten more than he'd hope for from tonight's visit with Laura. Maybe too much for his own good. Besides telling her a final goodbye, he'd found out that, after they had split up, she'd tried to contact him at one point in her life. He wished she hadn't told him that.

Knowing he could've possibly had Laura back, only added to his emotional pain. But then again, he knew, soon after their breakup, that he and her were doomed forever. That was because he'd begun his career in killing.

With the garage door fully open, Charlie drove in and cut the engine.

As he listened to the pings and pongs of the engine cooling, he considered the totality of the failure of Laura and him, as a couple.

Sure, Laura broke up with him, explaining she was too damaged from watching her mother's marriage of violence to maintain a lasting relationship. But Charlie figured that it was he himself who was to blame for their breakup. More specifically, he thought it was his father, not hers, who was to blame.

And despite feeling weak for blaming his father's departure from his life for his own failures, Charlie knew it couldn't be tossed from the equation of him and Laura's relationship. The damage his father had done to him and his mother by deserting them changed his personality. It'd made him much less likely to contribute happiness to a marriage, he figured.

More to the point, he figured that Laura sensed the buried troubles that were lurking deep inside him. Combining this with her own crumbled insides, due to her father, she must have consciously or subconsciously seen the writing on the wall—her and Charlie would be doomed from the start of any marriage.

Charlie pressed the remote and began to hear the garage door jerk and screech its way down. As the door closed behind him with a boom, he forced himself to close his mind to any thoughts of his long-ago lost-cause love life. Laura would always be part of his past. For now, he had a busy 48 hours ahead of him, and he needed to focus.

Still, seated in the stillness of the garage, he struggled to let go of Laura's face. A face he hadn't been able to enjoy looking at for thirty years, until tonight.

Charlie told himself to take it one task at a time until he was out of the country. That was the only way to get moving and to escape his thoughts of Laura.

And the first move was to exit his car, which he did. He walked to his garage house door and twisted its handle, just as the light of the garage went out.

As he was opening the door, it hit him—the laundry room light was on which he'd always left off. As soon as that thought was completed, it was too late. He was facing Laredo and a gun he was holding.

Laredo's hefty frame nearly took up the opposite doorway of the laundry room. Stealing a peek over Laredo's shoulder, Charlie could see a couple more men staring at him. They were dark complected, probably Mexican nationals and had a blank look about them, and both needed a shave.

Charlie stood still, awaiting death. Laredo spoke.

"You're probably wondering why you're not dead. Well, Charlie I'll explain why after we take a little drive to your sleeping quarters for tonight." The cartel enforcer dipped his head. "I hope you don't mind if we use your Toyota. If something happens, and we are seen leaving a crime scene, it's your car that would be spotted."

Five minutes later, the four of them were all loaded into Charlie's Corolla. Charlie was seated in the back with plastic handcuffs tying his hands behind his back. Laredo was next to him and still had a gun pointed at him. The two associates of Laredo were up front. One of them reached back and outfitted Charlie with a blindfold. Charlie soon heard the car start and felt it backing out of his driveway.

As the Toyota began its journey to whatever destination Laredo had planned for, Charlie knew this could be his last car drive. With Bennie and Scott dead, Charlie realized he was the only loose end left that Laredo needed to eliminate in his Los Angeles killing operations. More specifically, Charlie was Laredo's last living contractor tied to the disastrous kill job on the money launderer, Alejandro Vargas, and the whole Hollywood Hills murder fiasco.

And with the Hollywood Hills murder spree continuing to dominate the news, Charlie knew that Laredo's cartel bosses had to have ordered him to clean up his LA mess.

As the car moved along in silence, Charlie realized Laredo was right about what he said tonight. Charlie was indeed wondering *why am I not dead yet*?

Inside his 23rd floor condo unit, just inside West Hollywood, Sal Maginn was enjoying a view of the mansion-sized homes of Beverly Hills. His enjoyment turned to concern when he saw his phone screen light up. It was showing the movements of Charlie's Toyota. Sal saw the time was 1:20 a.m., and he felt something turn in his stomach.

He grabbed his keys and headed out of his unit while his face was glued to Charlie's movements. And while his eyes may have been watching Charlie's car moving along on a map, Sal's mind was on what his best friend had told him back at his beach house some 3 weeks ago. There, over some beer, Charlie had told him that the cartels would "be hunting me down."

Taking the elevator down to the underground parking, Sal thought about all the news he had been hearing about the killings. The ones that began in the Hollywood Hills. The ones that Charlie had told Sal he committed. The ones that Charlie said had upset his cartel employer. The ones, Sal knew, could get Charlie killed when his cartel bosses had had enough of the news coverage of the killing spree. Stepping out of the elevator, Sal walked towards his car.

Soon, Sal was driving away from his condo building. Sal pulled over when he saw, from his GPS screen tracking Charlie's car, that the car had come to a stop. He quickly established that Charlie's Toyota was parked in a sprawling industrial area.

Sal sensed he needed a backup. One that was much younger, physically strong, and possessing a unique set of skills that included breaking and entering. He placed a call to an Armenian man with a barrel chest that could meet his requirements—Artie Abalian.

CHAPTER 45

After what Charlie figured was a 45-minute drive, he was taken out of the Toyota and guided inside a building. Once inside, his feet told him he was walking on cement floors. He sat down on a metal chair. The only noise he was hearing were the voices of Laredo and his men, all speaking in Spanish.

Charlie was instructed, by Laredo, to remain still as his feet were now going to be tied together. Within minutes, his blindfold was removed but not the handcuffs keeping his hands together behind his back.

Charlie found himself facing Laredo. The cartel enforcer was seated about ten feet from him with his hands folded. He was no longer holding a gun. Still, Charlie saw that Laredo's two associates, one on each side of him, were each holding guns at their sides.

Using only his eyes, Charlie stole a few glances around. He was inside a small enclosure made up of stacked pallets of bagged material. The pallets formed a horseshoe, with Laredo's back to its open mouth.

Things quieted down between Laredo and his men. Charlie eyed Laredo, who addressed him.

"Charlie, we had to get to Bennie and Scott before the police did. You were too slow." Laredo paused. "Bennie did tell us something before he was…well, he did tell us something. He told us that you needed a passport to be updated. Obviously, you have travel plans."

Charlie offered no response.

"Well Charlie, we got worried. You're now in the same category as Bennie and Scott were. Loose ends with a lot of knowledge and no particular loyalty. Such people are dangerous to my organization."

Charlie looked around.

"Don't worry Charlie. We're not planning to kill you."

Laredo stopped talking.

Charlie broke his silence with, "Okay. If you're not planning to get rid of me, then what is all this trouble about?"

Lifting his head up, but keeping his eyes on Charlie, Laredo answered him.

"I have an important job for you." Laredo unfolded his hands. "In exchange for doing it, you get to live. And, you get to move away or retire. One or both of which, Charlie, you had apparently been planning."

Charlie said, "I'm listening."

"What we will be doing is shipping you off to South Africa, tonight. Charlie, you'll have to earn our trust back by doing us a few delicate jobs over there."

Looking at Laredo, Charlie knew there was never going to be any retirement option. Once he did whatever Laredo wanted him to do in South Africa, the cartel enforcer would order him killed. For now, he would go along with the plan.

"Laredo, I'll go to South Africa."

A smile crossed Laredo's face and he said, "Let's go over some details."

It was past 2:00 a.m. by the time Sal Maginn arrived at the industrial warehouse location. He was led there via the GPS tracking device on Charlie's Toyota which he spotted in front of the warehouse. Sal knew the car had stopped moving 20 minutes ago, per the GPS tracking.

Charlie's car was parked in front of a door that, by all appearances, led to the main office of the building. The door was surrounded by windows that showed inside lights were on. Wanting not to tip anyone off that he was there, Sal drove around the building's corner and parked at the back of the building.

Next, Sal texted Artie Abalian, who was driving to meet him, to let him know where to park his car. And though Charlie's Toyota was the only car Sal saw in front of the building, he didn't believe Charlie came here alone. Sal felt a growing knot in his stomach.

A couple minutes later, Sal watched as Artie Abalian's car approached. Sal grabbed his pistol and quietly got out of his car. He then waved to the Armenian and motioned him to park alongside him. Within a minute, the two had developed a plan to get into the building. All for the purpose of checking on Charlie's well-being.

Two minutes later, Sal and Artie, who was wearing a tool belt, were standing next to the building's door. Sal let Artie take the lead. Artie tried to turn the doorknob but looked at Sal while shaking his head in silence. The Armenian would have to implore his locksmith skills. He grabbed some items out of his tool belt and went to work.

Artie quickly had the door unlocked.

Sal indicated he would go in first. But then Artie held up a finger and whispered to Sal, "My job is done…this is as far as I go."

After eyeing the man he'd known and worked with for years, Sal nodded. Artie turned and walked away. Sal refocused, as his old professional mindset kicked in and wouldn't allow him any mental distractions such as feelings of disappointment. He took out his gun. Next, he slipped inside the building and eased the door closed.

Immediately Sal was hearing voices. Following the voices, he made his way past a few office cubicles. He found an opened door and went through it and stopped.

Sal found himself on cold cement and looking at multitudes of pallets with bulky bags piled on them. There were columns of these stacked pallets that were spaced out, forming tiny passageways. He stood still and picked back up on the sound of the voices. They were louder now.

Sal followed the voices while squeezing between the rows of stacked pallets. He stopped again when he realized one of the voices, though fainter than a second one he was hearing, was Charlie's. Ahead he saw a clearing. He figured these were lanes for forklifts and warehouse workers.

Stopping just before the clearing, Sal ducked down a bit to hide between a couple of single pallets. These single pallets were at the end of the two rows of pallets he was between.

Sal heard the voices, again. They were within feet of him and to his right. Holding the gun, he peaked around the corner. He could only see a huge Mexican man sitting on a chair, facing the mouth of another small clearing in the stacks of pallets.

He figured the big man was addressing Charlie, who he couldn't see, since he heard his friend's voice in short bursts. The stranger was talking to Charlie in an unfriendly tone.

Sal stood still and looked down for a second. He recalled Charlie telling him, a few years back, about a man named Laredo. The man was a cartel enforcer and was Charlie's main contract client. Sal had remembered one thing about Laredo—Charlie hated him. As Sal peeked once more around the pallet, to his right, at the huge man in the chair. He knew it had to be Laredo.

Sal noted that Laredo wasn't holding a gun. Still, Charlie could be guarded by other men who Sal couldn't see from his vantage point. No matter, Sal figured that Charlie and company wouldn't be in the middle of the warehouse if this was a friendly meeting.

Thinking for a split second, Sal figured Laredo was calling the shots. And Sal thought if he pointed a gun at the boss, he'd have enough leverage to extract Charlie out of the situation. He was not going to wait any longer to make a move.

Sal came around the pallet he was behind. He walked straight to Laredo and pointed his gun at him.

Looking to his left, Sal saw Charlie, ten feet away, seated in a chair. They eyed each other, and Sal felt his chest sink. He gathered that Charlie's hands were tied behind his back. Sal saw Charlie's feet were bound together, too. A man was on each side of Charlie pointing a gun at him. Charlie and the two men guarding him were in a small alcove made from walls of pallets.

To Sal, everything seemed to freeze for a split second. Continuing to point his gun at Laredo, Sal addressed him with, "Tell them not to shoot or you're dead."

Laredo showed Sal a bored look and spoke.

"If you kill me now, my boys will kill Charlie." Laredo shrugged. "Why wouldn't they."

A few seconds passed.

Nodding, Sal put down his gun on the cement floor. Laredo motioned to his two associates, and they both walked over to Sal. They stood behind Sal and indicated to him not to move and to put his hands behind his back. One of the men put his gun in his back pocket and pulled out a set of plastic handcuffs. The other man stood near his partner, still holding up his gun.

Laredo watched all this in silence.

As the man finished putting on Sal's handcuffs, he stood up straight to stretch his back.

Sal began to fiddle with his hands to test the tightness of the cuffs. But something from the corner of his right eye caught his attention. He looked to his right and saw a 3-foot-plus long bag flying towards the back of him. His eyes went wide when he saw that it was Artie Abalian who had hurdled the bag.

Next thing Sal knew, to his left, between Charlie and himself, one of the gunmen was on the ground screaming in pain. The man was covered in a white beady material. Sal gathered that the flying bag had split open after hitting the gunman.

Turning around, Sal saw the man who cuffed him. The man was frantically reaching back to pull out the gun in his back pocket only to drop it. Sal managed to kick the gun into the white substance. The man went after it and fished it out of the white material that had spilled out of the broken bag. But when the man grabbed onto the gun he let it drop back into the white substance. All the while yelling in pain and shaking his gun hand.

Turning back around, Sal saw Laredo reaching to the cement floor near his feet. Sal quickly kicked his own gun, that he'd placed on the cement floor, away from Laredo. The gun disappeared into a space between a wall of pallets. Sal saw Laredo raise his massive frame and try to squeeze a hand into his tight-fitting pocket for his own gun, but he was too late. Artie was upon the cartel man and holding a box cutter, from behind, to his throat. Laredo's face acknowledged the gig was up. And he relaxed his body.

Artie eased Laredo back down into his chair, while keeping the box cutter to his throat. The Armenian instructed Sal to step towards him and turn around. Sal did as he was instructed, and soon Artie had split his plastic handcuffs apart with the box cutter. Laredo didn't try anything after getting a look at the bulky Armenian.

Once freed, Sal quickly went and retrieved his gun from between some pallets. He initially pointed it at the two gunmen. But they were still on the floor moaning and holding onto parts of their skin that'd been exposed to the white material. Both their guns were still covered in the menacing white material.

Sal then pointed his gun at Laredo and spoke to Charlie.

"Are you okay, kid?"

"Now I am."

Sal reacted with a smile while keeping his eyes on Laredo. He instructed the cartel enforcer to stand up. Sal then had Artie grab Laredo's gun out of the man's pocket.

Then Artie took the lead and grabbed some wiring out of his tool belt. He quickly had Laredo's hands tied behind his back. Once that was done, Artie walked over to Charlie and cut his hands and feet loose. As Charlie stood up, Laredo's voice was heard.

"Charlie?"

The two men locked eyes and Laredo continued.

"Are you going to kill me?"

Charlie gave the cartel man a blank look and answered.

"I'm done with killing."

Laredo held Charlie's stare for a split second and looked away.

Sal caught Laredo's attention with, "Who has Charlie's car keys?"

Laredo indicated he had them. Artie fished the car keys out of one of Laredo's pockets and tossed them to Charlie.

Sal's eyes took one final look around and he said, "Let's go."

Artie waved his hands at Laredo's men on the floor. Sal answered the Armenian's concern while looking at the men.

"Those men can't grab their guns. Their hands are still burning." Sal then looked up at one of the pallets and focused on the labeling on the bags. "Whatever caustic soda beads are, I think these men are done trying to fish their guns out of it."

Then Sal looked over at Laredo.

"And by the time they manage to free their boss, we'll be gone."

A minute later, Charlie, Sal, and Artie were outside the warehouse. The men paused. Sal smiled at the Armenian who smiled back.

"What gives, Artie?"

With a shrug, Artie looked at Charlie and then back at Sal.

"I couldn't walk away. Both of you have been good to me."

Charlie caught Artie's eyes and said, "Thanks."

Artie turned and walked towards his car. With a smile, Charlie turned towards Sal.

"You've been following me."

Sal let out a laugh.

"Kid, I followed you for my own selfish reason…I missed the action."

Charlie, still holding his smile, said, "I don't believe you."

"Kid, I'm just glad to know I can still tail a pro around without him noticing. So much for my good teaching skills back in the day."

"I'm just a lousy student." Charlie dropped his smile. "You're blood to me, Sal."

DAY 21

CHAPTER 46

After leaving the warehouse, the next 16 hours were busy for Charlie. All without sleep. Having a plane to Mexico to catch, he'd raced to complete many personal and business tasks. These included taking care of the people who took care of him.

Charlie gave his cars away to Lew Holt, who he knew had a fondness for Porsches. He sent a large cash gift to Artie Abalian, who saved both Charlie and Sal last night by risking his life by going into the warehouse. And despite Bruce William's refusal to take the money help Charlie offered him, he made arrangements for him to get some cash to help start his new, straight life.

As for Sal, Charlie didn't dare offer anything of value to his friend, who ultimately was responsible for saving Charlie last night from Laredo and his men. A gift would've insulted Sal.

But finally, Charlie was seated in a single-prop Cessna's passenger chair. The flight would be his first of several he would be taking to get to where he was headed to in Mexico.

As the plane lifted off the ground, his thoughts were mixed about leaving his home and his friend Sal. But Charlie had no concerns about leaving his career as he leaned back his chair. As he watched the desert landscape sink below him, he fell into a slumber.

THREE DAYS LATER: DAY 24

Harris could think of no meeting that he'd ever had in his superior's office that turned out to be a positive experience. This, as he walked through the open office door of his LAPD commander.

The commander was at his desk. With the top of his thinning white head of hair showing, the commander said, "Come in, have a seat, Harris."

Harris sat down in one of the three chairs in front of the desk. A few seconds went by before the commander lifted his always-red face and eyed him. The commander put aside his reading material.

"Look, Daniel, I'm taking you off the Deadbeat Killer case."

Harris threw a shoulder back and shifted in his suit coat. He wouldn't bother protesting. It'd do no good. He'd learned that from past interactions with the man. Besides, he knew one day the commander would pay him back for disobeying his order, some 3 years back, not to go into an apartment where a woman was being held hostage by her husband. The commander was steamed at the time, but Harris had become such a big overnight local hero for saving the woman's life that he couldn't punish him. He had to let it drop. But today was payback time. And, the commander finally had a perfect excuse that nobody would call him out on.

"You see, Daniel, you're dating the ex-girlfriend of the still-at-large killer—Charlie Casey. The case is now personal to you." The commander exhaled. "I feel bad about this. You've worked hard and made progress on the case."

Harris got up from the chair. He didn't want to give the commander any more enjoyment than he had to. He eyed the commander and took his leave.

ONE YEAR LATER

CHAPTER 48

Clicking off from her daughter, Velinda Valdez ran her hands through her hair. She felt her stomach tighten after hearing her daughter talk about the dinner she'd enjoyed with her father last night. He'd flown in again from Mexico for another visit and to attend their daughter's high school graduation.

For reasons unknown to her, Velinda's ex-husband had started flying in to see their daughter. Jorge's visits began about a year ago. Velinda knew his visits were good for her daughter, but she'd found herself angry and jealous over the situation. Putting her phone back down on the counter inside her flower shop, she paused.

She had been praying for several years for her ex to become active once again in her daughter's life. It had broken her girl's heart when her daddy left the two of them for Mexico, some 7 years ago.

Realizing her own selfishness over the visits, Velinda turned and walked over to her work bench. She stopped and vowed to herself never to wonder or worry about her ex paying visits to her daughter, anymore. Smiling, she resumed cutting and arranging her flowers.

A bell rang, signaling a visitor had entered her shop.

Looking up, Velinda saw a tall man dressed in a pinstripe suit walk in. Removing her work gloves, she met the 30-something looking man at the counter.

"May I help you?" she said.

The man tilted his head forward and slid an index card across the counter toward her and said, "I have an invitation for you."

She looked down briefly at the card and looked back up to ask, "What is this about?"

The man held her stare and answered, "There's a package and a business card awaiting you at the law firm listed on the card."

Velinda stepped out of the elevator and onto the 21st floor. As the elevator closed behind her, she held tightly to the index card the shop visitor had given her the week before. Turning toward the quiet hallway, she stopped while looking at a couple of bronze wall plaques with numbers and arrows on them. Making a right, she began to walk, growing more uneasy with each door she passed.

She came to door 2111 and read the name on the door—*Law Offices of Dean, Reynolds, Collette, and Benjamin*. After hesitating, she opened the door. The hum of a large copy machine greeted her ears. She spotted a woman wearing reading glasses sitting behind a receptionist desk, a few feet ahead of her.

Walking up to the desk, Velinda said to the woman in glasses, "I'm here to see Mr. Wallace Reynolds."

The receptionist looked up at her without moving. Velinda handed her the index card, with a half-smile. As the receptionist pressed some buttons in front of her, Velinda stole a look around. She saw nothing but dark wood walls and carpeted floors. Nothing about this office felt welcoming. Maybe she'd made a mistake coming here.

A minute later though, Velinda found herself seated in a leather and wood chair inside a spacious office. The only thing cheerful about the room was a window allowing a terrific view of a huge swath of the coastline of Newport Beach. Setting across from her, and behind an imposing desk, was a lawyer named Wallace Reynolds. Given his frail figure and thinning snow-white hair, she guessed he was past 75 years of age.

After offering her a few words of dry pleasantries, Reynolds looked down at Velinda Valdez's index card, which was placed before him by the receptionist. He then looked back up and eyed Velinda.

"Ms. Valdez, one of my clients asked me to give you a gift. This client was a customer of your flower shop for many years."

Raising her eyebrows, Velinda continued to listen.

"His name was Charlie."

Throwing her head back, Velinda said, "Yes, I know him."

Reynolds nodded while reaching into a drawer and pulling out a notepad. He looked it over and placed it next to the index card on his desk.

"Ms. Valdez, I am required to ask you a security question." He eyed her. "This, to insure you are the intended recipient of Charlie's gift."

Velinda met his eyes and waited for the question.

The lawyer tightened his lips and said, "What is the flower count?"

She smiled and said, "It's probably 31 since the last time I saw Charlie, it was 30. And Charlie hasn't been to my shop for about a year."

Ignoring her answer, he said, "Can you tell me what the question means?"

Nodding, she said, "Yes…yes I can. It means the number of years since Charlie's mother passed away."

With that, the lawyer pushed away from his desk and swiveled his chair. With his back to her, he began to fiddle with a wall safe that

Velinda hadn't noticed before. He quickly retrieved something from it. When he swiveled back around, the lawyer was holding a small box.

"This is Charlie's gift to you, Ms. Valdez," he said, handing the small box over to her.

Taking the box, she noticed it weighed more than she had anticipated. She put it on her lap.

"Thank you," she said. "But, what's this about?"

Reynolds wet his lips and said, "I don't know."

Velinda looked down at the box she was holding. "What's in the box?"

The lawyer looked down and back up at her.

"I do not know. And Charlie requested that you not tell me. He said to inform you it is simply a gift."

Reynolds then opened his top drawer and grabbed a business card. He handed it over to her. Before she could examine it, he folded his hands and started to explain the card.

"That is the business card of Margaret Tolson. She is the administrator of the college trust fund that Charlie set up." He paused and said, "I believe your daughter will be aiming for medical school."

Velinda's mouth dropped open as the man continued his explanation.

"Your daughter's schooling will be provided for via the trust fund. When you contact Ms. Tolson, she will explain how it works."

Try as she did, Velinda couldn't help but to tear up.

Reynolds ignored her watery eyes and said, "Any questions, Ms. Valdez?"

She wiped an eye with a tissue the man offered her.

"How can I contact Charlie to thank him?" She managed a laugh. "I don't even know his last name."

Reynolds looked out the window for a few seconds before turning back to her.

"I'm afraid my job is done." He stood up. "I will show you out the door. And, I wish to say that our firm appreciates you coming here for this visit."

Ten minutes after leaving the law firm office, Velinda was in her car, driving. She was thinking about how happy she was for her daughter. Her girl's college education was secure now with the trust fund. Nothing would be keeping her daughter from attaining her dream to become a doctor.

Velinda soon found herself thinking about the giver of the college trust fund—Charlie. For months she'd been wondering about him. Why had he stopped coming by her shop for flowers? She shook her head. Maybe the romantic crush she'd had on him showed too much during his last visit, she thought.

Glancing at her passenger seat, Velinda saw the box that Charlie had gifted her through the lawyer. A sadness came over her. She prayed that these gifts were not part of Charlie's will. Turning back to the road ahead of her, she hoped she'd see the man again. She wanted to not only thank him for his generosity but also ask him why he'd given the gifts to her daughter and her.

Pulling over into a familiar strip mall, she found a tree-shaded spot and parked. Grabbing the box, she lifted the top up and gasped. There were three side-by-side bundles of one hundred dollar bills.

On top of the money packets, there was a folded piece of paper with some writing on it. Unraveling it, she read the hand-written words—*Thanks for the flowers*. It was unsigned.

Velinda never noticed her tear drops that had fallen on the note, as she finished staring at it. Looking up, she now knew in her heart that she'd never see Charlie again.

But Velinda smiled as she rubbed at her blurry eyes. She was somehow happy for Charlie, her daughter's new guardian angel.

CHAPTER 49

Harris stepped into Laura's apartment. He was picking her up for what was to be a romantic night out in Santa Monica. A date made up of dinner in one of the many boutique eateries on Main Street. Afterwards, they'd go for a stroll on the pier.

Laura walked Daniel into the dining room and asked him to sit down for a moment. *This must be important*, he thought. The two usually sat in the living room to have a pre-night out chat.

He faced her and she smiled.

"Daniel, we have been dating for a year now. And, engaged for three months."

He nodded.

"And Daniel you told me that you were raised by your grandparents. You said your father is deceased and you didn't know him."

Holding her eyes, he listened while resisting the urge to ask where this was going.

She hesitated before beginning again.

"You also told me that your mother left you as a toddler. And, that you have never tried to find her."

She stopped for a reaction.

He swallowed and said, "That's right, Laura."

"Well Daniel, we are heading into marriage. I want this piece of your past, an important piece that is, to be settled. I've learned the hard way that parental issues should, if not resolved, be at least clarified…dealt with as best we can." She renewed her smile. "Besides, I want to meet your mother."

She slipped a small, square piece of paper across the table. He saw it was a phone number. He jerked his head back. Then felt ridiculous for fearing a phone number. One he knew to be his mother's.

"Daniel, your mother's been clean and sober for over 20 years. She told me that she was just too scared to contact her *little teddy bear*."

Daniel reached out and took the paper.

SIX MONTHS LATER

Harris was arm in arm with an elderly woman. He was letting her pace their walk down the nave of the church. She was smiling, head held up, and wearing a long dress with a matching purse.

When they reached the front pew, she leaned her head into his arm. She then looked up at him.

"You're now my big teddy bear." She wiped a tear away. "And, I cannot believe I am here, at your wedding. I love you and Laura both."

Harris smiled and helped his mother get seated. He then took his place at the altar next to his best man, Alex Garcia.

Standing at the altar, Harris waited as he glimpsed Laura and her father, both with beaming smiles, arm in arm, making their way towards him.

CHAPTER 51

A barefoot Charlie Casey walked out of his open front doorway, careful not to catch a splinter in his feet. He really had to get his old weather-beaten wooden deck sanded down or, better yet, replaced.

Taking in a deep breath of the salty ocean-scented air felt refreshing. He took a moment to appreciate the midday glistening waters of the warm Caribbean Sea, just feet from him.

A small wave broke on the shore, and a realization of happiness came over him. A year after leaving Los Angeles, Charlie had finally begun to feel settled in. He was glad he'd taken his friend's suggestion to move to Ambergris Caye. Whenever Charlie tried to thank Sal Maginn for the recommendation, his friend would laugh and remind him that he'd be getting free stays in Belize out of it.

Besides changing homes, Charlie also had made a career change. He'd left his former hitman days behind and had recently become a local business owner. Charlie was the proud, and busy, owner of a juice shop in San Pedro Town. The shop was a mile away from his beachfront house.

He turned to go back inside.

A moment later, Charlie was seated in front of his laptop on his wooden desk. He decided it was time to know if it all worked out for

Laura Hadley after he'd visited her at her father's home. He googled her name.

Looking at his laptop screen, his internet search results showed several news headlines linking to articles on the continued hunt for the Deadbeat Killer. As he scrolled down, one link caught his attention. He clicked on it.

Charlie read the brief public wedding announcement for Daniel Harris and Laura Hadley. The announced wedding date had passed. He closed the laptop, and, with it, a long chapter of his life.

Next to the laptop, he spied a book he was trying to finish. It was one of the few poetry books of his mother's collection that he'd managed to bring with him when he moved from LA. He gently padded the book and silently asked for his mother's forgiveness for his continued dislike of poetry.

He got up and looked over at his recently purchased drafting table. Charlie had taken up drawing, a hobby he'd last left off as a teen. And, like when he was a teen, drawing was therapeutic for him.

Walking over to the drafting table, he looked down and studied a simple pencil drawing he'd recently completed. It was his father. The drawing was Charlie's best recollection of him. And though his father was a deadbeat dad that had deserted him as a kid, the few times Charlie did see him, his father was always nice to him. Charlie had decided that was all he wanted to remember about his father.

Picking up the drawing, Charlie realized that he never knew, and would never try to know, what had become of his deceased father. But that was okay.

Charlie would frame the drawing that represented, to him, his father. Another chapter in his life had been completed.

As he put the drawing back down, he turned his head. A new chapter in his life was smiling at him. Angelika was in a sundress and sandals. Her thin frame was half shaded by the coconut trees surrounding the wooden deck behind her.

Charlie offered Angelika a smile back. The two had met on the sand in front of his home, only a couple of months ago. They were already making plans for a cove side wedding.

Charlie Casey will return in

REVENGE RETURN

Five years ago, hitman Charlie Casey found himself contemplating the question—*What made me possible?* He realized the anger inside of him was the answer.

Charlie was chased out of the USA, settling in Belize. He married. Became a small businessman.

But his happy life in Belize came crashing down. The passing of a loved one brought Charlie back to a soulless and directionless life. And he found himself contemplating a new question—*What is my purpose?*

Then he read about a murder. In that instant, Charlie had a purpose. He was alive once again. And revenge was his only focus. Charlie would return to Los Angeles to seek it.

Acknowledgements

My mom read an early version of my first attempt at a Chalie Casey novel. She suggested that I change genres with it. It was changed.

Author Pam McCord pointed out a useful character reaction. It was implemented.

Aunt Patty caught something while hearing a scene described. Her suggested addition was added.

Dan Elsner provided technical advice and personal encouragement.

Lea Vickery had her mind in the novel when reading/editing it. This was comforting.

Siân Hyleg was my author services coordinator. I would not have anyone else guide me along in the publishing process.

All the folks at Between the Lines Publishing/Willow River Press were responsive. And I am thrilled they offered publication of the Charlie Casey series.

After numerous non-fiction books, Michael Oldham turned to fictional novels. THE VALENTINO FORMULA was his first novel. THE DEADBEAT KILLER, A CHARLIE CASEY Novel is his second. Oldham lives in Irvine, CA. He is at work on the next installment of the Charlie Casey series. Oldham can be reached at mikeoldham344@gmail.com.